The
LONG-AWAITED
CHILD

TRACIE PETERSON

The
LONG-AWAITED
CHILD

BETHANYHOUSE
MINNEAPOLIS, MINNESOTA

Published by Bethany House Publishers
A Ministry of Bethany Fellowship International
11400 Hampshire Avenue South
Bloomington, Minnesota 55438
www.bethanyhouse.com

Printed in the United States of America by
Bethany Press International, Bloomington, Minnesota 55438

Library of Congress Cataloging-in-Publication Data

Peterson, Tracie.
    The long-awaited child / by Tracie Peterson.
       p.   cm.
    ISBN 0-7642-2290-2
    1. Adoption—Fiction. 2. Childlessness—Fiction. 3. Foster parents—Fiction. 4. Teenage pregnancy—Fiction. 5. Juvenile delinquents—Fiction. I. Title.
    PS3566.E7717
    [L66 2001]
    813'.54—dc21   00-012968

To women everywhere who know
the heartache of loss and the
desire for hope and joy.
You are daughters of the King.
The best is yet to be.

BOOKS *by* TRACIE PETERSON

Controlling Interests
Entangled
Framed
The Long-Awaited Child
A Slender Thread
Tidings of Peace

WESTWARD CHRONICLES

A Shelter of Hope
Hidden in a Whisper
A Veiled Reflection

RIBBONS OF STEEL*

Distant Dreams
A Hope Beyond
A Promise for Tomorrow

RIBBONS WEST*

Westward the Dream
Separate Roads
Ties That Bind

SHANNON SAGA†

City of Angels

YUKON QUEST

Treasures of the North

*with Judith Pella   †with James Scott Bell

TRACIE PETERSON is an award-winning speaker and writer who has authored over forty-five books, both historical and contemporary fiction. *City of Angels*, a recent collaboration with James Scott Bell, highlights the courtrooms of 1903 Los Angeles. Tracie and her family make their home in Kansas.

Visit Tracie's Web site at: http://members.aol.com/tjpbooks

Chapter

1

"Tess, I'm sorry. There's never an easy way to give a patient this kind of news."

Tess Holbrook stared at the bearded man in strained silence. It seemed like she'd been coming to the doctor—this doctor—for nearly all of her adult life. She sighed.

She'd been so hopeful, so positive that this time the news would be different. Hope now faded into resignation and then to a painful urgency that left Tess almost breathless. Thoreau had been so right when he'd penned that resignation was confirmed desperation. Tess and desperation were life-long companions.

Tess gripped the arms of the chair. "So there's nothing to be done?" she finally asked, her voice strangely hollow. "This is the end of it?"

"We've pretty much exhausted all the known scientific possibilities," the man replied. "Medicine has its limitations."

Tess knew Dr. David Zeran was one of the best in his field. If he could no longer give her an answer—a hope—what chance did she have of finding it elsewhere?

"Look, I know this is hard to hear," the doctor said as he leaned back against his immaculate mahogany desk. "You aren't the first one I've had to give this kind of news to, but it hurts no less each time I'm required to say the words."

"What am I supposed to tell Brad?" she asked, tears misting her vision. "We had so many plans. . . ." her voice trailed off.

"Tess, I've known you and Brad now for some time. We're friends. We go to the same church and are grounded in the same spiritual beliefs. You can't give up; with God, all things are possible." He paused and eyed her. "I can tell by the expression on your face that you're letting go of hope."

"And why not?" Tess questioned with a bit of defiance in her tone. "You can't give me any."

"Maybe the scientific world has failed you."

"That's putting it mildly," Tess said, pushing back long brown ringlets. It was too late to have hope that she would ever conceive a child. She was infertile. Barren. The word echoed in her mind.

"I'm thirty-six and Brad and I have been trying to have a baby for the last ten years. The medical community from here to Kansas City has poked and prodded me, tested and medicated me, and infringed upon my privacy in ways I don't even want to discuss. Why should I have any hope? I can't get pregnant."

"Maybe not right now," Dr. Zeran agreed. "But maybe in the future. Tess, I've seen people totally give up on ever getting pregnant and then *voilà*! They find themselves expecting and suddenly their dreams are realized."

Tess stood up and shook her head. "That's not going to happen for me. I just know it. I wouldn't have spent all our spare money on in vitro and fertility drugs if I had believed it was possible to conceive on my own. Now, many thousands of dollars later—dollars we should have invested in a house or the business—you chide me for having no hope. Well, you're right. I have no hope of ever getting pregnant." A bitterness borne out of years of disappointment seemed to take possession of her heart.

David Zeran put out his hand to stop her from leaving. "Tess, wait just a minute. Don't leave just yet. I know you're upset, and I don't want you out in traffic this way."

She sniffed back tears and tried to remain calm. "I'm fine. Truly. I'm disappointed, but I've been disappointed for years on end. This is no different." But it was. This was the end of the road. David had said as much. There was nothing left to try.

Tess had tried hard to be brave and strong. *"Never let them see you down,"* one of her college business professors had told her. But that had been at least a hundred years ago and she had been a younger, more courageous soul back then.

David spoke compassionately. "But you're not fine. You don't need a degree in medicine to see that. You said it yourself. You see no reason to have hope. I've always seen a glint of anticipation—a personal challenge, if you will—that demanded the odds work with you instead of against you. Now I just see defeat."

Tess shook her head. "I'm tired, David." She put aside his profession and the formalities and turned to him as a friend. "Brad is tired. We've spent most of our marriage trying to have a baby and it's taken all the romance and fun out of our relationship."

"Why not adopt, then? Put all of this behind you and call up an agency."

"We've been through all this before," Tess replied. "I'm adopted. And I don't want to put the idea down—I'm so grateful that someone chose to adopt me and give me a home. But I have no one else in this world to whom I'm related, that I share that blood bond with. Don't you under-stand?" Tess knew her tone was pleading, but that was how she felt. She was begging for someone to comprehend her feelings. Even Brad failed to grasp them in full.

"I want a child of my own. A baby who is flesh of my flesh. I want to know there are other human beings out there who carry my blood. I feel so isolated." She allowed her tears to fall. "I feel there is no one in the entire universe who is a part of me in that way."

"But why should that be so important, Tess? Can't you love an adopted child? You loved adopted parents."

An exasperated sigh escaped her lips. "Yes, I loved them. I would have done anything for them. I loved my adopted sis-ter, Elaine, as well. We were as close a family as any in the neighborhood, but Elaine and I always felt the need for some-thing more."

"Elaine was also adopted?"

Tess nodded. "She was even younger than me when she came to our folks. She has no memories of her childhood, but I do. I was nearly six. I remember." The painful truth of those words hung in the air for a moment before Tess dissolved them with her next statement. "I don't want to seem ungrate-ful, David. I know the benefits as well as the downside of adop-tion. I just want my own baby."

"I know, Tess. I wish there was something more I could do."

She turned away from him and picked up her purse. "Well, that's that. I guess we just go home and suffer through the truth of the matter." She looked back at David's sympa-thetic expression. "I'm sorry for taking this out on you."

"You don't need to apologize. I completely understand."

Tess nodded, but she doubted he could ever fully understand her misery. He was a man and the father of two beautiful children. How could he possibly grasp her pain?

Intent on composing herself, Tess decided to concentrate only on her business and the tasks she had yet to complete before evening. Work was the way she'd always bolstered herself and forced herself to move forward. Concluding there would be no real chance for productivity, Tess buried her emotions and arranged her day on mental note pads. With any luck she'd be able to beat the rush-hour traffic and get home well ahead of Brad.

Unlocking her car door, Tess kept thinking at least two steps ahead. *I'll take the Palmetto, swing by the country club, and pick up that packet for the Caraway couple in Minneapolis. Then I'll drive by the bank and pick up the papers for the Davidsons.*

As a Senior Relocation Coordinator, Tess dealt with elderly people all over the nation. It was her primary responsibility to give them a safe and easy transition from their old locations to their new retirement homes in Florida. Tess had dreamed up the business after seeing a television special on the needs of retiring senior citizens. She'd still been in college then, safely living back home in Kansas City and making the commute to the University of Kansas in Lawrence.

"I didn't have a clue back then," she muttered and started the car. It wasn't until she checked her reflection in the visor mirror that Tess's willpower left her. Staring at her reflection, Tess recognized the unmistakable devastation in her expression. Her eyes welled with tears.

The emptiness in her heart threatened to blot out every other point of reality. There would be no baby. Her flat abdomen would never bulge full with a growing infant. The gift she so longed to give her beloved husband would never take form—never be born.

"It's not fair," she told her reflection. Refusing the pain, she allowed anger to rise up within her. "It's not fair!"

She slammed her fists against the steering wheel and let her tears wreak havoc with her mascara. Her mind warned her to stop—to think of something else. But this time her heart pushed logical thinking aside.

"Teenagers get pregnant every day. Inconveniently pregnant women select abortion as if they were choosing party dresses. Everybody can get pregnant at the drop of a hat except for me!"

The flames of bitterness grew as Tess fueled the fire with her thoughts. Confirmed desperation. It permeated her very soul. After years of disappointment and heartache, it was the only emotion left to her. The only emotion that didn't completely rob her of the will to go on.

She threw the car into gear and pulled out of the parking lot with much less discretion than Miami traffic usually demanded. Her anger kept her edgy and tense as she darted from lane to lane. Yet soon her anger dissipated and her fears and sorrows overwhelmed her until she was reduced to a sobbing mass of emotionally raw nerves.

Knowing the danger she posed, Tess attempted to compose herself. She tried to force her mind to go over a detailed list of what she needed from the store, but it didn't work. Finally giving up, Tess pulled into the parking lot of a fast-food burger place and parked the car once more. She didn't bother to turn the engine off. Nor did she make any pretense of hiding the fact that she was having a breakdown. She simply put her head against the steering wheel and cried.

Oh, God, I'm so ashamed, she struggled to pray. *I have a good life here in Miami. I have a wonderful, loving husband.* Thoughts of Brad only made her cry harder. He deserved a wife who could bear him a child. He deserved the children he so much desired. Hadn't he been the first one to bring up having a baby?

They had hardly been married a week when he brought up the subject one morning over breakfast. Tess had been thrilled. She knew before marrying him that Brad wanted children, but she hadn't realized he'd be quite this eager.

"I've . . . ruined . . . everything, God." Her voice came in ragged little spurts. "I feel . . . so . . . useless."

Her mind wandered back in time to one of her last memories of her birth mother. Severely addicted to alcohol and cocaine, the woman often had Tess run the streets for her well into the night. Tess knew the local pushers like other children knew their extended family members. J.J. could make her the best deal on coke. Slick Boy had the best weed, and Big Daddy carried a large assortment of amphetamines.

The life she'd come from was harsh and cold, a dismal beginning for a child.

But Tess's memory had to do with something entirely different. This memory had started out good. She had been allowed to go to kindergarten after turning five years old that August. School had been a wonderful alternative from the life-style she'd known with her mother.

At school the shades were left up to let the light pour into the room and chase away the shadows. The teacher smelled good and dressed in beautiful clothes that had no holes in them. Tess could envision her teacher standing at the front of the room, smiling, instructing, and always caring. And on this day, she had praised Tess's accomplishments and sent her home feeling that nothing in the world could be as wonderful as school.

Upon arriving home that day, Tess had called out excitedly, "Mommy! Mommy! Look what I made you!"

The kindergarten class of Grant Elementary had labored since Thanksgiving to create Christmas gifts for their mothers. They had been required to bring a plastic jar or container to school in order to make a vase for flowers. Tess couldn't find a jar to bring, so her teacher had found a spare glass jar in the janitor's closet. They weren't supposed to use glass, but the teacher had sized up Tess and remarked on how mature she was and how she was certain Tess would be careful with the glass. And Tess had carried that jar around as if it contained the very essence of life. And in some ways, for her, it did.

They took yarn and saturated it with glue, then wrapped it round and round the jars until they were covered from top to bottom. Once dried, the yarn caused the jar to look like a coiled, colorful rope. The appearance and feel fascinated Tess. And she had brought it home as a Christmas present— her very first chance to give something to her mother.

"What are you yelling about?" her mother asked, stumbling into the living room wearing torn sweat pants and a T-shirt advertising her favorite beer.

"I made you this for Christmas," Tess declared proudly. "Teacher said mine was the prettiest." She presented the vase to her mother and waited. Surely this would cause her mother to smile, to approve of her. Oh, how she wanted to please her mother. More than anything in the world, she just wanted her mother to love her and be proud of her.

Tess waited eagerly, her tiny arms outstretched, the vase teetering in her hands.

"What's that ugly thing?" her mother questioned, her contempt quite clear.

"It's a vase for flowers. You put flowers inside."

Her mother stared in disbelief for a moment. "Do you see any flowers around here?"

"No, but we could get some," Tess suggested, certain that this made perfect sense.

"I can't afford to buy food," her mother said angrily. "Where do you suppose I could come up with the money to buy flowers? You are, by far, the stupidest child ever born to this earth. What ever made you think I could use a vase?"

The anticipation of approval faded quickly in light of her mother's condemnation. Tess's lips began to quiver as she fought to keep from crying.

"We made them in school," she tried again. Hope faded from her voice. "Teacher said mine was the best."

Her mother swept the vase from her hands in one fluid motion. For a brief moment, the vase seemed to be suspended in midair, and then it slammed against the wall. The dried yarn kept the glass from shattering all over the room, but it broke into pieces nevertheless.

"There!" her mother declared. "That's what I think of your teacher. Now clean up the mess while I go find some cigarettes. You are the most useless, good-for-nothing brat." Her mother stormed off into the kitchen, muttering expletives all the way.

Tess crept to the place where the broken peanut butter jar lay mingled with the glue-matted yarn. What once had been lovely and purposeful now lay as ugly trash. Her mother had a talent for turning beauty into rubble.

"Lady, are you okay?"

Tess tried to place the voice and quickly realized it was coming from one of the fast-food employees as he tapped on her window. The present was little better than the past, yet she let the images of her mother fade away.

Rolling down the window a fraction, Tess nodded. "I'm fine."

The kid eyed her suspiciously. "You sure you don't want me to call someone? The police? An ambulance?"

"No," Tess reassured him, reaching into her purse for a tissue. "I'm fine. I just had some bad news."

The kid shrugged and went back to picking up trash in the parking lot. Tess dried her eyes and watched him work. He was a sweet kid. Hispanic in looks, tall and slender. He couldn't have been any more than sixteen or seventeen. His mother had obviously raised him to have manners and concern for other people.

Looking heavenward with heartfelt imploring, Tess whispered, "I would teach my child to be just as good. I swear I would. I wouldn't be like my mother. I wouldn't destroy and maim—I would love and cherish. I would never let my child feel anything but love. You have to know that, God. You know everything—you must know that."

Chapter
2

"Tess, are you home?" Brad Holbrook called from the foyer of their high-rise condominium. He frowned when there was no response. Where could she be? He'd phoned several times that afternoon but had only reached the answering machine.

"Tess?"

Giving his suit coat a toss as he entered their bedroom, Brad saw every indication that Tess was home. Her purse sat on the dresser, her shoes were sitting by the bed. She had to be here.

"Tess?"

He glanced in the master bath but found it empty. Then he spied the balcony curtains blowing ever so slightly. *She must be outside,* he reasoned.

He pushed back the partially open sliding-glass door. There on the chaise lounge, his wife dozed peacefully. He smiled. It was unusual for her to take any time out to rest, but he knew business had been especially stressful of late.

Sitting down on a chair beside her, Brad watched his sleeping wife for several moments. She stirred his heart with a love and desire that he thought would have surely diminished after eleven years of marriage. He reached out and toyed with a long brown curl. He smiled when he thought of her insecurities after perming her hair. He liked the effect—liked the way her hair seemed to bounce and dance when she walked. Tess, however, was always quite critical with herself. She forced herself to walk a narrow line, always seeking ways to improve herself in one manner or another.

But to Brad, she was already perfection. He'd fallen in love with her from the first moment he'd laid eyes on her. They'd met at her church. She was twenty and he was twenty-four. He had just finished a bachelor's degree in marketing and she was knee-deep in her sophomore year at the University of Kansas. He had teased her about majoring in social work, joking that she was too pretty to be one of those dowdy women who wore thick glasses and pulled their hair back into tight little buns. She had laughed at his stereotype and pointed him to three very attractive women at the church party who were already working for the state as social workers.

He shook his head. The years had passed so quickly, and yet Tess still looked as young and beautiful as she had on their wedding day.

She shifted a bit in her sleep as if coming awake, so Brad took the opportunity to nuzzle a kiss against her ear. She came awake slowly, opening dreamy eyes of chocolate brown to meet his smile.

"Wake up, my pretty little sun maiden," he whispered.

"Hello," she said, smiling sleepily. Yawning, she stretched her arms over her head, making it simple for Brad to pull her close.

"I worried when I couldn't reach you," he said, kissing her cheek in a lingering manner. "I called but you weren't here. I even tried your cell phone." He put his lips to her closed eyes, then trailed kisses down her nose to her lips. Kissing her with the promise of a shared passionate moment, Brad felt his wife tense.

Pulling back, he eyed her with concern. "What's wrong?"

Tess opened her eyes. The sleepy look diminished and one of serious reality took its place. "I saw David today."

Brad nodded. "That's right. You were supposed to get back some test results. So what happened?"

Tess shook her head. "Nothing happened. Nothing is going to happen. David can't help us anymore. He said we could keep trying in vitro and the fertility drugs, but he knows it's costing us a small fortune. He suggests we stop trying so hard to have a baby and just enjoy each other and life."

Brad licked his lips and nodded. "He's probably right." The years of doctors studying and recording their love life was beginning to get on his nerves.

"You do know what this means, don't you?" Tess questioned him with a pained expression.

He reached out and took hold of her hand. "It doesn't mean that it's impossible. David has always said he can't find a real reason for why we aren't conceiving."

"It's impossible enough," Tess said, pulling away. "It's hopeless."

"No," Brad said, shaking his head. "With God all things are possible."

"David said the same thing, but you have to admit that possibility might also include the fact that He doesn't want us to have a child," Tess countered.

"I suppose that's possible, but I doubt that's the reason. The timing just isn't right."

She looked at him in disbelief. "I'm thirty-six years old. The right timing is rapidly slipping by us, Brad."

"Women have babies into their fifties," Brad threw out. "I

mean, look at all the actresses who are waiting until their forties to have their first child."

"Don't!" Tess demanded, getting to her feet. "Don't try to make this something it's not. We aren't opting to wait until our forties for children. We aren't opting for any of this. We *can't* have a baby. The sooner we accept it, the better we'll be."

Brad went to where his wife stood. She looked so hurt—so lost. He reached out and pulled her to him. She refused to yield, remaining stiff and distant.

"Sweetheart, I love you. It doesn't matter to me that you can't get pregnant. For all I know, it's all my fault. We can't play the blame game. I want children—your children—but I wouldn't trade a house full of kids for the love we share. Don't let this become a wall between us. I thought we agreed we were in this together."

She softened, as he'd hoped she would. He could feel the tension ease just a bit as her shoulders rounded toward him and she buried her face against his neck.

He held her there for several minutes. The ocean breeze blew gently against them, the warmth of the sun fading to leave a hint of a chill in the air.

"It'll be all right," he whispered against her hair. "You'll see. One day we'll have a child. I just know it."

She looked up at him, her eyes brimming with tears. "I'd like to believe that."

"Then do." He smiled and brushed back a stray curl. "You are the most beautiful woman in the world, and you're mine. I'm a lucky man."

She put her arms around his neck. "Oh, Brad, I love you so very much. I'm sorry for taking my pain out on you. You deserve something better than my anger and frustration."

"I can think of many things you have to offer that could replace those less-desirable feelings," he said, grinning. She melted against him, showing a willingness for whatever he had in mind. "Ah, Tess," he murmured before touching his lips to hers. Her kiss held all the promise and encouragement he needed. Surely God would make things right for them.

Tess caught the ringing phone just before the answering machine picked up the call. "Tess Holbrook."

"Tess, I don't know if you remember me or not, but this is Laura Johnson in Kansas City."

Tess laughed. "Of course I remember you. You had Elaine and me call you Aunt Laura. How are you?" Tess shuffled the tax papers she'd carried with her from the living room to one side and pulled forward a tuna salad sandwich that she'd been trying to get to for the last hour. This call would give her the perfect opportunity for lunch.

"We're doing well. Darren has finally decided to retire from being the world's busiest architect, and now we're ready to do some serious planning for our future. That's why I called. We want to use your services."

Tess pulled up a note pad and grabbed a pencil. The sandwich would have to wait a bit longer. "What did you have in mind?"

"Well, I know you work with people to relocate them. I just didn't know what all was involved."

Tess laughed. "Just about anything you want to be involved. I've done cases where the folks involved wanted me to take complete inventory of their lives and include every imaginable detail in the move. Then I've had cases where I did little more than help newcomers find a good doctor and hospital. Do you have a retirement location in mind?"

"Well, we had thought of the Southwest. We knew your sister Elaine was handling relocations in the Phoenix area," Laura began, "but then we decided we liked the idea of the ocean and such. Cruises would be easy to enjoy, and you know how Darren loves to fish."

"Those are all good points," Tess said, making notes. "What kind of place did you have in mind?"

"Well, certainly something a whole lot smaller than this monstrosity. We should have downsized after Adam and Aaron left home. Somehow we just never got around to it and since Darren had designed the place and put so many additional renovations into it, we hated to let it go."

"And now?"

Laura chuckled. "Now our son Adam fancies that he'd like to buy the place for his family. They're in Chicago right now, but he can easily transfer to Kansas City. He loves the house and it would be a relief to both Darren and myself to know we could come back and visit."

"Well, it's also nice to know that you wouldn't have to worry about getting a buyer," Tess replied. "I have a list of great retirement communities. Was that what you were thinking of, or were you preferring something more private?"

"No, we like the idea of a retirement community. We're both afraid of getting old and lonely and hiding ourselves away from life. I think a community feel would be just right for us."

Tess nodded and reached over to pull out a huge notebook of senior retirement listings. "Now, are you wanting the eastern coast of Florida or the western? I have connections in both places and we can work out just about any location you have in mind.''

"I think it would be nice to be near to where you live. We miss your folks so much. It seems like they've been gone forever. If you wouldn't mind a visit now and then, we think it would make our transition to Florida much easier.''

"I wouldn't mind that at all. There are plenty of places to consider. I'll send you copies of the literature and some information on each place. I'll also send you a package of information on what I do and how I might help. This has my prices and all the details of time scheduling and so forth. You just check off the areas in which you think you'd like my help and then I can give you an estimation as to what it will cost.''

"That sounds wonderful. It's such a relief to know we can trust you to help us through this,'' Laura replied.

"No problem. I love this business for that very reason,'' Tess answered. Her second line began ringing. "Look, I have another call. I'll have the information in the mail today.''

"Thanks again, Tess. I'll look forward to hearing from you.''

"Oh, let me have your telephone number and address,'' Tess said, suddenly realizing that she had neither one. Laura rattled the numbers off quickly and bid Tess good-bye without a thought to keep her even a moment longer.

Tess hurriedly picked up the second line just as the answering machine began to take the call. "Tess Holbrook.''

"Hi, sweetheart.''

"Brad, what's going on? It's not like you to call at this time of day.'' She checked her watch and saw it was nearly two o'clock.

"Well, I need a favor. We're working with several area business people on a tourism package. I need to have them over

25

for dinner tomorrow night. Will that be a problem?"

Tess picked up her pencil once again. "No, it's not a problem. How many?"

"Probably ten," Brad replied. "It shouldn't take all night, but we discussed it among our own team here and thought the more homey setting might work to our advantage."

"Did you have something in mind for dinner?"

"Why don't we just get it catered and have Esperanza come to serve?" he suggested.

Tess knew her housekeeper was due to come yet that afternoon. It would be easy enough to see if Esperanza wanted to earn some extra money keeping their kitchen for the party.

"All right. I'll take care of the details," Tess replied.

"You're a doll. I'll probably see you around seven. I'm playing racquetball with Justin after work."

Tess nodded, seeing she'd noted Brad's game on her calendar. "Have fun."

"Say, do you want to go out to dinner tonight?" Brad questioned. "Kind of my way of making up for springing this business dinner on you at the last minute."

"Sure. Sounds like fun. Do you want me to make reservations?" Tess questioned.

"Nah, I'll take care of it. We'll do something special."

"Trying to cheer me up?" she asked, half teasing, half serious.

"Just letting you know how much you're appreciated."

She smiled. "Ah, bribery."

He laughed and denied it. "See you at seven."

Tess hung up the phone and tapped her pencil on the notes she'd made. It would be short notice, but she was certain she could get Evangeline's to cater her dinner. The owner had been so grateful for Tess's help in relocating his mother to Ft. Lauderdale that he practically fell all over Tess whenever she appeared in his shop.

Then the notes for Laura and Darren Johnson caught her eye. Laura had been a dear friend to Tess's mother, while Darren and her father had begun their relationship through business. Tess's father, Rudy Hersh, had been a big name in construction in the Kansas City area. It only seemed fitting that he should befriend an architect when he decided to bid on one of the city's biggest renovation projects. It would be nice having Laura and Darren in the area, Tess decided. Almost as nice as having her folks around again.

Rudy and Stella Hersh had been gone longer than Tess liked to remember. Her father had succumbed to a heart attack nearly a year after Tess and Brad had married. After that, her mother's health had gradually gone downhill. Tess believed her mother had died of a broken heart, never having been quite able to find her niche after Rudy had died. How Tess missed them.

Gathering up some information, she tried not to think about her parents or her desire to have a baby. *There are just too many sad things in this world,* she concluded. *I hardly need to add to them with my own poor spirits.*

This was the way Tess generally did business. This was how she kept herself from sinking too low in self-pity. Her demands on herself were always greater than those anyone else placed on her. Other people might have allowed for her to have hurts and sorrows, but Tess refused to allow herself the luxury of such feelings. At least not for long.

Chapter

3

"The flowers are on the table, Mrs. Holbrook," the fifty-something housekeeper announced as Tess emerged from her bedroom.

Securing a diamond stud to her left ear, Tess nodded. "Esperanza, would you mind zipping me up?" she questioned, turning her back to the woman.

Esperanza quickly slid the zipper into place. "The food is ready and the table set. What time do you want me to serve?"

The concierge from the downstairs lobby buzzed Tess before she could answer.

"Yes?"

"Mr. Holbrook is on his way upstairs."

"Thank you, Carlos," Tess replied and turned to Esperanza. "I suppose we'll want to eat in about thirty to forty minutes. Let's give the men time to discuss their racquetball games and Wall Street victories before stuffing them with Evangeline's seafood salad and tortilla soup." Tess knew her husband and his business dinners well enough to know that this would be sufficient time for all formalities to be set aside.

The condominium went almost instantly from its routine calm to a kind of overwhelming onslaught of activity. Tess found herself glad for the dressy appearance of her black sleeveless Donna Karan creation. With her high-heeled strappy sandals and simple diamond earrings, she looked neither too extravagant nor understated.

"Mrs. Holbrook, I am Bartolo Aznar. I've long wanted to meet you," an older, salt-and-pepper-haired man spoke as he took hold of her hand. "Your husband has told me much about you and your business."

Tess smiled. The man's dark-eyed gaze was fixed intently on her face. "I'm flattered. What was it that so intrigued you?"

The man flashed brilliant white teeth. "I must confess, I saw your photograph on Brad's desk. We started to talk about you and he told me of your business in helping senior citizens."

Tess nodded. "It's a challenging but rewarding career." She turned to find Brad making his way to where they stood.

"Ah, I see Bartolo has already cornered you." He leaned forward and gave Tess a kiss on the cheek. "You look fantastic," he whispered against her ear before straightening.

"Mr. Aznar—"

"Please call me Bartolo, as your husband does," the man interjected.

Tess smiled and nodded. "Bartolo tells me my business became the topic of office conversation."

"Yes, he's very excited about what you've been able to accomplish," Brad replied. "He and his wife have been in business for themselves for nearly as long as they've been married. They have two teenagers and live here in Miami."

"How did you two meet?" Tess asked.

"We share a common interest in tourism," Bartolo told Tess. "Along with other things. Retirement communities and such. That's why I found your business fascinating. I would very much like to discuss it more, if the evening will allow," the older man replied.

Tess couldn't imagine why the man found her work so exciting, but she quickly agreed. "I would be honored."

"Perhaps after dinner," Aznar suggested before giving her the slightest hint of a bow and taking his leave.

"What a pleasant man," Tess said, gazing up into her husband's eyes. "Not as pleasant as you, but very nearly."

"You may not think me pleasant at all when I tell you what I've done. I hope you don't mind," Brad said, putting his arm around Tess's shoulder, "but I've invited Justin to join us this evening."

Tess laughed. She was used to Brad's last-minute additions and always ordered at least three extra portions of food. "I suppose we'll fit him in."

Brad kissed her again. "You're awfully good to me, Mrs. Holbrook."

Laughing, she walked away, but she looked over her shoulder to answer playfully, "Yes, I am. Just don't forget it."

Tess quickly explained the addition to Esperanza, who merely nodded and went to set another place at the table. She couldn't imagine why Brad had invited his best friend to join a tourism business meeting. Justin Dillard was a lawyer by trade, so perhaps there were legal matters to be considered. Nevertheless, Justin was always a pleasure to have at their table. Tess also figured it did the man good to be around other people. His wife had been killed only four months earlier in a car accident. Justin had been devastated, and had it not been for his active role in the church, Tess was certain he would have locked himself away in his grief.

"Tess, you look wonderful," Brad's supervisor, Mel Grommet, declared. "But then, you always do."

Tess smiled. The man was old enough to be her father, yet she knew him to be married to a woman at least ten years her junior. "How are you, Mel?"

"I'm hitting four under par and making a fortune on those technology stocks Brad clued me in on," the man replied with a devious twinkle in his eye. "Now, if I could just get this deal wrapped up tonight, I could take Kelly to the Keys for the weekend. She been dying for a little excitement."

Tess nodded, imagining the shapely wife of this aging business executive prancing about one nightclub after another while Mel struggled to stay awake past ten.

"If you'll excuse me, Mel, I have to check on dinner."

Tess hurried away before the man could reply and rolled her eyes heavenward at the thought of spending the entire evening with him anywhere nearby.

But worries about having to keep company with Mel soon faded as the evening progressed. Justin arrived with a bouquet of flowers for Tess and a new tan, which suggested he'd spent some R and R time at the beach.

With Justin to her left and Bartolo Aznar on her right, Tess found herself pleasantly occupied. She learned all about Aznar's Cuban and Spanish background, as well as his avid interest in building a retirement community on some newly held property to the north. Justin was just as good company as Aznar. He talked of his vacation to Marco Island and a long-overdue visit with his parents. Tess was glad to hear that things were going so well for him.

Brad, too, seemed pleased with the turn of events. From time to time he looked to her and smiled. *He seems so content,* she thought. Almost as if their inability to conceive had never been an issue. The weight of that reality suddenly weighed heavy on her shoulders.

Smiling tolerantly as Justin related some amusing story about jellyfish, Tess struggled to take her thoughts captive. This dinner was important to Brad and she didn't want to ruin it for him by appearing less than happy and full of confidence.

When dinner concluded, and Esperanza and Tess had cleared away all but the coffee and dessert, the men got down to discussing the details of their business. Tess knew very well how these things could go into the wee hours of the morning, and so after paying Esperanza, she dismissed the woman and saw to the final kitchen work herself.

"You are not interested in what we stuffy old businessmen have to say?" Aznar questioned as he came up behind Tess unannounced.

She turned and shook her head. "There's always some new angle to Brad's work in tourism. I'm sure to hear all about it after the meeting concludes."

"I had hoped we might speak more on your business," Aznar replied. He waved Tess off when she offered him coffee. "I would very much like for you to consider a proposition I'd like to make."

"Related to your planned retirement community?"

"Somewhat," he replied. "You see, not only would I like for you to help me to arrange clientele for the community, but I'd like to propose an expansion of your business."

Tess cocked her head back a bit and raised a brow in question. "An expansion?"

"Yes. I realize you currently run everything out of your home, but I would like you to consider allowing me to invest in your business and see it grow. I have the perfect rental property that would make a wonderful location for your business and allow for additional staff."

"I like working out of the apartment," Tess replied. "I

don't want to keep hours and answer to someone else."

He chuckled. "I would imagine you are already answering to a great many someones in dealing with your numerous newspaper ads. Brad was saying that you often get called in the middle of the night."

It was true, Tess had to admit. People were not always very considerate of the time zone differences. The multiple ads she ran in northern metropolitan city newspapers across the nation gave her a variety of customers, as well as calls at all hours of the day and night.

"It just seems to come along with the business," Tess replied.

"With my proposal, you needn't disturb your sleep," Bartolo said with a smile. "I only ask that you consider my proposition. We could further discuss the details, and you could of course continue to name your own hours and responsibilities."

Tess shook her head. "I don't see it working that way. Whenever you add staff, there are always added problems. Right now, when someone calls with a need, I know what I can and can't do for them. I won't have some overzealous nineteen-year-old promising some pension-bound retiree the moon when I can't deliver it."

"You are a thoughtful woman."

"I'm a realistic woman," Tess countered. "I'm also a Christian businesswoman. Two things that do not always go together very well. I have a deep concern for the elderly and their needs. I have seen many of them taken advantage of by major corporations and our own government. I don't wish to add to that problem. Rather, I'd like to be a light through that dark tunnel."

"I admire that and would never want your goals to change."

"But you don't understand," Tess replied. "Increasing the number of employees and making the location a fixed business will only impersonalize this service. People feel comfortable because they are only dealing with one person instead of the thirty or more that might otherwise be needed for such a major move. I won't even employ a secretary for that very reason. I take only so many cases a month and I heed well my limitations."

"But if your heart is in helping the helpless," Aznar said rather firmly, "would it not be better to train additional people and help even more? Why not train a staff to be just as personal? You could assign cases to each person and let them be the one sole contact for each client. Give them individual pagers and phones. Arrange it as it is now, with you to supervise the entire situation—approve all the final decisions."

Tess nodded. "I suppose something like that could work, but at this point I'm just not ready for expansion."

"At least think on it," Aznar requested. "The timing might not work just now, but perhaps later." He handed her his business card.

She took the card and shrugged. "Perhaps."

Tess felt a tremendous sense of relief when the last of the businessmen, with the exception of Justin, had departed with Mel for one of the more popular nightclub spots. Mel could always be counted on to show his people a good time. Miami wasn't really the kind of town known for its late-night activities, but such events could be had if a person knew where to look. And with Mel married to the vivacious Kelly, he had no trouble in locating a party.

"I thought they'd never leave," Brad said in an apologetic

tone. "I'm really sorry. I figured it for being two, three hours tops."

"It's really no problem," Tess said, picking up glasses from the living room.

"Why don't you just leave those for a minute and come sit down? Justin and I have something to discuss."

Tess looked at her husband's eager expression and began to run through a mental list of anything he'd hinted at over the last couple of weeks. There were no men's retreats planned or church parties that would require her attention. She couldn't remember Brad planning any getaways for fishing or other activities that might spell complications for her own very organized life. Smiling, she put the glasses down and straightened.

"All right, what are you two up to?"

Justin looked to Brad. "Do you want to tell her or should I?"

Brad grinned. "You go ahead."

"Well?" Tess questioned. "Somebody tell me."

Justin shrugged. "I guess the responsibility falls to me. I know how badly you and Brad have been wanting a baby."

Tess felt her stomach tighten. She hadn't expected Justin to speak on this matter.

"Well, I was telling Brad that I know of several unwed mothers who are expecting. You know I'm involved with the Christian Crisis Pregnancy Center. Some of these mothers-to-be are just kids themselves and they come from good families who are Christian and want to see the babies adopted rather than the sad alternative."

Tess held up her hand. "I've told you both how I feel about adoption. I think it's a wonderful option, but I don't know that I can do it. I really want to have my own baby."

"And if you can't?" Justin questioned softly.

Tess felt as though he'd struck her. Her cheeks grew hot. "I don't know."

"Look, Tess," Justin began, "I've been friends with you and Brad for a long time. I know what you've been through with all the doctors and trying over and over again to get pregnant. I just want you to know there's another route to consider."

"I appreciate that," Tess said, reaching again for the glasses. "I know very well that this is a viable choice for many people. My own friend Kim is adopting in this manner. I think I've told you about her." Tess straightened and met Justin's compassionate gaze.

He nodded. "She's the one who had the hysterectomy, right?"

"Yes. There's no possibility of her getting pregnant. She's worked through an adoption agency and attorney, and within the next few weeks she expects to have a baby."

Justin nodded again and moved closer. "Is she happy?"

Tess thought back to Kim's animated phone call a few days earlier. *Happy* seemed a weak word to describe the woman's jubilant enthusiasm. "She's ecstatic."

"You could be too."

Tess felt overwhelmed by the turn of events. Adoption was the last thing she had figured to deal with this evening. Looking to Brad she questioned, "Was this your idea?"

Brad got a sheepish expression on his face that answered her without words. "I just thought it was time to . . . well, to think about a new approach. It actually seemed like it might be something God was steering us to consider. I mean, Justin is the one who came to me with the idea, and this came after I'd spent most of the day praying about having kids."

Tess softened, feeling an abundant love for her husband. He had prayed about their need. He had cared enough to consider the situation throughout the day.

"Look, it's just not an easy situation," Tess said. "Adoption is a wonderful thing. I cherish the parents it gave me. I've known many blessings because I was adopted."

Brad's eyes seemed to light up at this. "*Blessing* is just the word I was thinking. Perhaps this is God's way of blessing us with a child."

Tess hated causing him pain and she didn't want to take away from his otherwise very successful evening by causing a scene. "I'll think about it," she finally said. "But please don't pressure me. I'm doing well just to consider this."

Brad and Justin exchanged a look. "There's plenty of time," Justin finally said. "Most of the cases I know about aren't going to be having their babies for several months."

Tess tried not to let her emotions take control. "Good" was all she managed to say before heading to the kitchen. She might have fooled her husband and his friend, but inside, the tight band that wrapped itself around her lungs, threatening to cut off her air, proved that she hadn't fooled herself.

"Do you think she'll come around?" Justin asked as Brad walked him to the door.

Brad drew in a deep breath and let it out slowly before answering. "She's been so focused on getting pregnant that I don't think she's ever allowed herself to seriously consider that adoption might be her only chance to have a family."

"Why is she so against adoption?" Justin asked as he opened the front door.

"Like I said, for years she's thought only of having a child that would be her own flesh and blood. I don't think she's so much opposed to adoption as she is fixed on the idea of bearing a baby herself.

"Then, again," Brad added, remembering some of the conversations he'd shared with Tess, "I think she's terrified of trying to adopt a baby. Every time there's something on television about adoptions gone bad, Tess is right there to watch the story. Usually it's some situation where the biological parents come to realize that they made a mistake. There was a story on a couple of nights ago about a mother who had given her baby up at age seventeen because the father skipped out on her. Then when the father came back into her life four years later, they married and wanted their child back."

"I saw that too," Justin admitted. "Sad case. The judge actually ruled that the mother had given the baby up under duress and that the adoptive parents had taken advantage of her state of mind. Things like that seem to be creeping up all over the country."

"Exactly. And it scares Tess to death."

"But it doesn't scare you?" Justin asked softly.

Brad knew it did. He had battled his fears and disappointments as best he could, trying hard to never burden Tess with them, but he wouldn't hide them from Justin.

"It does scare me. It scares me to think of growing attached to a baby, only to lose him or her years later from some strange trumped-up technicality. It scares me to watch Tess grow more disappointed and empty. I want to believe that God has a reason for all of this, but it sure doesn't make much sense to me."

"God's like that sometimes," Justin said with a smile. "He

just doesn't seem to think it necessary to give us all the details of His plan."

Brad grinned. "If I thought I could coax it out of Him, I'd sure give it a try."

Justin smiled rather sadly. "Try just trusting Him for the outcome. I never thought I could say those words again and truly mean them—not after the accident. But God is good and He's making my way better every day. He can do the same for you and Tess."

"I know He can. It's just a matter of the details."

"Well, let me know if Tess changes her mind. Maybe once she considers the magnitude of this opportunity, she'll want to give it a try."

Brad hoped she would but wasn't about to count on it. "I'll let you know."

Closing the door behind Justin, Brad leaned back against the heavy oak wood and stared down the hall. Could she be persuaded? Could Tess ever give up her dream of pregnancy now that the doctor had deemed them unable to conceive?

She doesn't understand, he thought and shook his head. *She only knows how empty her own arms are, but she never thinks about my arms being just as empty.*

Chapter 4

"But I don't understand why you're so opposed to adoption," Kim Cummings said as she sampled the coffee Tess had just poured. They had agreed to catch an early breakfast at Tess's home and now the conversation had turned less favorable.

With a glance toward the bedroom where Brad was still getting ready for work, Tess tried to gather her thoughts. "I know you're happy with your choice. I think you should be. In fact, I'm happy for you."

"But?" the soft-spoken blonde prompted.

"But I just don't think I can go that direction. Not yet."

"Not until you're as desperate as me?" Kim asked. She toyed with a bagel, cutting it into four pieces before attempting to smear it with cream cheese.

"That's not what I meant and you know it," Tess replied. "I know you have no other choice. You can't very well conceive after having a hysterectomy. But I remember how much you wanted your own baby."

"Yes, I did. And now I'm getting my own baby," Kim said quite seriously. "Travis helped me to see that it's all a matter of heart. If we take this child and love him or her as we would our own, then it *will* be our own. Blood accounts for very little

41

when you really think about it."

"I don't expect you or your husband to understand," Tess said rather dejectedly. "I don't expect anyone to."

"Oh, don't sound so maudlin," Kim chided. "We've been friends for too long for you to take that attitude with me. Just tell me what's on your heart."

Tess poured a generous amount of cream into her coffee and considered her words carefully. "Kim, I don't want to bring you down about this adoption. That wouldn't make me a very good friend." She attempted a smile, but the result was feeble. "I really am happy for you. I'm happy that this satisfies the longing inside you. Honest.

"But for me, it's different. You know who your mother and father are, who your siblings and grandparents are. You have a family. You can point to a long line of deceased people and you know that you are tied to them by blood. I can't do that." Tess held up her hand as Kim opened her mouth to speak. "All of my life I've wanted to belong to someone. I thought marriage . . ." She glanced over her shoulder and lowered her voice. "I thought marriage would fill that desire, but it didn't. I love Brad—just as you love Travis—but husbands are one thing and children are another. Children are the culmination of the love shared between a husband and wife. They join the blood lines of both with an inseparable tie."

"I think you're too hung up on blood relations. I have a great many of them I wouldn't give you a dollar for," Kim said, trying to lighten the mood. "Believe me, Tess, I know how important this is to you. I've heard all your arguments and they all make sense—to a point. But past the point where you either deliver a baby from your own body or never have a child, never know what it is to mother someone, it makes no sense at all. I think you're just being stubborn."

"Morning, ladies," Brad said, coming into the room while adjusting his tie. "Did I hear the word *stubborn* mentioned?"

Kim laughed. "We were just discussing Tess's more obvious attributes."

Brad leaned down and kissed his wife. "I assume you already covered beautiful and charming."

Tess rolled her eyes while Kim spoke. "Well, we hadn't gotten that far. Guess we were just waiting for you."

Brad grabbed a mug and poured himself a cup of coffee. Joining Tess and Kim at the table, he eyed his wife. "So what is this really about? I can tell by the expression on your face that the topic is much heavier than just your good points."

"We were discussing the idea Justin posed last night," Tess finally admitted.

"And what did you conclude?"

Tess grew uncomfortable as both Kim and Brad trapped her with an intense stare. "Look, you both know how I feel." Still they continued only to stare. Tess grew even more restless. "Okay, okay," she said, holding up her hands. "I'm stubborn and selfish and wrongly focused."

Brad grinned and jabbed Kim playfully. "We should be detectives, huh? Confessions like that don't come easy."

"I'm serious," Tess said, shaking her head. "I know how much you want me to accept this idea. Believe me, I lay awake half the night considering all the aspects of adoption. But you need to understand that to me, agreeing to adopt is like giving up the fight."

"I didn't know we were at war," Brad said softly.

"Well, we are," Tess replied. "It's a war against our bodies. A war against time."

"A war against God?" he questioned.

Tess was taken aback by his words. "Why would you say that?"

"Because only God can create a life and obviously He hasn't created one through you and me. Are we warring against Him as well?"

"You know we aren't." She knew she didn't sound very convincing.

"Sweetheart," Brad said, reaching out to touch Tess's arm, "I want to do whatever is right. I want you to be happy. But I can't lie to you. I want children. Our own, somebody else's—it doesn't matter. We're quickly reaching middle age. Most of our friends are battling teenagers and what colleges to choose. I don't want to wait until it's too late."

Tess wiped the corner of her eye. She wasn't going to break down. "Neither do I."

Tess knew Kim was trying to make herself invisible as she excused herself and headed to the bathroom. Tess felt bad for instigating such a negative conversation about adoption. Here Kim was due any day to receive the baby she'd so long dreamed of, and Tess was spoiling it.

"I'm sorry," she said, looking long into Brad's eyes. "I really will think about it, okay?"

"Pray about it, too."

Tess nodded but secretly wondered if she could trust God with such a big matter. After all, she'd prayed so many times before and He'd never chosen to answer her. Well, maybe He had answered, but it had always been no.

"Look, I've got to get to work," Brad said. He quickly gulped down the coffee. "I shouldn't be too late tonight. Will you be here all day?"

"I think so," Tess replied. "I have some packages to put together and I have all the materials I need. You can always reach me on the cell phone if I'm gone."

"Will do." He kissed her again, this time on the top of the head. "See you later, Kim," he called as he headed for the door.

Kim had just returned to the kitchen. "Bye, Brad." She eyed Tess cautiously. "I didn't want you to feel ganged up on."

"It's all right. I love you both enough to tolerate your harassment," she joked, then buttered a piece of toast and tried to think of how to apologize to Kim. "Look, I want to say something. It's important that you hear me out."

Kim nodded and sat down. "All right."

"It has not been my intention to take away from your happiness in this adoption. I know you are doing the right thing for you, and I know you will be deliriously happy and you will be a wonderful mother. I've never meant to imply otherwise."

"I know that," Kim said.

"I can even admit that I'm being rather foolish in all of this. I'm working on it, however," Tess admitted. She caught Kim's sympathetic smile and knew her friend understood. Kim's nature was so gentle. It matched her soft features and unpretentious heart. For a woman so strikingly beautiful, Kim hardly seemed to consider her looks important at all.

Tess drew a deep breath. "It's just that it's so hard. People think that because I was adopted, I should automatically believe adoption to be the perfect solution for my problem." She fell silent for a moment and quietly chewed on the toast.

Finally she continued. "I had good parents from my adoption. They were a far cry from the life I'd known. They offered me safety and security and that was something I couldn't remember ever having. I slept under the bed instead of on top of it for the first two months, but finally I accepted that nothing bad was going to happen to me." Tess smiled. "They were good parents—the best. I know adoption was my salvation. I would probably be dead now, just like my biological mother, if the social services hadn't taken me out. She cared for no one but herself, doping up so much of the time, she didn't know what she was doing. She used to send me out to pick up the stuff for her. Talk about scared. I wasn't half as afraid of the drug dealers as I was of her—of what she'd do to me if I didn't get back with her stuff."

Kim only listened and picked at the bagel. Tess knew Kim had never known too many of the details about Tess's background. She was probably mortified—as were most people when they heard of the horrors Tess had endured.

"Anyway, I'm telling you this because I completely support adoption. The young mother who is giving birth to your child made the right decision. She could have had an abortion—so many do. I'm glad she chose you instead. I want you to be happy with your decision, and believe me, I'll be happy with you. This is a time to rejoice and I intend to be there with you every step of the way."

Kim grinned. "Auntie Tess, huh?"

"You bet," Tess replied, though her heart was no lighter than when she'd started the conversation. Why couldn't she be free of her demons? Why couldn't she just forget the sorrow of her past in the love of the present?

Just then Kim's pager went off. She looked wide-eyed at Tess. "Oh, this could be it!" She hurried to the telephone. "I hope you don't mind."

"By all means."

Tess knew she was waiting to be paged to come to the hospital for the baby's delivery. In this day and age of very complicated adoptions, the birth mother had chosen adoptive parents who allowed her a time of bonding. Kim and Travis were supposed to be in attendance for the baby's delivery, and Kim could hardly wait.

"Yes. Yes, I'm on my way," Kim spoke into the telephone and then slammed the receiver on the cradle. "It's time! She's in labor and waiting for us at Mt. Sinai."

Tess couldn't help but laugh. "You'd think you were the one about to deliver."

"I feel like I am. I even think my stomach hurts," Kim said, grabbing her purse.

"Godspeed, then," Tess replied, getting to her feet. She hugged Kim, then hurried with her to the door. "Let me know if it's a boy or a girl."

"Oh, you know I will. We'll have the biggest party this town has ever known!"

After Kim had gone, the house seemed unnaturally quiet. Tess walked out onto the balcony and surveyed the blue-gray Atlantic. She loved Miami. Loved the smell of the ocean, the feel of the sun. She loved the palm and mangrove trees and the fresh fruit. She was happy here, at least reasonably so.

"Why can't I work through this one?" she questioned aloud. "I want to trust you, God, but it's so hard." She looked up to pale blue skies. Cobweb clouds touched the scene from place to place. "I know I haven't been much more than a pew warmer at times. I know I have a long way to go in understanding spiritual matters. But I'm trying. I'm trying to understand and I'm trying to trust that you know more about this than I do.

"I don't want to be bitter, but I know I'm hurting in a way that only encourages bitterness. I don't want to be that harsh, angry woman who has everyone's pity but no one's love."

She turned and walked back into the living room. The

browns and beiges were complemented with cream and gold accents, but the room seemed very drab—almost cold. Her sister, Elaine, had chided Tess on one of her visits that this was no place to raise a child. The Lalique crystal would never hold up to an inquisitive toddler, she had insisted. But even that wasn't as bad as what followed. Tess could hear the conversation as if it were yesterday.

"Maybe you're not suited for motherhood," Elaine had said. *"It is a big commitment, and with your business and entertaining, a child might not fit in."*

Tess had been livid. It was one of the only times she had gotten ugly with Elaine. She had actually screamed at her sister for those painful words.

"How insensitive can you be?" Tess remembered saying. *"You have three children. Your own children. You live the way you want to, and I'll live the way I want to, but don't ever think you can come into my house and tell me I'm not cut out for motherhood."*

That had been just the tip of the iceberg. After that, no matter how much Elaine tried to apologize or explain her words, Tess had simply gotten more and more angry. Finally she had asked Elaine to leave—to go back to Phoenix and her perfect life and her kids. Brad had tried to help them patch up the argument, then finally agreed to drive Elaine to the airport. The sisters hardly spoke again until nearly two years had passed. Even now, there was a sort of tender treaty between them.

"Elaine is right," Tess said, looking around the room. "This is a showplace, not a home. We do business here, we entertain here, but we don't really live here."

The thought saddened her.

Chapter
5

"Well, you beat me again," Brad said, wiping sweat from his face.

"Racquetball is not for the faint of heart," Justin countered, his breath coming in heavy pants. "Nor for those whose minds are otherwise preoccupied. Wanna tell me about it?"

Brad gathered his things and went over to the bench. "It's just this adoption thing. Tess isn't herself. It's been almost a week since we mentioned the idea to her, and she's grown more despondent by the day. I think she knows it would be a good solution, but she's terrified to admit it."

"Well, parenting is a big responsibility," Justin said, packing his racket away. "Maybe it's just kind of overwhelming her."

"Not Tess. It wouldn't be the tasks or the responsibilities that would overwhelm her."

Justin sat down beside him. "Look, I think you've both been so focused on this one issue, that there's been little time for anything else."

"I know that's true. Between the doctors and the fertility shots and charting temperatures and making love when all the elements are just so . . . well, frankly, the romance has gone out of our marriage. I love Tess. I love her dearly. And I want children. But if I could only have one or the other, I'd take Tess, hands down."

"Does she know that?" asked Justin.

"I'd like to think so," Brad replied, twisting his towel. "I suppose I should be more vocal about it."

"Sounds like you could both use a vacation—just the two of you."

"I can't argue with that. It's been a while since we did anything just for the fun of it. Tess has to travel from time to time with the business, and the same goes for me, but we haven't gone anywhere together for at least four years."

Justin smiled. "It might just do the trick. You know, get Tess out of her normal environment and maybe the world will look completely different to her."

Brad ran a hand through his sweat-soaked hair. "I just want her happy. She means the world to me."

Justin nodded and sounded rather sad. "I know."

Brad suddenly thought of Justin's loss and felt guilty for having gone on about his problems. "I'm sorry, man. I wasn't thinking."

Justin's expression grew thoughtful. "I miss Cindy so much. Some days I almost forget she's gone. I'll pick up the phone to suggest we go out to dinner or to tell her about a case I've just finished, and then I realize the truth."

"I don't think I could bear it if something happened to Tess. How do you get through something like this?"

"My faith is all that's sustained me," Justin admitted. He looked at Brad for a moment, then stared up at the ceiling. "I know that God is in control. I know He has a plan—even if I can't figure out what that plan is."

"I believe He's in control," Brad began. "I just don't know that I could be so strong in my faith."

"Faith has to be grown. It doesn't just blossom overnight. Life gives you all sorts of ups and downs, and usually those issues are small enough that your faith gets tested and stretched and hopefully produces even more faith. But the big things, things like losing your wife or . . ." He paused and looked back to Brad. "Being unable to have a baby when you want one so desperately, those are things that sometimes challenge your beliefs to the very limit of your ability."

"What then?"

Justin smiled. "That's where you rest in God. That's where you let Him take the full burden, because believe me, buddy, there's no way you can shoulder that load on your own."

Brad's brow furrowed. "Isn't that like giving up? I mean, you're essentially saying, 'I can't deal with this. I don't have the ability to see this through.' "

"And what's wrong with that?" Justin asked quite seriously.

"I don't know. I guess it just sounds like copping out."

"Quite the contrary. Having faith requires us to have action behind it. That much we can all agree with. Sometimes that action comes in taking things in hand and doing for ourselves. But sometimes the action is simply to take it to Him. Because, Brad, there are some things that only God can see you through."

"I know you're right. I just feel so ill equipped. I mean, I do all the basics—I go to church and try to read the Bible regularly and pray, but I guess I'm starting to feel the need for something more."

"So why don't you join us at church for the men's Bible study on Thursday nights?"

Brad shrugged. "I've never really thought much about getting into a regular study. My job keeps me working late sometimes."

"So come in late or miss a week and come the next. We're pretty laid back."

"Do you really think it would help?"

Justin got up and slung his gym bag over his shoulder. "I know it helps. It's gotten me through the last four months."

"Then it must work," Brad replied, gathering up the rest of his things. "Seeing you is all the convincing I need."

"No, don't look to me, Brad. I'll disappoint you. Look to Jesus. Fix your sight on Him and don't take it off. The road to either side might hail you with all sorts of promises and charms or terrify and threaten you with all sorts of horrors. Jesus is the only one who can get you through this."

Brad considered Justin's sorrowful past and held this statement as a testimony of the highest order. "I always like to quote the verse about how all things are possible with God, but I don't think I really believed that until just now. Funny how you can know of the Bible and God and yet not really understand at all."

"Then ask Him to help you understand. There is a light at the end of this tunnel, and as corny as it might sound . . . that light is Jesus Christ."

"It doesn't sound corny at all," Brad said, feeling at peace. "It sounds very right."

"Oh, Kim, she's beautiful," Tess said, gazing at the week-old infant.

"She is, isn't she?" Kim replied excitedly.

The tiny newborn yawned and blinked dark blue eyes up at Tess and her new mother.

"We finally decided to call her Laney Rose. Rose is her

birth mother's name, and the girl is positively darling."

"How old is she?" Tess asked curiously.

"She's almost eighteen. She's anxious to finish high school. She's going to graduate in two months."

"How did she ever keep up with her studies during the pregnancy?"

"They have some special classes set up. She's done really well. She wants to go to college next fall."

Tess watched as Kim carefully lifted Laney into her arms. "I'm just so new at this and I always worry that I'll do something wrong."

"I would imagine all new parents feel that way," Tess replied. She knew that if it were her, she'd be just as worried.

"Do you want to hold her?"

Tess smiled. "Absolutely. That's why I'm here. I have to spoil her for you."

"Well, you've certainly gotten a good start," Kim said, bringing Laney to Tess. "I can't believe all those clothes you bought her. I've got so much stuff I could change her five times a day into a different outfit and still have plenty of clothes left over."

Tess held out her arms and took the baby. A current ran through her as Laney settled against her breast. *Oh, God, help me not to fall apart,* Tess prayed.

"She's just perfect," Tess whispered, tears misting her vision. Raising Laney up, Tess bowed her head to kiss the baby's forehead.

Soft. So very soft. Tess marveled at the feel and the smell—a sort of baby sweetness that wafted up to meet her senses. Running her index finger along Laney's cheek, Tess was surprised when Laney turned her face to suck on her finger. The action caused Tess's emotions to crescendo. Forcing

53

down the lump in her throat, Tess bit her lower lip to keep from crying.

"We're going to have her picture taken on Saturday," Kim said as she buzzed around the nursery. "What do you think of this outfit?" She held up a lacy miniature dress of pink dotted Swiss.

Tess nodded, not trusting herself to speak. She gazed into Laney's face and felt an iron band wrap itself around her chest. The tightness threatened to cut off Tess's air. The desperation of ten barren years rose up to haunt her in a fit of jealousy. *Why can't you be my child? Why should some seventeen-year-old be able to give birth, but I can't?*

"Tess?"

Tess looked up to find Kim staring at her rather quizzically. "What did you say?"

Kim grinned. "I was asking you about the dress for Laney's pictures. Travis and I figured we'd have some taken of Laney alone and then have a family picture taken. Won't that be wonderful? Afterward, we're going to my mother's and the family is getting together for a party. I'm just so happy I can hardly stand it."

Her animated voice and beaming smile were Tess's undoing. *I have to get out of here. I have to leave . . . now!* Tess gently placed Laney back into the crib. As she straightened back up, her arms ached at the sudden emptiness.

"I'm sorry. I just remembered an appointment I have. I'm going to have to leave."

"But you just got here," Kim said, disappointment in her voice.

"I know. I'll come back. I promise," Tess said, heading out of the room and down the hall. She knew her self-control would only hold out another minute—maybe two, but certainly no more. She had to leave before she said something she would regret.

"Well, you know you're always welcome," Kim said. She caught up with Tess at the door. "Now, don't forget about the baby shower that the girls from work are giving me. That's Thursday night at seven. You don't have to bring another gift, but I want you there for the fun."

Tess nodded. "I should be there. I haven't talked to Brad yet, so I'll have to let you know for sure tomorrow."

She didn't even wait to hear Kim's reply. Instead, Tess hurried from the small but stylish two-bedroom house and nearly ran to her car. She turned as she opened the door and gave Kim a wave. "I'll call you," she promised.

She ignored the stunned look on her friend's face and started the car. *I should never have come. I knew this was going to be hard. I just had no idea how bad it would be.*

She threw the car into Reverse and backed out of Kim's driveway. Jealousy overwhelmed her as she pulled onto the street. "It's not fair!" she declared. "I can't take it anymore. It's just not fair, God."

She could barely see the street for her tears. Grateful that Kim lived in a quiet neighborhood, Tess took a shortcut that led her to a small park. She pulled the car to the side of the street and let her tears fall in earnest.

"What are you trying to teach me, God? What is it that I've missed that keeps you so distant?"

She remembered a sermon several weeks earlier on the patriarch Jacob. Jacob and Rachel had been unable to have a child, but Jacob had no trouble producing heirs with his other wife, Leah, Rachel's sister. It was bad enough that Rachel was barren, but that her own sister should be able to give their husband so many offspring was more than Rachel could bear.

Tess remembered reading the verses in Genesis where Rachel cried out in her jealousy and told God to give her children or else she would die.

"That's how I feel, God. I can see myself coming to you in my jealous spirit, pleading to give me a child or I will die. I just know I'll die. I can't bear this emptiness anymore, Father. I just can't."

Tess thought of all the times she'd lingered in the baby department of certain stores. She thought of the cradles and bassinets and sweet little lamps with laughing moons and dancing stars. Even now she could see the people in the park. One couple swung a toddler between them. The little boy laughed in pure rapture and the joy on his face only made Tess feel worse.

Bowing her head, she hugged her empty arms to her chest. "It hurts so much, God. I hate myself for feeling jealous of Kim. I know I have the same opportunity. I could adopt. I could give up my selfish agenda and . . ." Her words trailed off. Was that the answer? Was God merely waiting until she was ready to purge herself of having to have her own way?

Tess sniffed back tears and searched through her purse for a tissue. If that was what it took, then she was ready to give it a try. The pain of trying to orchestrate things her way wasn't worth it. It wasn't working, for one thing, but beyond that, she felt as though she'd alienated the only other person in the world who really loved her: Brad.

"All right, God, I give up. I yield. If this is the only way to have a baby, then let me stop wasting time and give Brad the answer he wants to hear."

She had thought a sense of peace would fill her heart, but nothing felt any different. Had God heard her? Or was it too late?

Surely it wasn't too late.

Chapter

6

The file on the judge's desk read *Sherry Macomber*. Glancing up, Judge Barbara K. Woodsby eyed the slender teenager over the rim of her reading glasses.

"I'm not happy to see you here, Sherry," she began. The indifference on the face of the teenager made it difficult to proceed. How many times had it been? Sherry was in and out of the court so often it was joked that she should have her own office. But this was no joke to Barbara.

"Sherry, what did I say to you the last time?" Barbara questioned, pulling her glasses off to hang from a chain around her neck.

The girl toyed with her long blond hair, twisting it around her finger as she rolled her eyes toward the ceiling. "I don't know. I don't remember."

Barbara knew better. Why was this child so much more difficult than the rest?

"I warned you that the foster-care system had reached its limits with you. No one wants you in their home, Sherry."

The teen shrugged. "Their loss."

After years of working with foster children, particularly the older kids, Barbara found herself better able to interpret them than most of her peers. She saw the fleeting look of pain in Sherry's eyes. But she also knew the teen would readily deny having any feelings on the matter whatsoever. Unless, of course, that feeling was anger.

Barbara continued to study the child. At fourteen, Sherry was already wearing too much makeup and dressing too immodestly. She had no idea how Sherry got the makeup or the clothes. She'd probably shoplifted them, as Barbara had already talked to the current foster parents about finding a lot of other things that didn't belong to Sherry.

Barbara could have wept for the girl. She was pretty and her school grades proved she was smart. In fact, the psychologist who did the most current case study on Sherry said she was exceptionally bright. So why couldn't the girl see that she was ruining her life?

With a sigh, Barbara put her glasses back on and opened the folder.

"You have been in foster care roughly since birth," she announced as if Sherry had somehow forgotten. "You've been listed as abusive to your foster parents. I have notes here showing everything from theft to vandalism to verbal tirades and physical fighting."

"Yeah," Sherry replied. "So what?"

Barbara ignored her question. "You have been taken from one home to another, always at the request of the foster parents." She looked at Sherry and for a moment locked glances with the girl. "I want to know why," Barbara continued, "when you finally had a decent place to stay, a place, by your own admission, that was acceptable to you, did you go and pull a stunt like this?"

Sherry looked away. "Why are you blaming me? Joey had just as much to do with this as I did."

Barbara looked again at the latest complaint against

Sherry. It seemed that the Delberto family had come home to find Sherry in bed with their fifteen-year-old son. Upon investigation, the parents learned that their son and Sherry had been an item for some time. It was the final straw as far as they were concerned.

"Sherry, I realize that Joey Delberto had equal responsibility in this situation. You're both just kids and you're bound to make stupid mistakes, but in this case, you've just lost yourself another home."

"So what else is new?" Sherry looked down at her hands and picked at her chipped nail polish.

"Sherry, I have the results of your lab work. Your drug testing proved clear, but your pregnancy test came back positive. You're pregnant."

The girl looked up at this announcement. Barbara read the fear in her eyes and for a moment Sherry appeared to forget her façade.

"No way," she said, shaking her head in disbelief. "No way."

"I'm afraid so," Barbara said, leaning back. "I can see this comes as a surprise to you." She watched the teenager try to collect herself, but apparently this news was more than she could cope with. "I've asked the Delbertos to come here today. I've asked them to bring Joey. You're going to have to decide what you want to do about this, and because Joey is the father—"

"I'm not pregnant!" Sherry screamed, jumping to her feet. "I'm not! You can lie to me about everything else, but I'm not going to buy this one."

"Sherry, I wish I were lying about this. I had the tests run through twice, however, and the results are the same."

The girl raised her tight midriff top to show even more of

her stomach. "Do I look pregnant?"

"Sherry, surely you know enough to know that it takes months for a baby to grow and change your physical shape. You've probably already suspected you were pregnant, but you just didn't want to admit it to yourself. My dilemma is first to figure out what you want to do about this pregnancy. Next, I have to figure out what to do with you."

"I just want to be left alone," Sherry said, flopping back down in the chair. "I don't understand why you all don't just leave me alone. I can take care of myself. Why don't you just let me sign some papers and I'll be out of here."

"It doesn't work that way, Sherry, and you know it."

The girl said nothing more. She chewed on her nails instead and stared out the window.

"I'm going to ask the Delbertos to come in now. They have no idea why I've asked them here, but I will expect you to be civil."

Still Sherry said nothing.

Barbara picked up her phone and dialed her secretary. "Yes, send the Delbertos in." She replaced the phone and within seconds the door opened.

First came Mrs. Delberto, a petite redheaded woman with a haggard expression. Her eyes looked swollen and red as though she'd been spending a good deal of time crying. Judges in the juvenile court system saw a lot of red-eyed mothers.

Next came Mr. Delberto, a short, stout man with a clean-shaven face and balding head. Behind him came the lanky-framed Joey.

"Thank you for coming," Barbara said. "Please take a seat and we can get down to business."

"What's she doing here?" Mrs. Delberto questioned,

throwing a look of disdain at Sherry.

"She's here because I've asked her here," Barbara replied. "If you'll take a seat, I'll explain."

"We're not taking her back, if that's what you have in mind."

"I have no such plan in mind. Please just take a seat and we'll discuss the matter at hand," Barbara instructed.

The trio sat down almost in unison, and Barbara gave them a moment to settle into the leather seats before continuing. "I've been given this case and it is my desire to help all of the parties involved to reach the most amicable and beneficial solution."

"The solution was to get that little hussy out of my house," Mrs. Delberto ranted. "I have other children, you know. Young, impressionable children—three of them are foster children. I've been caring for foster kids for most of our marriage, but this piece of work . . ." She pointed at Sherry. "She takes the cake."

"Be that as it may," Barbara replied, "we now have another issue at hand."

Before Barbara continued, she looked over at Sherry, recognizing that she was pulling deep within herself mentally. She saw the distant look, the blank, expressionless eyes. This was Sherry's trademark way of dealing with pain and problems.

"I'm afraid that after having Sherry undergo routine drug testing and other lab analysis, the results reveal that she's pregnant."

Joey slid down in his seat and stuffed his hands in his pockets while Mr. and Mrs. Delberto looked at each other in astonishment.

"That doesn't mean the baby is Joey's," Mrs. Delberto

snapped. "Obviously the girl has no morals. She could have been running around with half the school for all we know."

Barbara fixed her gaze on Sherry. "Sherry, were you with anyone else? Is it possible this baby belongs to someone other than Joey Delberto?"

Sherry said nothing, her shoulders hunched forward ever so slightly, almost as if Barbara's words were blows.

"Sherry, I want you to answer me on this," Barbara pressed.

Sherry shook her head. "If I really am pregnant, then it's Joey's. I wasn't with anyone else."

"What does she mean, if she really is pregnant?" Mr. Delberto finally spoke.

"I just broke the news to Sherry," Barbara admitted. "She hasn't taken the news much better than you have. It's just as much a shock to her as it is to you."

"I don't believe any of this," Mrs. Delberto declared.

"We can have DNA testing done," Barbara countered.

"The kid is mine," Joey said in a grave tone that sent all eyes, including Sherry's, to the fifteen-year-old's ashen face.

"You don't know that, son," Mr. Delberto declared. "You know, we should probably talk to a lawyer. Those two are probably in this together and it's some mixed-up way to milk us for money so the state doesn't have to pay child support for the baby."

"I'm not having this baby," Sherry said angrily. She got to her feet and faced the Delbertos. "Since everyone is so certain I'm pregnant, I'll take care of the matter myself." She turned to Barbara. "I want an abortion. It's my constitutional right. We learned that much in sex-ed class."

Barbara looked past Sherry to the very uncomfortable family. Finally she settled her gaze on Joey. "What about you?

Do you agree to sign away any rights to this child and allow Sherry to have an abortion?"

"He'll sign whatever we tell him to," Mr. Delberto answered for his son. "He's just a child."

"A child who has fathered a child," Barbara reminded them. "He has certain rights as well."

Joey looked almost apologetically to Sherry before looking back at the floor. "I'll sign whatever I have to to get this over with."

Barbara realized that even if the kid had had any other thought on the matter, his parents would have rapidly seen to a change of mind.

"There's always a possibility that Sherry will change her mind," Barbara added. "Would you also agree to waive your rights in case Sherry desires to put the baby up for adoption?"

"Surely she wouldn't actually consider such a thing," Mrs. Delberto replied.

Barbara cringed inwardly, wishing with all her heart the woman had remained silent. The one thing Sherry couldn't stand was any adult implying what she should or shouldn't consider doing.

"This is completely up to Sherry," Barbara replied, desiring nothing more than to put an end to the discussion. She hoped that by saying this, Sherry would still feel as if she had some control and say over the events that were to take place.

"Well, I don't care what you say," Mrs. Delberto said, getting to her feet. "I want this thing settled. My son isn't going to be responsible for anything connected with her. She's trash and that's all she'll ever be."

"Are you sure about this?" Brad asked Tess in an animated voice.

Tess felt a wave of pleasure at his joy. His eyes were alight with anticipation and hope. She hadn't seen him look like this in months—years, really.

"Yes. I've prayed about it and thought it through. You go ahead and tell Justin that we'd like to adopt a baby from one of those unwed teenagers."

Brad came from around the breakfast table to pull Tess into his arms. "I'm so happy you've decided to do this."

"*We've* decided," Tess corrected him. "It was your idea, after all. I would never have thought of it if you hadn't been so supportive of it."

"You won't regret it," Brad said, kissing her passionately.

Tess wrapped her arms around Brad's neck and returned the kiss. She prayed she wouldn't regret it, but deep in her heart she still held nagging doubts. Maybe it would be all right. Like her doctor had told her, often people adopted and when they stopped trying so hard to have a baby, voilà—they were pregnant. But then, Tess had read extensively on the subject of infertility and knew full well that many couples never conceived—even after adopting.

Brad pulled away abruptly. "I have to call Justin. Better yet, I'll go by his office." He twirled Tess around and danced a few steps with her in the kitchen. "We're going to be parents!"

Tess laughed at his antics, but inside her heart ached. How she wished her news could have been that the doctors were wrong—that she was pregnant. If only his excitement were due to her having conceived.

I want to be happy about this, Lord. I know you can give me a peace about this. I know you can show me how to let go of my own desires and seek yours instead.

Hours later, with Brad gone, Tess made her way across town to pick up some floor plans and color photos for the Johnsons. She thought of Laura Johnson and knew she would be pleased to have her parents' old friends nearby. Laura was the motherly sort and Tess knew she could easily be the grandmotherly sort as well. Maybe once Tess and Brad adopted, Laura would be a good source of advice on raising children. With Brad's mother passed on and Elaine living so far away, Tess took comfort in the idea that Laura Johnson might well become a mentor.

The real estate office was in a small strip mall not far from Tess's home. Familiar with the shops there, Tess was rather surprised to see that one of her favorite knickknack shops had been replaced with a store boasting every possible type and style of bedding.

She didn't really give it much thought until after she'd picked up the package for the Johnsons. Then she saw the sign again and the storefront window seemed to beckon to her. Tossing the package in the car, Tess made her way back to the store. She walked inside and was immediately overwhelmed by the sweet mulberry scent.

"Good morning," an older saleswoman announced. "May I help you?"

"I just came in to look around. I didn't realize this store had changed."

The woman smiled. "We've only been open for a few days. Feel free to look around. We carry the finest linens and bedding. If you see something you like, just ask for help."

Tess nodded. "Thank you."

Tess spent several minutes studying the layout of the store. To the far right the entire wall was a shelf of various comforters and to the left were wall displays showing various bedding combinations. Then something in the very back caught Tess's eye.

The display was done in such a fashion that without even questioning it, Tess knew the area held designs for children and infants. Maneuvering past rows of printed sheets, Tess made her way to a section that read *For Baby's Comfort.* Tess found herself inexplicably drawn to the rows of hand knitting and muted pastels.

And then she saw it. A white hand-crocheted baby afghan, so lacy and fine that she couldn't help but pick it up. The softness amazed Tess. She could only imagine cradling a newborn in the creation.

"Are you expecting?" the saleswoman questioned.

Tess glanced up. She shook her head, then remembered her agreement. "Well, in a way. My husband and I are going to adopt."

"How wonderful. Have you begun plans for the nursery?"

Tess shook her head. "No, I don't suppose we've even thought of that."

"Well, I have some books here that might help. You see, once you pick a theme, it's much easier to decide on the things you'll need."

Tess refused to put down the blanket. "I like this," she said. "I don't suppose that's exactly a theme, but that's a start for me."

The woman nodded. "It's a lovely piece. Would you like to purchase it today?"

Tess had planned to return the afghan after studying it a bit longer, but the idea of leaving it behind was unthinkable. In some ways it represented her willingness to move forward instead of letting herself go on being wrapped up in the past.

"Yes," Tess declared. "I want to buy it now."

When she got back out to the car, Tess opened the box. The saleswoman had carefully sandwiched the blanket between two pieces of white tissue paper. Once again, Tess touched the baby softness, but this time she drew the afghan to her cheek. A surge of energy burst to life inside of her.

"This blanket is for my baby," Tess whispered. The idea seemed too impossible to believe. "We're really going to do this."

The excitement of the idea finally took root in her heart and began to grow. With a look of wonder, Tess replaced the blanket and sat in silence for several moments. "We're going to adopt a baby."

Tess giggled. "I'm going to be a mom."

She thought of Laney and Kim and how happy they were. Kim and Travis had planned so long for Laney's arrival. Tess easily remembered being dragged from one store to another, looking for things for the nursery.

"We've got so much to do," she declared to herself. There was the nursery and furnishings. Then she would have to baby-proof the house.

"What about names?" she declared, even as she realized it was rather premature. "We'll have to figure out a name for a boy and a girl."

The excitement of motherhood took over the final visages of apprehension in Tess's heart. Surely this was the peace and happiness she'd originally waited for.

She started the car and headed for home, but just as she started to turn, Tess remembered a wonderful little baby shop that Kim had taken her to. It was no more than another mile, maybe two, up the road.

Laughing to herself for being so silly, Tess headed to the store. "I'm going shopping for my baby," she said with little-girl delight. "I'm really going to do this!"

Chapter 7

For the second time in five weeks, Tess sat down to coffee and homemade cinnamon rolls in the Kansas City home of Darren and Laura Johnson.

"I have always loved your name," Laura said as she poured coffee into her husband's cup. "Tessera has such an appealing ring to it, and I always thought it fascinating that the word came from those little pieces in a mosaic. Who knew they even had a name?" Laura questioned with a grin.

"Your mother must have known you were going to be a special child," Darren said, spooning sugar into his coffee.

"I suppose it's the only thing my biological mother ever did right," Tess replied, stirring cream into her coffee. "I love the name, but on the other hand, I've certainly never had much luck finding it on any of those cute knickknacks you find at souvenir stands. Lots of Sarahs and Marys, but no Tesseras." She tapped the spoon against the cup, then placed it on the saucer.

"Well, I disagree about your mom. She had you, so she did at least two things right," Laura replied. She smiled at Tess as she tested the temperature of the coffee with the briefest sip. Completely changing the subject, Laura said, "You remind me so much of Stella."

"Why?" Tess asked curiously. Being adopted, Tess had never really thought of being compared to either of her parents.

"Your mom always liked a little coffee with her cream and I've noticed you're the same way. Half a cup of creamer and half a cup of coffee."

Tess laughed. "Guilty as charged." She sampled Laura's cinnamon rolls and gave a sigh. "I wish I could make something that tasted like this."

"I'll teach you after I move to Florida," Laura replied. "Darren can go out fishing and golfing with his friends and you and I can make cinnamon rolls."

"Speaking of golf," Darren said, eyeing his watch, "I'd better get going. We're teeing off in half an hour and you know how traffic can be at this time of day."

Laura waggled her finger at him. "You should know better than to plan a morning rush-hour game. Would it have hurt you to wait until ten or eleven?"

"Yup," Darren replied, leaning over to kiss her before he got to his feet. "Would have just about broken my heart if I couldn't have had an excuse to get tangled up on I–35 in the morning rush. I do some of my best praying in traffic jams."

"Then you ought to love Miami," Tess teased. "Especially the Palmetto from four to six-thirty."

"I'll remember that," Darren said with a grin.

"You'd better wear a jacket. It might be May," Laura told him, "but you know this weather can turn cold without warning."

"Yes, ma'am," he said, giving her a little one-fingered salute off his rather bulbous nose. "Don't let her ever tell you that I'm in charge," Darren said to Tess.

Tess couldn't help but smile. She had forgotten how much

she liked Darren and Laura Johnson. Her parents had been friends with them for practically forever, but once Tess and Elaine passed from the child stage into the teenage stage, they seldom shared events with their parents' friends.

"Well, at least with him gone," Laura said, "we can get down to business."

Tess pulled out a pencil to take notes. "Is Adam still determined to take over the house?" She fervently hoped Laura would affirm this earlier suggestion. She had no desire to have to arrange for the sale of this fashionable estate.

"Yes. We've already begun the arrangements. Our lawyer is taking care of drawing up a contract. Adam is working from his end with our banker and hopefully the entire matter can be resolved by the end of the month."

"So have you decided how soon you want to make the actual move?"

"The sooner the better. We certainly don't need to stick around for all the details up here. I'm leaving Adam a good portion of the furniture and bric-a-brac. I'm sending several pieces of furniture and art to Aaron—along with half a dozen boxes of memorabilia and more knickknacks."

Tess nodded, looking around the room. "I thought things seemed a little more barren."

"Well, I figured if we were going to get anywhere, I was going to have to take some initiative or it wouldn't get done. I swear, for a man who made a living drawing out the finer details of various architectural masterpieces, Darren would never get any of this accomplished. Sometimes I think he believes little fairies come in at night and see to these things."

Tess laughed and felt lighter in spirit than she had in months. "It's going to be so good having you close by."

Laura patted her hand. "I feel the same way. Now tell me,

what do you hear about adopting a baby?"

Tess put her pencil down and took up the coffee. "Well, generally it takes some time and doing to get an infant, especially a healthy infant, but we have a good connection with a lawyer—a Christian lawyer and good friend. Seems he has several prospects. All unwed mothers. All from good families. Most are girls who simply didn't think and found themselves in trouble. Nothing too perilous or ugly. Nothing like my background."

"Well, that's probably good," Laura said, pushing up her glasses.

Tess met the woman's steely blue eyes. "Yes, I know I carried an awful lot of emotional baggage because of what happened to me as a child. I don't know that I would ever want to deal with those kinds of traumas again."

"Not to mention there might be health problems if the baby's mother was a drug addict."

"True," Tess replied. "It's just going to take some time to work out the details. Most of these girls are in the early months of pregnancy, so there's plenty of time. Then again, some of them may yet change their minds. The last thing I want to deal with is that."

"You must be anxious."

"Of course. There are a lot of variables, but I've prayed about it and feel that this must surely be the way God is pointing us. I've been putting together a nursery, but I have no baby and have no idea when I might get one," Tess replied. "Brad is beside himself with joy. It's all he can talk about. He wants to name the baby Thomas Michael if it's a boy."

"And if it's a girl?"

"We haven't really settled on anything," Tess admitted.

"We go round and round with the baby books and nothing really seems to fit."

Laura poured herself more coffee. "It's always that way."

"So," Tess said, drawing the conversation back to business, "we need to get some of these last-minute details figured out if you still want to move as soon as possible."

"Fire away."

"Well, I need to have you contact your doctors—optical, dental, family, whatever. You'll need to give them the names and addresses of your new doctors in Miami so they can transfer your records. Since you have no pets, you won't have to worry about doing the same for them."

"Maybe once we get down to Florida we'll think about a small dog. You did say that the condo will allow for that, right?"

"Right."

"Well, we can worry about one thing at a time."

Tess handed Laura a checklist. "These are things that you need to take care of. You'll see there are suggested times for when you should have these accomplished."

Laura looked the list over. "It looks very complete. You certainly know your work."

Tess found a great deal of satisfaction in her ability to make these moves as painless as possible. She pulled out another list and with it, a map. "This is a numbered list that corresponds to the map. You'll be able to look at this and see where all the places are that we've discussed. For instance, you'll see number one is the retirement condo. You can go from that point to see where things are in approximation to where you're living."

"Wonderful!" Laura declared, reviewing the map and list. "This is going to be so helpful."

"I hope so," Tess replied. "Now, do you plan to drive down or are you going to fly and have the car shipped?"

"Oh, I think we'll drive the RV and pull the car. We love traveling and Darren hates to fly."

"Do you need me to arrange a trip agenda?"

Laura looked at her rather oddly. "You mean plan it all out for us?"

Tess nodded. "Sure. I can get you maps with the best routes. Routes that have the least roadwork and the best accommodations and services."

"You really are something, Tess."

"In this computer age, Laura, it really isn't that difficult." She smiled at the older woman and took another bite of cinnamon roll. "I'm telling you this, if you wanted to open a bakery in Miami, I'm thinking these would go over quite well."

"Your mom could make them just as good as I can."

Tess grew thoughtful. "I miss her. Dad too. You know, I've had such a phobia about adopting a baby, but it never had anything to do with them. They were good parents and I would never want anyone to think otherwise."

"So why are you afraid of adopting?" Laura questioned.

"Well, I've told you how much I wanted a baby that was my own, flesh of my flesh." Laura nodded and Tess continued. "I guess I just feel like I'm settling for second best. I can't have what I really want, so I'll take what I can get. And if that's the way it is, how do I explain that to my child? They're bound to grow up and find out how I feel."

Laura put down her cup and reached out to take hold of Tess's hand. "You aren't settling for second best. Once you realize that, the other problems will kind of fade away. You are making a choice to be a parent. You desire a child, and, Tess, let me tell you—once you've adopted and had that child with you, you won't know the difference. And if you do, you won't care. That baby will be yours because whether your blood is the same or not, your heart will be. That baby will be such an intricate part of your heart that the paper work will mean literally nothing."

"I'd like to believe that," Tess said softly. She wanted very much for Laura to be right.

"Believe it, then. I speak from experience."

"What? But I thought Adam and Aaron were your own children."

Laura laughed. "Sweetheart, they are my own children. Aaron I gave birth to and Adam we adopted."

"Do they know?"

"Of course. I wouldn't hide something like that. But I'm telling you, Tess, I don't love either one of those boys more than the other. I would die for either one. They are both mine just as surely as if they were both born from my body."

"Did you always feel this way?" Tess asked hopefully.

Laura shook her head and Tess's hopes fell. "No," Laura admitted. "There were about five minutes prior to walking into the orphanage and seeing Adam that I loved Aaron more." She grinned. "You'll see. We'll have another conversation about this in a few months and you'll know exactly what I mean."

"Sometimes I feel like no one can understand me. I'm not without a heart and I know how good adoption can be. I've benefited in every way from a good adoption." She paused for a moment, trying hard to make her feelings understood. "I guess it's just the way I've structured my thinking and planning all these years."

"But that can all be altered. Ask God to give you understanding and to direct your desires for a child, Tess. You'll see

His fingerprints all over your decisions and choices if only you'll yield your heart to Him first."

Tess clung to Laura's words, desperately wanting to believe them. She knew from her background in the church and hundreds of sermons on faith that this was the right path to take.

"Sometimes I think I'm just a baby Christian," Tess said, looking Laura in the eyes. "I feel weak and stupid and not at all the faithful follower that I want to be."

"We all suffer growing pains. You're not going to be any different than anyone else. No one's faith is born fully grown. These are testing times, Tess. Times that will either grow your faith or squelch it. Mostly, it's up to you, and it generally starts by yielding attitudes and desires that are steeped not in God, but in self."

Tess felt an immediate conviction in Laura's words. "I suppose I have a lot to consider."

It was late Friday evening when Tess finally walked back into her own apartment. The trip from Kansas City had seemed ridiculously long. Mostly because she longed to be home with Brad, but also because she was hoping to hear news of their adoption plans.

"Brad? Are you here?" she called out. She dropped her luggage at the door and continued calling to Brad as she walked through the apartment. Apparently he'd had to work overtime.

She went to the answering machine and saw the light blinking. No doubt there were multiple messages from prospective clients. Tess was enjoying—or perhaps *enduring* was a better word—a huge surge of interest in her relocation skills.

She'd signed on twenty new clients in the last month alone. Suddenly Bartolo Aznar's suggestion of additional help didn't seem so unreasonable.

Pressing the button and grabbing a pencil, Tess prepared to write down the messages.

"Tess! Tess, call me right away!" The voice belonged to Kim and the tone was rather excited. Tess smiled to herself. Maybe Laney rolled over or did some other new baby thing.

Tess waited for the next message and jotted down the name and telephone number of a prospect in Seattle. The next two messages were both Kim and each one sounded more frantic than the other. The final message truly worried Tess.

"Tess, it's Kim. I need you to call me as soon as possible. It's really urgent—something's happened. Oh, Tess, please call me."

Tess immediately picked up the phone and punched in Kim's number. The telephone rang and rang, but no one answered. The machine never even picked up, and Tess could only figure that maybe it was overloaded with messages or had broken down. She replaced the receiver with a frown. Something was obviously wrong with Kim and she hated that she hadn't been there for her friend.

Just then Tess heard the front door being opened. "Brad? Is that you?"

"Yeah, it's me."

He sounds tired, Tess thought. She walked into the foyer and helped him take off his suit coat. "I just got in myself."

He pulled her close and kissed her briefly. "I missed you," he said softly against her ear.

"I missed you, too." She lingered a moment at his side, catching the faint scent of his cologne. When Brad didn't try to kiss her again, however, Tess pulled away and saw the unmistakable look of worry. "What is it? You look upset. Has something happened?"

"I'm afraid so," Brad replied.

"Is it Justin and something about the adoption?" Tess asked fearfully. She held her breath and waited for his response.

"No." He reached out to take hold of her arm. "Why don't you come sit down with me."

"Brad, you're scaring me. What's this all about?"

He led her to the living room and motioned her to the couch. "Please sit down and I'll explain."

Tess shook her head and lowered herself hesitantly to the edge of the sofa. "So what's going on? You look as if you've lost your last friend. Oh, Brad, it isn't your dad, is it?"

"While you were gone, something happened. I didn't call because I just found out this morning. I figured you'd be on your way home and fretting all the way, and it just seemed more responsible to wait until you got back."

"What!" Tess nearly yelled in her irritation. "Don't keep going on and on."

"It's Kim and Travis."

Tess felt her stomach tighten. "I had three messages from Kim on my answering machine. She sounded horribly upset."

"She is."

"Is it Laney?" Tess questioned. *Please, God, don't let anything be wrong with the baby,* she prayed.

"Yes. It's Laney." Brad bit his lower lip and appeared to struggle for the right words. "The birth mother has changed her mind."

"What?" Tess had envisioned the baby sick or even dead, but never had this thought come to her mind.

"The birth mother has decided to take Laney back. You know there's always a length of time given the birth parents to change their minds. Well, apparently the mother acted upon that choice. She claims to have been forced into the adoption, and apparently the legal system is on her side."

"No," Tess said, shaking her head. "Laney is Kim's daughter."

"I know, sweetheart," Brad began. He took the seat next to her and reached out to take hold of her hand. "But the birth mother has rights, too. She and the birth father plan to marry and they want their child to be returned to their family."

"So just like that," Tess said, snapping her fingers for effect, "Kim and Travis have to give Laney up? They've bonded with this child for almost two months and now she's going to be ripped away from them?"

"She's already been taken. The social worker came today."

"No!" Tess said, jerking away from Brad. "This can't be right!"

"I wish I could say it wasn't, but I've talked to Justin. He says it's all perfectly legal. He says Florida adoption laws are chock-full of loopholes and problems. I didn't want to say anything because I didn't want to spoil our plans to adopt."

Then a thought of dread washed over Tess. She had agreed to set herself up for the same nightmare. "This could happen to us." She looked at Brad and instantly realized that the same thoughts had been on his mind. "You've already thought of this, haven't you?"

"Yes. I knew it would be one of the first things to come to your mind. I just don't want you worrying about it and giving up the idea of adoption because this has happened to Kim and Travis."

Tess jumped to her feet. "How could I not be worried about it? You sound like I should just wave this off as one of those things. I didn't want to consider adoption in the first place, but you told me it was our only real choice. Then seeing Kim and Laney together, and realizing how happy they were, I figured it might be okay. You were happy that I used Kim as an example to put my mind at peace. Why shouldn't this painful nightmare also serve to be an influence?"

"But what about trusting God for the outcome?" Brad questioned. "I truly felt that God put us together with Justin for a reason. Adoptions take place all the time without a single hitch. We have to trust that God has this under control."

"You mean like He had it under control for Kim and Travis?"

"Look, you're upset, and rightfully so. I don't want to argue with you about this. Kim and Travis will need us to help them through this."

"Yeah, well, who's going to help us through it?" Tess turned on her heel and headed for the foyer. "I knew this was too good to be true."

Brad followed her into the hall and interceded when Tess went to lift her own bag. "Tess, you shouldn't let yourself get all upset about our situation. Nothing has happened."

"Yet," Tess replied. "But it could. We could find ourselves in the same situation, Brad. Doesn't that worry you in the least?"

"I suppose it concerns me, but no, it doesn't worry me. I want a baby just as much as you do, but I would want it to be the right situation. Wouldn't you rather a child be with their birth mother and father if they could be?"

"No," Tess replied flatly. "Not if those parents are unfit. How can a teenager offer Laney what Kim and Travis could give that child? Those kids will probably marry and divorce within the next few years. You know the odds aren't with them. Kim and Travis are stable and solid. They have financial security and a home already established.

"And, as you well know," Tess continued, "I'm a prime example of a situation where a biological parent was not the better choice for my upbringing."

"Sweetheart—"

"Don't 'sweetheart' me!" Tess yelled. "I don't need to hear any more of this. I'm sorry you ever talked me into the idea of adoption. I want you to call Justin now and tell him we've changed our minds."

Tess ran to the sanctuary of her bedroom and slammed the door. There was no way in the world she was going to set herself up for the kind of pain Kim was enduring.

The image of Brad's pain-filled expression caused Tess to draw a deep breath. She'd shut him out again. She'd made this sorrow all about herself, her fears. When was she going to stop doing that?

But this is *about me. It's about me and my fears and my lack of faith.* She walked to the window and tried to focus on anything that would take her mind off what had just happened. *Oh, God, I'm so scared. I'm so scared for Kim and for myself and Brad. I feel so inadequate to handle this. I try to trust you, I really do. My faith is just weak. I've grown up attending church, but I've not grown up spiritually.*

Her biggest sorrow was how she'd treated Brad. She knew he wanted to adopt a child—knew that he didn't care if the baby was biologically related or not. Tess thought back to what Laura had said about her love for her boys. She said it didn't matter. Tess really wanted to believe that. She could almost persuade herself that it was true, but then the reality of Kim's situation darkened her dreams with a kind of hopelessness. And that hopelessness made her more angry with Brad than sympathetic. Adoption was Brad's idea, and it was easier to be angry with him for causing her to let down her guard than it was to trust that everything would work out.

"God, you can't leave me here," Tess whispered against the window. "You just can't leave me here. I'll never make it."

Chapter
8

For the next three days Tess barely spoke a single word to Brad. Hurting and confused, she wanted no part of his comfort or advice. In truth, she wasn't sure how to deal with her husband. She was such a contrast of emotions and thoughts. One minute she was certain Brad was right and that God would make their situation different, and in the next minute she was hopelessly mired down with a sense of discouragement that went clear to the bone.

Without the strength to fight it, a depression overcame Tess in such a manner that she found little interest in anything. Her work suffered as she allowed call after call to go unanswered. When the answering machine finally filled up, Tess simply removed the tape and turned off the machine. She didn't care what happened.

In her heart, Tess knew she was blaming Brad for her pain. He held responsibility, but only marginally behind the blame she assigned to God. Why wasn't God fixing things? Where was the peace He promised? Her anger and sorrow, combined with the guilt she felt for alienating her heavenly Father, only added to her depression.

Day after day, Tess sought solace in sleep. It was really all she wanted to do. She knew it was ridiculous to seek comfort in her dreams, however, as she spent more time in nightmar-ish memories than in peaceful slumber.

The bedside telephone rang several times before Tess could rouse herself enough to answer it. Rolling over to see what time it was, she was stunned to see that the hour was so late. It was already three o'clock in the afternoon.

"Hello?" she said, trying not to sound too groggy.

"Tess, it's Laura Johnson."

"Hi, Laura."

"You sound awful. Have you caught yourself a cold from your trip up here?"

"No," Tess answered and struggled to sit up. Yawning, she covered the mouthpiece and tried to think of what to say. "I've just been tired."

"Well, I know how that can be," Laura said with a chuckle. "Look, the reason I'm calling is because Darren thinks we can be ready to roll by the twenty-fifth of May. Can you go ahead and arrange for the movers?"

"Sure," Tess said without any enthusiasm for the discus-sion. "They'll want to come over and see what you have for them to move. Are you going to have them pack everything or just move boxes and furniture that's already been pre-pared?"

"I'd just as soon turn it over to them. Adam will be here by then and we figure he can help us condense everything into one or two rooms. The movers shouldn't find it too hard to take care of if it's all together."

"Okay." Tess rubbed her eyes. "I'll see to it."

"Tess, if you don't mind my asking," Laura began, "is something wrong?"

Tess fully intended to say no, but instead found herself suddenly telling Laura her woes. "My friend lost her baby.

The adoption went sour and the birth mother demanded the child back."

"I'm so sorry," Laura replied. "I'm sure this has caused you a great deal of trepidation."

Tess realized in that statement that Laura understood. She wasn't going to chide Tess as Brad had done, nor would Laura condemn Tess for her fears.

"I can hardly face the day, and Brad and I haven't spoken since I came home from Kansas City and he told me the news."

"How awful. He must be feeling his share of fears as well."

"I don't know about that. He thinks I'm being stupid. He doesn't understand why I refuse to go forward with our own adoption after seeing what's happened to our friends."

"You've put a stop to adopting a baby?" Laura questioned.

"I certainly don't want to go through what Kim did. She's a basket case. The doctor has had to sedate her. She won't see me or anyone else. I guess that was enough to send me to my own bed," Tess admitted. "I've been worthless since this whole thing started. I haven't answered the business phone or even bothered with clients."

"I figured there was at least a problem with the phone line," Laura told her. "I tried the business phone but it just rang and rang. That's why I called on your personal line. I hope you don't mind."

"Of course not," Tess said. "You're a friend."

"Am I, Tess? I'd really like to be."

Tess fidgeted with the telephone cord. The implication in any definition of friendship was that they would share certain aspects of their lives together. Right now, Tess didn't feel like sharing anything with anyone.

"I want your friendship, Laura. I just don't feel much like

a friend to anyone right now. I'm angry at Brad for talking me into adopting and I'm angry at myself for not having stuck to my original feelings. Then I get mad at myself for being upset with Brad, knowing that he was just trying to help us to have a child. On top of that I'm mad at God because He could have kept this from happening and didn't."

"So God's the bad guy because He allowed bad things to happen to good people, is that it?"

"Well, aren't we supposed to have some sort of guarantee when we accept salvation?" Tess asked earnestly. She'd battled with this thought for days now.

"We have a guarantee. We have Jesus and He's all the guarantee we need."

"But what about the evil in this world? Aren't we supposed to be protected from it? I remember hearing sermons that talked about God's protection from evil."

"How was this baby being returned to its mother an evil thing?" Laura asked.

"Well, maybe it wasn't evil, but it was very painful and very wrong," Tess replied. She swung her legs over the edge of the bed. "My friend Kim loved that baby more than life itself. She was happy. Her husband was happy, and I believe that baby was happy."

"Tess, we can't always know why bad things happen. Sometimes we see they happen from a clear case of disobedience to God's Word. Other times bad things happen because of poor choices and not seeking proper direction. But sometimes we just don't have answers.

"It's like one time when Adam and Aaron were little, they wanted to go on a ski trip with their youth group. I prayed about it and felt it wasn't the right thing to do. I told them no. They asked why and I had to be honest. I told them I didn't know. Darren even tried to change my mind, but I told him I felt strange about the entire matter. I don't know if you remember that incident or not, but the youth group went on the trip and several of the kids and two leaders were killed in an avalanche."

Tess nodded. "I remember."

"Darren was the first to say that I had saved the kids by acting on my feelings. He credited those feelings to God, but, Tess, in my heart I was weeping. Even though everyone who died was a Christian, I still cried at the injustice of it all. Why hadn't God simply warned everyone off of the trip? Why hadn't He interceded to save my friends' lives and the lives of their children?"

"And what conclusion did you come to?" Tess questioned, eagerly needing to know the answer.

"That God is God. He will save whom He will save, and He will take those He will take. It's not something I understand, but it's something I can live with. He has a plan for you, Tess. A good plan."

"I'd like to believe that, but given the circumstances of my entire life, I don't know how I can," Tess replied. "I was born to a junkie, enduring perils and dangers to keep my mother supplied with drugs. I suffered beatings and abuse, then left the only home I knew to go into foster care. I didn't know anyone there, I felt afraid and alone. Even though my mother was a nightmare to live with, at least I knew her—knew her patterns and her habits.

"I've lived through adoption and the fears that go along with it. I've lived through ten years of being unable to conceive a child. And even though I have a good job and loving husband, I just don't see my life as being that good."

"That's the anger and pain in you talking," Laura replied

softly. "You know very well that you are blessed. You simply don't want to admit to it right now because that would make you feel even more obvious in your temper tantrum."

Tess fell silent. How dare Laura accuse her of throwing a fit? She was hurting and her heart was nearly broken for her friend. How did that add up to be a temper tantrum?

"I know you probably didn't want to hear that," Laura continued. "I wasn't trying to hurt your feelings, but honestly, Tess, you can't always have your own way. I know you want a child and I want a child for you. But I believe God has a good plan for you. I believe He loves you no less today than He did three days ago when you were happy."

Tess felt tears come to her eyes. "But He seems so far away."

"If He does," Laura replied, "it's not because of any moving He did. If you've run away from Him in order to sulk and rage, you have only to ask for His presence and you'll find Him at your side. He loves you, Tess, and He wants the best for you."

"I do want to believe that." Tess wiped at the tears that now flowed down her cheeks.

"Then believe it. Jeremiah 29:11 says, ' "For I know the plans I have for you," declares the Lord, "plans to prosper you and not to harm you, plans to give you hope and a future." ' He wants to give you hope, Tess. But you have to be willing to take it."

"It's so hard."

"Nobody ever said it would be easy," Laura stated. "Look, I'm going to be praying in earnest for you and I want you to pray as well. I'm going to call you every day and see how you're doing."

"Why would you want to do that?" Tess asked, sniffing back her tears.

"Because we're friends, remember? You agreed to that idea and now I'm sealing the bargain. Friends stand by each other and they pray each other through the bad times and they rejoice in praise through the good."

Tess felt the older woman's love and concern wash over her damaged spirit. "All right, Laura," she finally answered. "I'll do what I can."

"That's all that's required. We do our part, and God does His. It's when we go trying to take on both roles that we get ourselves into trouble. Just remember that."

"I will," Tess agreed. "Although I'm sure to need a lot of practice in knowing the difference."

Laura chuckled. "No more or less than the rest of us, Tessera. Like your name, you are but one piece in a magnificent masterpiece. God has perfectly ordered this work—He won't forget about your part. He won't leave any space, no matter how large or small, undone."

Chapter
9

"Sherry, I have no choice but to put you into the county detention center," Judge Woodsby stated.

Sherry eyed the woman with great hostility. At three months pregnant, Sherry had been suffering from terrible bouts of nausea. The last thing she needed to hear was that she would be removed from her emergency foster home and put in detention.

Sherry shuddered. The thought of detention made her want to beg for mercy. Everyone knew that detention was where the criminal cases were put. Sherry might well be delinquent and on occasion a bit violent, but she wasn't a criminal. Not unless you counted the thirteen times she'd shoplifted or the money she'd stolen from her foster parents.

"Why can't I just stay at the place I'm at now?" Sherry questioned. She knew the temporary location was only for emergency cases, but it was a sweet deal. The woman and man were really pretty decent, although the woman fussed too much over Sherry and her pregnancy. Sherry couldn't understand why the woman should be such a pain about it when Sherry fully intended to abort the baby.

"Sherry, you know very well that the Holmes residence is an emergency site." The judge looked at her with one of those stares that was supposed to intimidate, but Sherry thought it almost amusing. Why were adults always trying to push their weight around with looks like that? Did they really think it mattered to a kid what kind of face they made?

"You'll be moved into detention this afternoon," the judge continued. "Your possessions will be taken from you and put into storage until such time when your permanent location is decided. You'll be issued a uniform and treated as the other girls are treated. You'll have no special privileges. Do you understand?"

The weight of the punishment was starting to sink in even more. Sherry tried to mask her fears, but she'd heard such hideous stories in school and elsewhere that she couldn't help being afraid.

"What about my abortion?" Sherry asked almost hesitantly. She kept thinking that maybe there was a chance she could be placed somewhere else. "Won't I have to be in the hospital?"

"We've set up an appointment for you with a local clinic. You'll go in, have the abortion, and leave in the afternoon. You'll then be taken to the detention center infirmary where you'll recover."

Defeated, Sherry sunk lower in the chair. "Why can't I just be emancipated?" She'd heard the term from one of her friends at school.

"Can you support yourself?" the judge asked seriously.

"As well as I need to," Sherry replied.

"How?"

"Well, I could work. I don't need a lot of stuff and I don't eat much. I could work just about any place and have more than enough money for everything I need."

"Sherry, you're fourteen years old. You aren't legally old

enough to work more than a few hours a week. Especially while you're attending school."

"So I'll drop out."

"That would be illegal without the court's permission and we aren't about to give it." The judge removed her reading glasses and shook her head. "Sherry, don't you care at all? Don't you see the severity of this decision?"

She did, but why should she acknowledge anything to this woman? What did it matter? She'd spent so much time being bounced from place to place that no place felt like home. Sherry honestly doubted she would ever find a place that did.

Finally Sherry spoke. "You don't have to give me your song and dance about how hard this decision was or how worried you are about my welfare. I'm just one more kid on the books to you."

The woman actually looked stunned at Sherry's words and it surprised the fourteen-year-old. Why shouldn't she accept that statement as truth? The judges in this state were overwhelmed with teenage hoodlums. Sherry couldn't imagine that anyone even gave her a second thought after the files were closed.

And for reasons that Sherry wished didn't exist, that bothered her more than anything else. No one cared. No one even knew she was alive, except for when that thick folder was brought out of the cabinet and opened for review.

"Sherry, you're wrong. I do care and you're not just one more kid on the books. Not to me. What I don't understand is how I can care, and yet you don't. You haven't got the slightest understanding of what you're up against, and yet from what you've already endured, I would think you would be doing everything in your power to change."

"Change into what?" Sherry asked without thinking.

Great, now I've done it. I've shown interest in what she's saying. Now I'll have to listen to a three-hour lecture on the legal system and all its benefits and downfalls.

"Change into a productive human being. Into a useful, loving adult who can go into society and make the world a better place."

Sherry said nothing. She didn't want to encourage a continued conversation.

Seeing that Sherry had clammed up again, the judge looked back to the file. "I've arranged for an officer to escort you to detention." She closed the file and took off her glasses. "I'm sure we'll find her waiting for us."

"For me, you mean," Sherry said rather snidely. She got up from the chair and folded her arms across her chest. "At least you'll be rid of me now."

The judge eyed her for a moment before coming around from behind her desk and crossing to the door.

Sure enough, outside in the small waiting area, a uniformed guard sat waiting for Sherry. The woman was tough looking. She looked Sherry up and down as if to decide how much trouble it would take to keep her in line. She looked Sherry straight in the eyes and scowled. Sherry immediately hated the woman and scowled back.

"This is Sherry Macomber," the judge announced. "Has my secretary given you her papers?"

"Yes, I have them," the woman assured her.

Sherry tried her best to remain indifferent, but the truth was, she was scared and growing more so by the minute. They were taking her to jail. Always before she'd been headed to someone's foster care. That care might be new and even a bit frightening, but it wasn't jail.

"Sherry, I wish you the very best. If you ever need me,"

Judge Woodsby said, "don't forget where I'm at."

I won't need you, Sherry thought to herself. *I don't need anybody.*

As a five-minute warning was called for lights out, Sherry tried to come to terms with her environment. Just as she had feared, the girls around her were hard as nails and twice as mean.

"What'd you do?" a heavyset girl with dirty blond hair questioned.

Sherry shrugged, not wanting to acknowledge the girl and yet not wanting to ignore her either.

Without warning, the girl slammed her against the end of the bunk bed. "I asked you a question. What are you in here for?"

Sherry pushed the heavier girl back, knowing the importance of asserting herself as not accepting such behavior. "It's none of your business," she retorted.

The girl looked surprised by Sherry's actions but stood her ground. "You better never do that again."

"The same goes for you," Sherry said, hands on hips.

"You gonna beat her up, Joleen?" one of the other girls asked.

"I wouldn't waste my time," Joleen replied.

Sherry breathed a momentary sigh of relief. Maybe she wouldn't have to prove herself any further. At least not tonight.

"Two minutes," a uniformed guard called from the door.

"You know where you can put your two minutes," Joleen countered before turning to walk away from Sherry.

"You'd better watch her," a slender girl about Sherry's same height said. Standing not two feet away, the girl barely whispered the words. "She'll take you out when you least expect it."

Sherry eyed the girl for moment, then nodded. "Okay."

Eyeing the bunk bed with some distaste, Sherry put her foot onto the rail and hoisted herself topside. The bed felt like a lumpy board and the blanket was itchy.

Having discarded the uniform pants and pullover shirt of navy blue, Sherry was dressed like every other girl in the place, in a simple white nightgown. They'd taken her personal effects along with her purse and its contents, but Sherry was good at concealing things and so had managed to slip a few things into her pants and bra when the guards weren't looking. Those things were carefully hidden inside her pillowcase, but tomorrow she'd have to find a better hiding place. For the time being, it would probably be best just to keep them on her person.

Quietly, so as not to draw attention to herself, Sherry pulled out a picture of Joey. She rolled onto her side and studied the photograph. She had really thought he loved her. He said he did. She sure wouldn't have slept with him if he hadn't said that he loved her.

The picture was her only link to her baby's father. The family had made it clear they wanted nothing to do with her or the child. Worse still, Joey hadn't been willing to talk to her when she'd managed to sneak in a phone call from the emergency foster home. He said they were better off going their separate ways and that he couldn't do anything more to jeopardize his future and college. Never mind that he'd gotten her pregnant and had totally ruined Sherry's chances at a decent home.

"Lights out!" The lights clicked off in rhythmic cessation.

Sherry put the picture safely back inside the pillowcase, but not before pressing it to her lips. Tears that she hadn't allowed earlier began to fall in silent, hot streams.

You said you loved me, Sherry thought sadly. *You promised we'd be together forever. You promised me a home and a life that would be just like the movies. You said we'd be happy. Oh, Joey, we could have been happy. I would have made you happy.*

Chapter
10

Sherry was relieved to find that the guard escorting her to the abortion clinic was a different, more amiable woman than the one who had brought her into detention.

Officer Riley actually smiled and made polite conversation with Sherry, even going so far as to compliment her long blond hair.

"Great," the woman said as she turned onto their destination street. "The holy rollers are here again."

"What?" Sherry asked, noting the crowd of picketers across the street.

"Oh, those are the holier-than-thou types who think they have a right to impose their views on the rest of us. They picket the abortion clinic as often as they can get a group together."

"Why should they care what I do?" Sherry questioned. She saw at least a dozen women, some with small children, standing with signs that declared abortion to be murder.

"They consider themselves to be lifesavers. You know, keep women from exercising their right to choice by telling them what to do. Just ignore them. They have to stay at least a hundred feet away from the clinic."

Sherry nodded. The scene was not something she'd expected. All she wanted to do was be rid of this horrible reminder that she'd been gullible once again. She wanted to get rid of the pregnancy and then figure out how to escape her current situation.

Officer Riley parked the car in the small clinic parking lot and motioned for Sherry to get out. She hadn't used any type of restraints on the girl, and for this Sherry was relieved. She wasn't a criminal and she didn't want to be treated like one.

"They're going to have plenty to say to you," Officer Riley announced, "so just keep your head down and keep moving to the door. For pity's sake, don't strike up a conversation or answer any of their questions."

Sherry nodded, but she couldn't help but wonder why they would be asking her any questions. She opened the door hesitantly. "They won't like . . . throw rocks or anything, will they?" Sherry couldn't help but ask.

The guard laughed. "No, don't worry about them. They'd have to get through me to hurt you."

Sherry felt only a moderate amount of relief. After all, there were at least twelve women across the street and only one officer.

Just as Riley had warned, the tirade began as soon as Sherry stepped foot from the car.

"Please don't kill your baby!"

"Let us help you. We know people who would be happy to adopt!"

"You can't be very far along," one woman called, "but do you know that at nine weeks, your baby already has fingers?"

Sherry faltered in her steps. Fingers? Somehow she had imagined nothing more than a lump of forming tissue. Something that would someday be a baby, but for now was just this mass of blood and veins and nothing more.

"Come on," Officer Riley said, giving Sherry a gentle nudge. "Don't pay any attention to them."

"You're taking the life of an innocent baby," another person called. "Think about what you're doing. A life is growing inside of you and those butchers are going to rip your child from limb to limb."

Sherry grimaced and kept her head down. Surely they were wrong. They didn't know everything. They were just regular people. Holy rollers, as her guard had put it. What did they know?

"Please listen to us. Please don't kill your baby. I'd be happy to adopt your child. Please don't kill him."

The voice tore at Sherry, but it was the next statement that got to her.

"Your mother could have killed you, but she didn't. She gave you life—now won't you please give this baby life?"

Sherry stopped in her tracks. Her mother had been killed in a drug deal gone bad. Sherry had only been a few months old when she became a ward of the state. No one knew who her father was. But she knew her baby's father. Had the circumstances been different, she might have relished this condition. Had Joey been honest about his love for her, they might have even married. So what if they were young, very young?

"What's the matter, kid?"

"I want to go back," Sherry replied. "I want to go back to the detention center. I don't feel very good."

"Oh, don't let them get to you."

"Is it true? Does my baby really have fingers?" Sherry asked, looking into Officer Riley's face. She'd know if the woman was lying by whether she'd look her in the eye.

The woman shrugged and looked away. "What if it does?

It's not like you want it. You're fourteen years old! What would you do with a baby?"

"Just take me back," Sherry told the woman again. "I need to think about this."

Cheers from the women across the street caught Sherry's attention as she moved back to the car. Officer Riley started the engine as soon as they were both belted in.

"Are you sure you don't want to just sit here and think about this for a moment?" the guard asked her seriously.

"Yeah, I'm sure," Sherry said.

They pulled out of the parking lot and Sherry could see the smiling faces of the women. One woman actually had tears streaming down her face. She blew Sherry a kiss and called out, "God loves you. He loves your baby. Seek Him."

"So why didn't you go through with it?" The question came from the same girl who'd warned Sherry about Joleen the night before. Her name was April and she was only about Sherry's height, though nearly seventeen years old.

Sherry shook her head. "I don't know. Guess I didn't feel like it."

"I couldn't figure out why you were doing it anyway," April said, sitting down beside Sherry. "You're going about this all wrong."

"Why do you say that?"

The girl smiled. "Well, I was once in your shoes. Pregnant and in juvey." She used the nickname for juvenile hall as if it were an old friend.

"What'd you do?" Sherry asked, genuinely interested.

"I sold the kid."

"Sold?"

April pushed her hair off her shoulder and leaned back lazily. "Yeah, that's right. I made a deal with the court and they found a couple who wanted to adopt my baby. I got the royal treatment for the rest of my pregnancy and even afterward. It was great. Everybody handled me with extra care. They didn't want me spoiling the adoption or getting upset or sick. I never had it so good."

"Really?"

The girl nodded. "I'm telling you the truth. Some rich folks took me in and went through the pregnancy with me. I had my own room and even my own TV. It was sweet. Then I had the baby and they even let me stay around for the first few months 'cause they wanted me to nurse her."

"You had a girl?"

April's eyes grew momentarily shadowed. "Yeah. I have a daughter somewhere. I get pictures once in a while."

"How old were you?"

"Fifteen. Jayceen is almost two years old now."

"Jayceen? That's your baby?"

"Their baby," the girl said firmly. "Look, my point is, if you want to make a better life for yourself, offer to choose a family for your child based on whether or not they'll take you in. After that, you can run away or do whatever you want."

Sherry nodded. She recalled Judge Woodsby's comment about if she ever needed anything. "Maybe I'll do that."

The telephone on Justin Dillard's nightstand rang at eleven-thirty in the evening. Putting down the book he'd been reading, he wondered who in the world was calling at that hour.

"Hello?"

"Justin? This is Barbara."

He smiled and closed the book. "So what's my older, wiser sister doing calling me at this hour? Don't you know folks generally try to sleep at night?"

Laughter erupted on the other end of the line. "You? Go to sleep before midnight? Not when we were kids and I'll bet not even now."

Justin couldn't help but grin. "Okay, so you know me pretty well, Judge. What can I do for you?"

"I have a case here," she began. "A young unwed mother whom I've recently put into detention. Not, I might add, for any criminal charges, but rather because she's pretty much exhausted the foster-care system with her antics. No one wants her."

"So how do I fit in?" Justin cradled the phone against his shoulder while he fought to push his pillows into a comfortable position for sitting against the headboard.

"She wants to arrange an adoption of her baby," Barbara replied. "She had asked for an abortion and legally I couldn't interfere, but now that she wants to adopt the child out, I want to do all that I can to help her."

"I see. How far along is she?"

"Just three months. She's only fourteen and a little bitty thing. She's had a hard life. Her mother died when she was only a few months old. Killed in a crack house when a deal went sour. She's never known any real security, and because of her attitude, she's been shuffled from home to home."

"What kind of attitude is she displaying?"

"Oh, you know, the regular hostility of being a teen, cou-

pled by the fears, sorrows, and emptiness of being aban-
doned. I think down deep inside, she's begging for someone
to love her. That's probably why she finds herself in her present condition."

"Is she an addict?"

"No, as far as I know she's experimented once or twice but
is basically clean. Her last four drug screens have come up
negative. I think she cherishes what little control she has over
her life and therefore won't jeopardize it with drugs."

"What about the father?"

"He was the son of her last foster family. The parents came
home to find the kids in bed together and that was the end of
that. They've signed a waiver to any rights regarding the child,
and since the girl originally planned to abort, there didn't
seem any reason for them to concern themselves overmuch
with her condition."

"And now?"

"I haven't talked to them. I'm sure they'll be upset, but
once I point out to them that they'll have no financial obligation to the girl or the baby, they're sure to calm down. My
question is, do you know anyone who might want to take this
on? It would require taking the girl into their home for the
duration of the pregnancy and some postnatal time as well.
The girl wants to make certain the family is a decent one and
wants to see them interact with her baby before giving the
child up completely."

Justin thought of Tess and Brad. Tess shared a common
background with the girl in question, but she was enduring a
horrific depression after seeing her best friend suffer from
just such an arranged adoption. She would probably never
want to consider an idea like this one.

"I'm not sure. I know a couple, but there's some current

complications in their lives. Let me do some checking around. I had a couple of other people who were interested in adopting. Why don't you fax me all the details. Maybe even include a photograph of the girl."

Barbara sighed loud enough that Justin could hear it over the phone. "Thanks, little brother. I appreciate your efforts. Let me know as soon as possible."

"Will do. Just be praying about it and then we'll be sure to get the right folks for this child."

"I've been praying ever since Sherry's folder turned up on my desk," Barbara admitted. "But I won't stop now."

Chapter

11

"So are you ready for the move?" Tess asked Laura as they discussed the final details over lunch. Laura had insisted on treating them to lunch on the Plaza at one of Kansas City's famous barbecue restaurants. Tess was glad she hadn't put up too much of a protest. The food was incredible.

"I'm ready for a change," Laura replied. "I've been ready for some time. It just took convincing Darren. He wanted to move, but he's always been a heel-dragger. Even in his work. He's one of those people who goes over every detail five or six times before he's comfortable with it."

"I can't blame him for being meticulous," Tess said, pushing back her plate of half-eaten blackened pork. "There are fewer surprises when you plan for all the possibilities."

"But sometimes surprises are good," Laura said. "Like today. I surprised you with lunch. It was worth it, wasn't it?"

Tess nodded enthusiastically. "Oh, definitely. But in other areas of life, I prefer no surprises."

"Bad or good?"

Tess pursed her lips and thought a moment. "Well, some good surprises are okay. But even some of those can be a terrible disruption. And I don't even want to talk about bad surprises."

"Like your friend and the baby?" Laura asked sympathetically.

Tess could read the sincerity in Laura's eyes. She truly cared about the situation. "Kim is still rather reclusive. She won't let Travis change anything in the nursery for fear the birth mother might once again change her mind and bring Laney back. It hurts so much to see her like that. I know I couldn't bear it."

"So you've given up the idea of adopting?"

Tess sighed. She'd been torn for days, battling within herself and trying to reason through her fears. She'd talked to Laura at least half a dozen times and still she couldn't bring herself to let go of the haunting images in her head.

"I just keep seeing myself in Kim's shoes. I see myself happy and bonded to a baby, finally having listened to everyone tell me how I could put my heart and soul into a child that wasn't biologically mine. I see myself watching that baby grow and change day by day. I envision making plans for her future and then having someone—someone completely outside of my control—change everything in a heartbeat."

"But that's life, Tess. It could happen even with your own child. Children get sick. Babies die. It happens. You can't truly live life in a bubble, never feeling or chancing anything."

"I know that's true," Tess admitted. "It just seems that because there are so many unpredictable variables, we ought to at least control the ones we can."

"Better yet, throw it all in the pot together and trust God for the outcome, as my mother used to say. Of course, she was originally talking about stew," Laura said with a smile and a wink, "but I think the application works here as well."

"You remind me so much of Mom," Tess replied. "That sounds just like something she might have said."

"Stella was a wise woman. So was my mother."

"So are you. Oh, Laura, I wish I could be more like you and Mom. I envy your confidence." Tess placed the terry cloth napkin on the table and shook her head. "But I have this void inside me, this great emptiness. I know it stems from childhood. I know the moment it hit me. I remember it like yesterday.

"My mother was stoned out of her mind and she caught the kitchen curtains on fire. The house filled up with smoke almost instantly. I can still taste it, smell it. It was so bitter and acrid. I remember grabbing my mother's hand and pulling her to the front door. She just stood there watching the fire. I'm sure in her drugged state she was fascinated by the flames." Tess took a long drink of tea and found herself transported in time as she continued to share the tale.

"The fire department came pretty quick. I imagine one of the neighbors saw the smoke and called it in. My mother kept screaming at everybody to leave her alone. To leave the fire and let it burn. The police came and saw that she was in no shape to deal with the fire or with me."

"You must have been terrified," Laura said softly.

"I was. You have to remember, I'd been taught from early on that the police were the enemy. They were the monsters in my closet and they were the people I most dreaded."

"But why, Tess?"

"My mother always told me that they would try to take me away if they found me. She made it sound like I was some sort of secret child who had been placed with her as a part of some bigger game. She warned me never to talk to cops and if I saw one, to walk away in the opposite direction. Never run—just walk. So when the police showed up and started hassling my mom, I was beside myself. I cried and screamed at them to leave her alone. I wrapped my arms around my mother's waist and when one of the officers tried to pry me loose, I bit him.''

"Oh my,'' Laura said, shaking her head. "Stella never told me any of this.''

"She never knew. I've never shared it with anyone but Brad,'' Tess admitted. "It was a scene, that's for sure. My mother got violent with the police. She screamed at them and when one finally managed to get me away from her, she attacked him with her fists.''

"So she must have loved you a little,'' Laura offered.

Tess shook her head. "She thought I was somebody else. She kept telling them to leave Sammy alone. I don't know who Sammy was. I don't know if that was the name of my real father or someone else she cared about, but it wasn't my name she called.

"I remembered crying for her over and over, pleading with them not to take me away. I promised to be good. I promised not to cry, but nobody was listening.''

"Oh, Tess. I'm so sorry for your pain. What a nightmare.''

"But at least Mom and Dad came to my rescue,'' Tess said, finally pushing back the memories. "In the long run they were a much better alternative.''

"But your emptiness was never filled?''

"I tried to fill it with them—with their love. I've tried to fill it with Brad and his love. But I think it has more to do with belonging to someone. That's why I need a baby of my own.''

"No, Tess, that's why you need a relationship with God,'' Laura corrected. "Your emptiness isn't going to be filled with anything here on earth. You need a closer relationship with Him. You need to let Him fill in those empty places.''

"But I go to church and I've been a Christian since I was

young. I suppose I should get more involved, do more things. . . ."

"I'm not talking about acts of service or works, although they both have their merit. Don't neglect an honest-to-goodness relationship with your heavenly Father by adding extra church activities."

"But I thought fellowship at church was important."

"And so it is. Working for the Lord is as well," Laura countered. "But fellowship with God, a real heart-to-heart, one-on-one friendship, is so necessary if you're to ever eliminate that void in your heart. You aren't going to find it anywhere else, Tess. I can guarantee you that, just as you can guarantee me the benefit of your relocation services."

"But I'm afraid," Tess finally admitted. She looked away and dug her nails into her hands to keep from crying.

"You're a child of God," Laura replied. "He hasn't given you a spirit of fear. The Bible tells us that in Second Timothy. If God hasn't given you that spirit, guess who has? Worse yet, guess who it serves?"

Tess didn't like the idea of serving anyone's purpose outside of God's and her own and sometimes Brad's. "I never thought of it that way."

"You have a source of power to call upon," Laura said with a smile. "Just like you have all those places and people you connect with to help you with your business, only this one is your heavenly Father, and His sources are limitless and eternal."

"You make it sound so easy."

"Why make it sound harder than it is?" Laura asked.

"I don't understand."

Laura leaned forward and patted Tess's arm. "It's like when the delivery man shows up at the front door. You can either open the door and take the package or refuse to answer the knock and let the package remain undelivered. It's that way for bad or good. You can refuse delivery on the things that you recognize to be harmful. The key is knowing what to look for."

"There's a lot of things I'd like to refuse delivery on," Tess said, finally offering Laura a smile.

"Then start now," Laura suggested. "Start by refusing to let the worries of this life overtake you. Start by opening the door and your heart to a closer walk with God. After you start to grow closer to Him, you might not feel so fearful about continuing with your plans for adoption. In fact, you just might find the confidence you need to take on the hardest job you'll ever have—that of motherhood."

"I'll really think about what you've said, Laura. I'm going to pray, too. I won't let this just slip by me." Tess put her hand over Laura's. "I'm so glad you're coming to live in Miami. I need you."

"Thank you, sweetheart. The feeling is mutual."

Chapter

12

Brad found himself greeted by a new woman when he came home that night. Tess stood at the door smiling and eager to talk.

"If you've got some time," she began, "there's something I'd like to discuss."

Brad shrugged out of his suit coat. "Okay." He felt almost fearful of saying anything more. Tess had been a ball of nerves since Kim had lost Laney. Whatever else happened, Brad didn't want to be in any way responsible for Tess going back into her depression.

Tess took his coat and draped it across a chair. "I had the most wonderful visit with Laura today." She held out her hand and Brad reached for it. "Come sit with me and let me tell you what we talked about."

Brad couldn't fathom what had brought the change in his wife's behavior, but he was grateful, nevertheless. Tess led him to the living room and quickly took a seat on the sofa. She curled her legs up under her as she often did when they relaxed together to watch television or a movie. Seeing her like this caused Brad to relax a bit.

"So what's this all about?" he questioned.

Tess positioned herself so that she could sit facing him. "I know I've been positively awful to live with and for that I'm sorry," Tess said, suddenly serious. "Seeing what happened to Kim was devastating. I kept seeing myself in her place."

"I know," Brad murmured.

Tess continued. "I told Laura everything. In fact, I've talked to her several times this week. I just couldn't work it all out in my mind and I needed someone to help me think it through."

Brad felt a twinge of jealousy. "I would have helped, if you would have let me."

She smiled sympathetically. "I know you would have done your best, but I guess I just needed a mother-type figure. With both our mothers dead, Laura was the closet thing I could find."

"So I take it she had all the answers," Brad said casually. He didn't want Tess to know that his feelings had been hurt by her rejection of him or his counsel. If Laura had managed to break through Tess's wall of pain, he knew his attitude should be one of gratitude and nothing more.

"No, not exactly. She did share some thoughts that I felt were very wise, but she made it clear that she didn't know why things had to happen the way they did. She didn't have the answers, even though I wanted her to. I really did. I wanted her to tell me why bad happens when people have prayed for good. I wanted her to explain how injustice could be allowed to destroy the lives of men and women who trust in God."

"So what did she tell you?"

"She basically said that I had to accept that God knew what He was doing, even when evil seemed to reign supreme. When she took me to the airport, she shared several accounts in the Bible of bad things that happened to innocent people, but she also showed me how God took the intended evil and made good come out of it."

"We were just talking about that in our men's Bible study last night," Brad said, taking interest in his wife's words. "We're studying the life of Joseph in the Old Testament."

Tess nodded enthusiastically. "That's one of the examples Laura gave. It made more sense to me when I looked at the examples she gave. I even studied them on the way home. The lady beside me on the plane even asked me if I was a preacher or Bible teacher." Tess smiled and it warmed Brad's heart.

"Anyway," she continued, "added to that, Laura told me my fears aren't from the Lord. She told me about a verse in Second Timothy that says God hasn't given me this spirit of fear. That got me to thinking. In a sense, by giving in to my fears, I'm serving two masters. On one hand, I love God and want very much to follow His ways and be pleasing to Him. On the other hand, I'm wrapped in the past and the fears and insecurities that those memories bring."

Brad could see the correlation. "But it isn't easy to just cast aside a lifetime of worry. I've always understood your longing for a child. I've even understood why you tried so hard to get pregnant. I never minded that it was important to you. We had the money to spend, and I couldn't think of a single thing I wanted more than to see you bear my child. I just didn't want it to be the final word. If we couldn't have a child naturally, I wanted to adopt."

Tess nodded. "I know. But I also know that my desires for my own baby were bred and born out of my fears and the empty places that people left in my life. My biological mother and father left a huge hole in my heart. I wanted to fill that hole with my own flesh and blood."

"But you don't anymore?"

Tess shook her head. "No. I want to fill that hole with God and His love." Tears came to her eyes. "Oh, Brad, I know I'm going to have moments when I take three steps back, but for now I feel as though I've run several miles forward. Can you forgive me for being so selfish?"

He opened his arms to her and sighed as she allowed him to cradle her against his chest. "You weren't selfish, Tess, you were just hurt. How could I ever hold that against you?"

"But I'm thirty-six years old," Tess replied, looking deep into his eyes. Brad had once said that he could lose himself in her gaze, and now was no different than the first time he'd felt that way.

"So what?" he questioned.

"So . . . I've caused us to waste a lot of time."

"But I thought we were going to accept that God's timing is perfect. If we were supposed to have a child by now, we would have one. I trust Him to be on time, even if you were still caught up in dealing with the past. There's nothing to forgive."

Tess reached up and took hold of his face. "I love you so very much. I can't imagine being happier with anyone or anything else. I just want you to know that—in case you might have doubted it these last few weeks or months." She smiled and added, "Or years."

"I never doubted it," Brad said, his heart racing. She was the light of his life. Beautiful and radiant, intelligent and efficient, everything he wanted in a wife.

He tightened his grip on her and pulled her closer. Pressing his lips to hers, Brad felt the overwhelming desire to take the phone off the hook, deadbolt the front door, and pretend the rest of the world didn't exist. Just him and Tess. Nothing more.

Tess sighed and put her head on his shoulder. "Do we have to go anywhere tonight?" he asked, his voice husky and low.

"No," she said softly. "Tonight is ours."

"Good," he grinned.

She raised her head. "Any ideas how we might busy ourselves?"

His grin broadened into a roguish smile. "I might have some thoughts on it." He pressed a warm kiss against her neck, pleased to see how eagerly she responded.

"Mmm," she sighed, reaching up to run her hand through his hair. "I'd love to hear your ideas."

"Better yet, why don't I show you," he said. He surprised her, causing Tess to squeal in delight as he lifted her in his arms and got to his feet.

Just then the telephone began to ring.

"Let it go," Tess suggested.

"Is the answering machine on?"

She nodded.

He started for the bedroom and had reached the door at the precise moment the machine picked up the call.

"Tess? Brad? This is Justin. Look, I have something important I need to talk to you about."

Brad stopped and looked at Tess. The romantic enthusiasm seemed to drain away with the excitement they perceived in their friend's voice. At Tess's nod of agreement, Brad put her down and went to the telephone.

"Justin, this is Brad. What's up?"

"Brad, I have a case to discuss with you. I know Tess wanted to drop the idea of adoption, but my sister has an unwed mother who is seeking a family to adopt her child. Can I come over and share the particulars with you?"

Brad felt a cold tingle run up his spine. He looked at his wife, who had been so very vulnerable and hurt for the past few days. Dare he ask?

"Ah, just a minute," Brad said, stalling for time. He covered the receiver even as he issued a silent prayer. "Tess, Justin wants to talk to us about adopting. Seems his sister—you know, the one who's a judge?" Tess nodded, her eyes growing wide. "Well, she has an unwed mother who wants to give up her baby for adoption. He's asked to come over and talk to us about it."

He saw the color drain from Tess's face and knew her answer would be no. Now the evening would be spoiled, and unless something or someone intervened, Tess might well sink into another depression.

But to his surprise, Tess nodded very slowly. "Tell him to come over," she said, her voice soft but not in the leastwise hesitant.

"Are you sure?"

She nodded again. "If I'm to trust God for the details, I have to start somewhere."

Brad had never loved her more. "Justin, Tess says to come over."

"Great! I'll be there in half an hour."

"See you then." Brad hung up the phone and looked to his wife. "He'll be here in thirty minutes."

"This is her picture," Justin said, holding out the photograph of a young blond girl.

Tess took the picture in hand and looked at it for several silent moments. The girl's expression haunted her. She knew that look—the pain mixed with anger.

"What's her name?"

"Sherry. Sherry Macomber," Justin replied. "She's been a ward of the state nearly from birth."

Tess nodded, suddenly feeling strangely connected to the child. "She looks too young to be pregnant."

"She's only fourteen," Justin replied, shaking his head. "But I had one who was just twelve, not six weeks ago."

"Twelve?" Brad asked in disbelief. "What is wrong with this world?"

"You and I both know very well what's wrong with it," Justin replied.

"So tell us everything," Tess said, taking her gaze off the photograph and placing it solidly on Justin. "Everything. The bad parts and the good."

Justin laughed a little nervously. "Why, Tess Holbrook, what makes you think there are any bad parts?"

Tess grew very serious. "Because you're here with information about a fourteen-year-old who has no one in her life to even care that she's gotten herself pregnant. A better question might be, what makes me think there are any good parts."

"You're a pretty wise lady," Justin replied.

"No," Tess said, shaking her head. "I'm simply being practical. I know this child. I could have been this child."

"Well, given what Brad's told me about your background, you aren't far from the truth."

"Her mother was a drug addict," Justin began.

Nearly an hour later Justin concluded telling what Barbara had been able to share with him about Sherry.

"She hasn't really done a lot in the way of violent acts. She did get out of hand with the family before the Delbertos, but that came from the fact that they were very strict and believed in corporal punishment. They've been taken off the foster-care program because of this, but it still resulted in Sherry being labeled as physically violent. Barbara assures me, however, it isn't the child's general nature. She's been on this case for many years now and has paid an undue amount of attention to Sherry."

"Why?" Tess questioned.

Justin shrugged and reshuffled the papers he'd been reading from. "She told me she saw something of value in Sherry. Something she didn't think most people saw. She felt the kid was worth saving, as all of them are, but that Sherry would have to be convinced of it first."

Tess looked again at the photograph of the girl. She saw it, too. She knew exactly what Barbara Woodsby was talking about. There was something in Sherry's eyes that stared out from the photograph like an animal in a cage. Only the cage in this case was a self-imposed isolation that Sherry had created for herself.

Drawing a deep breath, Tess handed the photograph back to Justin. "I think we should meet her."

Brad looked at her questioningly. "Are you sure? I mean, this isn't going to be easy under any circumstances, but with a troubled child it'll be just that much harder. What if you decide you want to go through with this and the kid changes her mind?"

"If I might add something here," Justin interrupted. "Sherry doesn't really have a whole lot of options. She can't have the baby with her where she's at right now, and Barbara isn't entirely sure what's going to happen to Sherry in the future.

"Sherry has done some petty thievery, but she's never

been caught or charged. Still, no one wants her in their foster home, and Barbara is feeling rather pressed to keep her in local or state detention. The baby would therefore go into foster care after its birth. I think Sherry has seen enough trauma in that area to last her a lifetime, and I don't think she'll want it for her baby.

"She's already assured Barbara that all she wants is the right to pick her baby's parents and to have a home for the months of her pregnancy and for a short time afterward to see how the baby and parents respond to each other. It's a big demand, we know, but she agrees to sign all papers up front. Barbara doesn't feel she'll be a risk to harming herself or the child, as she already contemplated an abortion and couldn't go through with it."

"And the expenses and care for Sherry would be our responsibility?"

"Her state funding from foster care would be available. But that doesn't amount to much. She'll have to start immediately with an obstetrician."

"But she's healthy, right?" Brad asked.

Tess was surprised to find that suddenly Brad was the one who seemed hesitant.

Justin nodded. "The medical reports show a healthy pregnancy just starting the tenth week."

Tess nodded. "How soon can we meet her?"

"If you're both willing, I'll set something up as soon as possible," Justin replied.

Tess looked to Brad and smiled. "We agreed that we had to start putting all of the details in God's hands, right?"

"This is testing that pretty hard, don't you think?" Brad asked.

"I think that Justin wouldn't be here if God didn't want us

to at least consider the situation. Maybe the answer is no, but we should at least see the situation in its entirety."

Brad nodded and then looked to Justin. "Go ahead and make the arrangements."

Chapter

13

Sherry watched the couple intently through a two-way mirror. They seemed nice enough and the paper work she'd been given to read through indicated they were financially well off. The woman was really very pretty. Sherry liked the way her hair had been pulled back off her face with a barrette. Sherry had tried to do things like that with her baby-fine hair, but it never looked as good.

The man was nice looking. Not movie-star handsome, but he had a nice smile and expressions that seemed sincere. Sherry had dealt with enough phony people to last her a lifetime. Maybe that was the only reason she was willing to work with Judge Woodsby. The judge had always been honest with her. She had warned Sherry about detention, and while Sherry had tried to walk the narrow line, she knew when she made the wrong choices that Judge Woodsby would keep her word. And as much as she hated detention, she would have hated even more if the woman would have simply smiled and suggested another foster home.

Maybe that's why I did what I did, Sherry thought as she watched the couple. *Maybe I just wanted to get it over and go to detention. After all, that's where everyone was always threatening to send me.*

"Are you ready to meet the Holbrooks?" Justin Dillard asked her as he came into the small room. He was the lawyer assigned to the Holbrooks, Sherry had learned. He was also Judge Woodsby's brother.

Sherry looked at the man and nodded. "I guess so."

She tried not to sound nervous, but her stomach was tied in knots. What if they didn't like her? Judge Woodsby had said they were the only couple to show interest in her proposition. If they didn't like her and decided against allowing her to come into their home, then Sherry would have to start all over in figuring out what to do.

Justin opened the door and held it for Sherry. "After you," he said in a polite yet casual manner. Sherry was unused to such treatment.

She came into the room and met the gaze of the woman first. Warm brown eyes and a welcoming smile were Sherry's first face-to-face impressions of the woman.

"I'm Tess and this is my husband, Brad. You must be Sherry."

Sherry nodded and took a seat opposite them at the conference table. Justin took his place at the head of the table and within minutes, Barbara Woodsby joined them.

"Tess, Brad, this is my sister, Judge Woodsby," Justin introduced.

Tess and Brad shook hands with the woman while Sherry watched in silence. She found adult games to be the most time-consuming of chores, but she had no other choice.

"I'm glad you both could come. I'm sure it wasn't easy to drop everything and fly up, but since the matter is a timely one, I felt it imperative to push toward an immediate resolution," Barbara Woodsby said. "This isn't a routine situation and I've gotten a lot of rules bent on Sherry's behalf." She eyed the girl for a moment, then smiled. "But I think she's worth the trouble."

Sherry was surprised to hear the woman make such a statement. She was equally surprised to hear that someone had altered the rules for her. That had to be a first.

"I know these things can be full of legalities and problems," Tess said quite openly. "I was apprehensive for that very reason. However, Justin is a good friend and he's promised to leave no stone unturned in resolving conflict and problems related to this arrangement."

"I feel the same way," the judge replied.

Sherry listened only halfheartedly to the conversation. She had already decided she would go with the Holbrooks, if they liked her and the idea of adopting her child. She didn't like the idea of having no other options; after all, what if she positively hated the Holbrooks? But there were no other choices. At least not reasonable ones.

"You've both been given information to read on the other party or parties involved. Do you have any questions?"

Tess nodded. "I do."

"Then why don't you go ahead," Barbara suggested.

"I'm wondering what kind of parents you're hoping to find for your child?" Tess questioned.

Sherry shrugged. "Good ones, I guess."

"So what constitutes good?" Tess pressed.

Sherry hadn't expected to have to answer a lot of questions. In fact, she had figured she would be the one asking the questions.

She studied the Holbrook woman for a moment. She wasn't nearly as old as Sherry had figured. Somehow thirty-six seemed awfully old, but this woman looked pretty young, like she exercised and maybe even jogged. She was classy, too, and nothing like any of the foster mothers Sherry had dealt with.

"I want someone who will love my baby like their own kid," Sherry finally answered. "I don't want someone who's just looking for a trophy. Kids need to be loved and cared about."

Tess nodded. "I couldn't agree more."

Sherry tried to think of all the things she had wanted to ask, but nothing was coming to mind. All she knew for sure was that she had to find a way out of her current situation. And quick. April had relayed information that Joleen had plans to hurt Sherry, and that in turn could hurt the baby.

"I'm about three months pregnant," Sherry stated as if it were a secret. "That means for six months before the baby is born and for at least three months afterward I'll be living with you. What kind of place do you have?"

Tess smiled. "We live in Miami and have a two-bedroom condo in a high-rise on the beach. We've already converted the second bedroom into a nursery, just hoping and praying that God would send the right person to us."

Sherry frowned and shifted uncomfortably in her seat. "Sounds like you're religious."

Tess looked to Brad. "We love God and serve Him, if that's what you mean," Brad replied. "We'd expect you to attend church with us."

Sherry shook her head. "I don't think I'd like that much."

"How could you know until you try it out?" Tess suggested. "We have a lot of neat youth activities going on all the time. You might really enjoy it."

Sherry didn't know a whole lot about religions but she couldn't help but remember the woman at the abortion clinic. She had said that God loved Sherry. The words had made her feel funny, but she didn't have a clue as to why.

Not willing to delve any further into religious idiosyncrasies, Sherry surprised them by blurting out, "Why do you want my baby?"

She watched Tess Holbrook carefully, certain within her heart that she'd somehow see the truth in her eyes.

"I've always wanted a baby," Tess replied. "I can't have children and the doctors aren't sure why. Brad and I would love to have a big family, but so far that just hasn't happened."

"But why do you want *my* baby?"

The woman was undaunted. "I read your profile, Sherry. You and I have a lot in common."

"Oh, sure." Sherry suddenly felt like bolting from the room. This woman was probably going to try to spin some tale about how hard her life had been growing up poor or how she'd lived in the bad part of town.

"I was the daughter of a drug addict. My mother used to send me out to buy her stuff because she was too drunk or weak to go for it herself." Tess eyed Sherry with a steady, unblinking gaze. "I knew all the dealers and their prices. I knew which ones could rob me, and I knew which ones would give me a candy bar because they felt sorry for me.

"I was taken from my mother, literally ripped out of her arms by the police, after she accidentally set our rat-infested house on fire. I was put into foster care and adopted a short time later, but the wounds went deep and scars are still there."

Sherry looked at the table. She'd heard adults lie to her all of her life. Lies about where she'd go if she didn't eat her vegetables. Lies about love and honor. Lies about truth and why it mattered. If there was one thing Sherry knew like the back of her hand, it was whether or not someone was lying to her. Tess Holbrook wasn't lying.

She glanced back up without lifting her face. The woman was watching her. Meeting her gaze was almost like seeing herself in a mirror. This woman knew how it was. How it felt to have nothing and no one. She could see it in her eyes, and instead of comforting Sherry, it frightened her. The awful truth of being understood, of having someone else know about the demons and monsters in her life, was more disturbing than she would have imagined. This was something entirely different and Sherry couldn't ignore it. This woman knew what it was to be alone.

The silence seemed to make the other people uncomfortable. Sherry didn't know what to say in response to Tess's statement, and Tess seemed perfectly content to let Sherry digest the news. However, Barbara Woodsby and the men grew restless.

"Sherry, these are the only applicants we have for your case. The Holbrooks live in Miami, as they've stated," Barbara said, interrupting the silence. "They are both professional people. Tess owns her own business, however, so she will make herself available to you and eventually to the baby on a full-time basis. Brad is involved with tourism and marketing. They are financially capable of taking you into their home and meeting all of your physical needs."

She paused and turned to Tess and Brad. "You do realize that this will include buying her a wardrobe to wear? She has no maternity clothes—not that she needs them yet. You'll also be responsible for anything else she needs. Foster children come with some state funding and assistance, but it isn't a lot, and Sherry is bound to have more than the average need."

"We understand," Tess replied. "We're prepared to do that and anything else that's required. I am curious about her education, however."

"Sherry is a very bright student. She's just finished this school year with all A's, and this is in spite of being taken from her foster home and put into the state facilities."

"I did read that in the report," Tess replied. "I was very impressed." She smiled at Sherry. "I was wondering, however, if she would attend school next year. From the report you've given us, I see that the baby is due at the end of November. I also note that she would like to remain in our care until at least three months after the birth. That's almost an entire school year."

Barbara nodded. "I do realize the dilemma. Sherry and I have discussed the situation, and she doesn't want to attend school while she's pregnant. I've shown her that many young women attend school and carry babies to full term, but she's adamant and I'm trying to make this more comfortable for everyone concerned. My suggestion is to do home studies with an accountability at a local level. We can arrange something with your school district," Barbara stated, looking back and forth between her audience.

"We hadn't approached the subject with you because we were allowing Sherry to get to know you and for you to better know Sherry, as well."

"I think it's a critical issue," Tess replied. "I would consider homeschooling, especially since Sherry has proven herself to be bright, independent, and self-motivated. She would probably do very well in home studies."

"This would be her first year of high school," Barbara said, looking at Sherry with an expression that seemed almost sorrowful. "The subjects would have to meet state requirements, but I'm certain Justin could help you figure out all of those details."

"Absolutely," the man replied. "There are even video

courses that would cover all of the federally suggested curriculum requirements."

Sherry felt as if they didn't even know she was in the room. Sometimes she used this to her advantage, but at this point she was more desperate. She needed answers and she needed them quick.

"I want a home for my baby that will be secure," she suddenly interrupted. "It has nothing to do with how rich you are." She flipped her blond hair over her shoulder and leaned back in her chair. She wanted to appear as mature and grown-up as fourteen years would allow. "I need to know that my baby will be loved. I won't give my baby to people who only care about making money."

"Sherry, I'm sure the Holbrooks are well aware—"

Sherry refused to be quieted. She stood up and gave Barbara Woodsby a stern look. "This is my baby, and I'll be the one to decide."

"Of course," Tess replied. "It's imperative that you feel comfortable with us. Would you like to spend some time with us tomorrow? Just Brad and me and you? We could do lunch together, couldn't we?" She looked to Barbara and Justin for the answer.

"I'm sure we could work that out, if Sherry is agreeable."

Sherry shrugged. At least it would get her out of detention. "Yeah, okay."

"I'll make the arrangements," Barbara said, noting something in her day planner. "I'll page Justin with the details."

Later that night, Sherry climbed into bed and relived the conversation with Tess Holbrook. She had to admit, she liked the woman as well as any. Tess didn't talk down to her and neither did she try to impress Sherry with any of her own credentials. Still, there was a fear in Sherry that gnawed at her heart. *What if they say no? What if after lunch tomorrow, they decide they hate me and never want to see me again? What then?*

The idea was terrifying. Sherry hated feeling so out of control, so frightened. Up until the last couple of months, she'd done a decent job of getting what she wanted. Well, with exception of finding true love. Sherry thought she'd had that with Joey, but now she could see it was just about the physical. Nobody loved her for herself, and even if the Holbrooks allowed her to come and stay with them, they wouldn't love her either. They would want her baby. They would tolerate her for the sake of the child she carried.

A tear slipped from her eye and trickled down the side of her face and into her ear. She hated when that happened. She'd long ago learned to never cry on her back unless she wanted wet ears. Rolling to her side, she drew her knees up to her chest and hugged them tightly.

"God loves you. He loves your baby. Seek Him."

The words of the woman at the clinic still rang in her ears. Could it be possible? And if so, why? Why would God even care that she was alive and drawing breath? Obviously He hadn't cared up until now. At least if He did, He certainly wasn't doing a very good job of showing it.

The aching in her heart threatened to pour out into a sob. Sherry buried her face against the pillow. *Never let them see you cry.* This was her own self-imposed rule. Tears suggested weakness. Weakness suggested vulnerability. And that was the one thing Sherry could not afford to be. Vulnerable people got hurt. Vulnerable people suffered at the hands of the strong.

Sherry forced herself to draw even, slow breaths. *I won't be weak. I won't let them hurt me.*

"God loves you." The voice sounded again in her memory.

Shaking her head from side to side, Sherry buried the thought. Thinking like that could only cause her trouble.

Chapter
14

"I'm glad you could have lunch with us," Tess told Sherry. They had just finished placing their order and Tess felt an eagerness to get the conversation rolling. "I feel there are so many questions you must have for us. I also figured you'd feel a whole lot more comfortable doing it here where we could just be casual."

Sherry maintained a look that wavered between indifference and minor curiosity. "I guess so."

"So do you have some things you'd like to ask?" Tess pressed.

The girl played with her water glass for a moment before answering. "What's Miami like? Does it ever get cold there?"

"Not really. Not like snow and winter weather. We have a pretty moderate temperature through the winter months."

"We get a lot of tourists," Brad interjected, "because you can go to the beach just about any time of the year. Why, Tess and I went swimming last February and the water was wonderful."

The comments on the beach seemed to interest Sherry. Tess saw the momentary spark of life in the young girl's eyes. She made a mental note to look for that more often.

"How far do you live from the beach?"

"We live basically on the beach," Tess answered. "Our high-rise owns a private beach area, as well as swimming pools. Do you like to swim?"

"I guess so," Sherry replied. "I used to swim quite a bit. One of my foster families had a pool."

Tess tried to promote the interest. "That's great. Swimming is good exercise and you shouldn't have any problem with the pregnancy interfering in that kind of fun."

Sherry shrugged. "So what else goes on around there?"

Brad jumped in. "We've got a gym, tennis courts, and a golf course. There are also malls and movie theaters close by and all sorts of nautical activities, such as scuba diving, boating, fishing—you name it. If it has water involved, we've probably got it."

The waitress appeared with their appetizer of potato skins along with their drinks. Sherry had ordered a lemonade, to Tess's surprise. She didn't know why, but she had pegged the kid for a die-hard cola fan.

Tess waited until the waitress had finished serving them before asking Sherry to continue. "You're bound to have other questions. Please just feel free to ask them. But first, could we have a moment of prayer?" She looked at Brad rather hesitantly. They'd never worried overmuch about such traditions, but the idea met with his immediate approval. He nodded and closed his eyes, leaving Tess to look to Sherry for some sign of acceptance.

"I used to think saying grace was just an action of habit—one I got out of when I left home, but now I'd like to get back into it."

Sherry shrugged and bowed her head. "Whatever," she muttered.

The prayer was simple and to the point. Tess asked blessings on the food and on their meeting. But lastly, she asked God to bless Sherry and her baby.

"Father, I ask that you make yourself real to Sherry. Please show her how much you love her."

When the amen sounded, Tess noticed that Sherry's complexion had paled a bit. She hoped the girl wasn't suffering morning sickness.

"Are you all right?" Tess questioned.

Sherry watched her almost warily. "I'm fine."

Tess smiled and decided to leave well enough alone. "So what else would you like to know?"

Sherry nodded and looked to the potatoes Brad was offering her. She picked one of the skins off the plate and right before taking a bite asked, "What would my room be like?"

Tess nodded. "We've already started converting the spare bedroom into a nursery. We did that because we wanted to be ready for whatever God sent our way. It's not complete, however, so you and I could probably spend some time finishing that task. There's a queen-size bed, and we thought it might be nice to put in a television and VCR." Again, Tess noted Sherry's interest.

"There are bound to be times when you just want time to yourself," Tess continued. "We thought if you had your own TV to watch, it might be easier for you. Then there's the issue of a wardrobe. We would want to take you shopping as soon as possible so that you could have comfortable clothes throughout your pregnancy. Obviously you aren't all that big now, but the time will come."

"Would I get to pick out the clothes?" Sherry questioned.

"Sure, within reason," Tess replied, picking up one of the potato skins.

"What does that mean?"

Tess spread sour cream on the potato before answering. "Well, it means that we can't have you dressing too provocatively." She looked at Sherry and refused to worry over whether this detail and others, like the issue of church, might cause the child to reject them as parents for her baby.

"Justin's sister told us that you tend to dress too . . . mature for your age. We couldn't allow that. We obviously don't want to dress you like a nun, either. There has to be a balance. Tasteful shorts and skirts, slacks, dresses—that kind of thing is just fine. Even a maternity bathing suit for swimming and such is completely acceptable, just no bikinis."

This actually made Sherry smile as she replied, "Like I'd be caught dead in one now."

Tess couldn't help but smile as well. "So you could pick things out, but if I felt they were too short or low cut, I'd have the final say."

Sherry nodded. "I guess that's okay."

They chatted about the weather, school, and just about anything else they could think of until their sandwiches finally arrived.

They ate in silence for several minutes until Sherry looked up at Tess and startled her with a question.

"Do you really believe God cares whether you bless the food or not? Are you afraid it will make you sick if you forget to pray over it?"

Tess smiled. "I never used to think it was a big deal. Routines seldom have the meaning that people assign to them. I mean, how many times do you hear people say 'I love you' and you can tell it's just a saying to them? I guess if we're being completely honest with each other, I would say that I want to pray over meals because my heart has changed. I

think God cares that I acknowledge Him and what He's pro-
vided."

"How do you know what God thinks?"

"Well, the Bible tells me what He thinks. At least part of
what He thinks is there. No one knows the whole mind of
God," Tess answered.

"So what does the Bible say about people like me?" Sherry
asked, surprising Tess.

Tess had just reached to take a bite of her sandwich, but
stopped with it midway to her mouth. She had the overwhelming feeling that this question was somehow more important
than any of the other questions they'd discussed up until now.
Maybe even more important than any of the other questions
that would follow. *Please, God, let me say the right thing*, Tess
prayed.

"I guess . . ." Tess began slowly, "no, I take that back. I
know that if I were to sum up God's message to you from Scrip-
ture, it would have to be that He loves you."

The color drained from Sherry's face so quickly that Tess
thought for sure the girl was sick. The stunned expression on
her face did nothing to relieve Tess's concern.

"Are you all right, Sherry? You got all pale like this earlier.
Are you sick?"

The girl shook her head. "I'm . . . I'm okay."

"Are you sure?" Tess questioned. "I don't want you to sit
here if you're ill. We can leave. The food isn't that important."

Sherry shook her head and appeared to regain her com-
posure. "I'm fine. Let's just eat."

Tess nodded but watched the girl carefully. Something
about her answer had upset Sherry, but for reasons beyond
her, Tess couldn't figure out why. Usually, whether they ac-

cepted Christianity or the Bible or anything religious, people didn't seem to mind someone telling them that God cared about them in a personal way.

The next day, Tess nervously paced her Miami condo. Justin had promised he'd call with any news about Sherry, and the wait was killing Tess.

"You're going to wear a hole in the carpet," Brad said as she made yet another pass through the house.

"I can't help it. I can't concentrate on anything but waiting for Justin to call."

Brad nodded. "I know. I feel the same way. Look, I'll be playing racquetball with him in about an hour. If we don't hear from him before I leave, I'll be sure to drill him at the gym."

Tess crossed and uncrossed her arms. "I know I shouldn't be so anxious. I've prayed and everything. But I just want to know what's going on."

Brad put down his newspaper and came to where Tess stood. She had dressed casually in jeans and a sleeveless white blouse, and she smiled when Brad ran his hands up her bare arms. His hands were warm against her cool skin, and his touch seemed to transfer strength to her weary heart.

"We're in this together, don't forget," he said softly.

"How could I," she grinned. Just then the telephone rang and Tess jumped a good six inches off the floor. "Oh, that must be Justin!"

"I hope for our sake it is," Brad declared. "I don't think we could take too much more of this waiting."

Tess hurried away from her husband and answered the

kitchen phone on the second ring. "Hello?"

"Hi, Tess. Is Brad there with you?" It was Justin.

"Yes, Justin, we're both here."

Tess motioned for Brad to join her. "So what did she say?"

"Well, it seems you made an impression on our little gal," Justin replied. "She wants to go ahead with the plan and allow you to adopt her baby."

Tess let out a squeal of excitement as she turned to Brad. "She said yes!"

"I kind of figured," Brad said, laughing.

"When will she be able to come here?" Tess quickly asked.

"Within the week. Barbara is going to push through all the paper work and red tape. She says this is a rather unusual situation, but that she's owed plenty of favors and is ready to cash them in to see Sherry down here with you and Brad."

"That's wonderful news. Oh, thank you, Justin. Thank you for talking us into this."

"I'm sure God has His hand in it all," Justin replied. "I'm just the go-between guy."

"Well, you handled your part admirably. Let us know as soon as possible when Sherry will be flying down."

"I will. There's the normal reams of paper to be filed and approved with the state. Technically you and Brad will be listed as a foster home—at least, that appears to be the way things will be handled. You'll be Sherry's guardians."

"I hope there won't be any snags," Tess said, drawing a deep breath. "I know if you and Barbara have anything to say about it, things will go off perfectly."

"That's the plan," Justin said confidently. "Now you two go and celebrate."

"Maybe this evening," Tess replied. "Brad has promised

some friend of his that he'll come and play a Saturday game of racquetball."

"Oh! I forgot all about that. Good thing I called you," Justin exclaimed. "Tell him I'll be about ten minutes late but that I'm on my way."

"I will. Talk to you later." Tess hung up the phone. "He'll be about ten minutes late but said he's on his way."

"Good enough. I'd better get going, too, or I'll be late." Brad took her into his arms and kissed her lightly.

Tess pulled back and smiled. "It seems like all of this is a dream. I'm just so happy. I only hope we can make a difference in Sherry's life. I think it would be so wonderful if she were to have a change of heart and soul by the time she leaves us. Wouldn't that be perfect?"

"It would indeed," Brad replied. "Why don't you get us some reservations for dinner tonight? Someplace special. We'll get all dressed up and celebrate."

Tess nodded enthusiastically. "I think I can arrange that."

"Good. I'll see you later." He gave her another quick kiss before heading off to meet Justin.

Tess sighed and looked around the kitchen. She'd been so scatterbrained all morning that she'd forgotten to wash the breakfast dishes. Now that she had her good news, the task seemed to practically do itself. She had the kitchen cleaned and back in its pristine state within ten minutes.

She tried to busy herself next with some client work, but that couldn't hold her attention. What she really wanted was to work on the nursery. After all, there was plenty yet to do.

Walking into the spare room, Tess opened the sliding blinds, allowing the sunlight to floor the room. Tess smiled. This would make a lovely nursery. Across the room and away from the window, Tess and Brad had set up a sweet little wooden crib. The clerk had assured them it carried all the proper safety standards and was one of their more popular models. Tess could understand why. With its soft white finish it seemed perfect for the innocence of new life. Tess had found this particular model appealing for the dainty artwork along the top of each end of the bed. There, sealed under a glossy finish, were little figures of puppies, kittens, lambs, and bunnies. These were accompanied by a garden of colorful flowers and emerald green grass. It was sweet and delicate and only needed a baby to make it complete.

Tess lightly fingered the white afghan she'd purchased weeks ago. The soft folds were carefully draped atop the crib. Thinking that she really ought to put it away, Tess went to the closet for its box but found herself distracted by the doorbell.

"Who could that be?" she wondered aloud as she went to open the door.

The visitor proved to be none other than her friend Kim. She looked to be at least fifteen pounds thinner, and for a woman who had no need of losing weight, it caused her face to appear gaunt and drawn.

"Kim! I'm so glad you stopped by," Tess said, reaching out to pull Kim into the apartment. "How are you doing?"

"I'm better," Kim said without any real enthusiasm. "I wanted to stop by and apologize for being so hard to reach. I just needed some time to myself."

"Of course. I completely understand. Come on in. Would you like some coffee?"

"No, I can't stay long. I'm actually heading down to the airport. I'm going back to work."

It was only then that Tess noticed Kim was wearing her old flight attendant uniform. "When did you decide to do this?"

"Well, after Laney left I didn't see any reason not to go

back to work. I can't bear being in that house alone."

Tess nodded. "Have you heard anything more from the lawyer?"

"He says it's pretty futile for us to fight any further."

"What about adopting another baby?" Tess braved the question, though she feared that now was probably not the right time.

"I don't want another baby," Kim replied rather harshly.

Tess nodded and tried to steer the conversation elsewhere. "So will you be flying or working the ticket counter?"

"Ticket counter for now. I don't really want to be there, but I hate the idea of going out looking for another job."

Tess thought of how busy she would be in the months to come, and without thinking about anything else offered, "You could come to work for me."

Kim looked at her strangely. "Why would you say that? You've never needed help before."

Tess realized she'd made a mistake. Trying to think of how to explain the things that were taking place in her life, Tess tried first to make light of it. "It was just a suggestion. I don't like to think of you having to work a job you hate. I've had more business than I can deal with and I'm even considering taking up an offer by one of Brad's business associates. He wants to come in on this and help me expand by taking on several employees and moving the business to regular offices."

"That doesn't sound like you, Tess. What's really going on?" Kim questioned, eyeing her suspiciously.

"I don't want to upset you," Tess finally said after a moment, not knowing how to avoid the truth. "I mean, I don't want to add to your sorrows."

"Just tell me what's going on," Kim replied. "I don't like

being kept in the dark. I don't need people walking around on eggshells."

Tess drew a deep breath. "All right. Brad and I have decided to go ahead with adopting a baby."

Kim's jaw tightened, but then she relaxed and nodded. "A newborn?"

"Yes," Tess answered. "Justin Dillard has put us in touch with a young, unmarried girl. She's going to come and live with us while she's pregnant and for a short time after the baby is born, as well."

"Oh, Tess, don't do it!" Kim said, shaking her head. "You don't know what that's like. I mean, we didn't have Laney's mother living with us, but she shared in our lives enough for us to know her pretty well. Don't do it. It's just too much to deal with."

"Well, that's why I didn't want to say anything," Tess replied. "I know this is hard for you to hear. Our case is different, however. This girl doesn't really have a lot of options. She needs us and we need her."

"That's what I thought, too. Just don't count on it."

Tess reached out to touch Kim's arm. "Please don't be upset. I want to be happy about my choice and I want you to be happy too. If not for me and Brad, then for yourself."

Kim shook her head. "It's going to take time for me to be happy again. I just hate to see you making the same mistake." She turned to leave. "I know you won't listen to me. I wouldn't listen to anyone, not even to you. Remember how against adoption you once were?" She didn't wait for Tess to speak, but added, "Just remember, I warned you."

"Don't go," Tess urged. "Stay and talk to me. I was serious about the job."

Kim shook her head. "It wouldn't work out, Tess. I'm sorry."

Tess let her go, wishing there was something more she could say. She hated seeing her friend in pain. And hated even more the thought that Kim was convinced that Tess was headed for the same pain.

Looking upward, Tess closed her eyes. "Oh, God, please protect us both. We can't take too many more heartaches. We just aren't as strong as we'd like other folks to think. At least I know I'm not that strong."

Chapter
15

Tess waited nervously for Justin and Brad to bring Sherry back from the airport. She had fully planned to accompany them for the homecoming, but at the last minute found herself escorting Laura and Darren to their new home instead. Laura had been very understanding about Tess's inability to stay.

"Call me when you have time," Laura had told her. "I want to hear about everything."

Tess knew Laura would be a great source of help in the months and even years to come. Laura was so supportive of their choice and decision about Sherry, in fact, that she'd insisted Tess bring Sherry over for a visit as soon as she was settled in.

"We're here!" Brad called as they entered the condo.

Tess nervously hurried out to meet them. Sherry stood to one side looking around the room. She seemed curious but not overly excited.

"Sherry, welcome to our home!" Tess declared. She thought momentarily that maybe she should have said "your home," but it was, after all, only a temporary situation. Sherry was quite used to going from home to home and never really having one to call her own.

"Did you have a nice flight?"

"Yeah, it was cool. I'd never flown before," Sherry said, opening up a bit.

"Why don't you come with me and I'll show you around," Tess said, pointing toward the living room. Sherry followed her, leaving a plastic bag of things by the door.

"This is our living room. We have an entertainment center in here," Tess said, opening the doors to a built-in cabinet of highly polished oak. The doors folded back to reveal a television, stereo, and VCR.

"Nice," Sherry said before fixing her gaze on a collection of crystal. "Looks like this stuff cost a fortune."

Tess worried only momentarily that Sherry might steal some of the Lalique crystal or other nice pieces they'd collected. She hadn't really considered the possibility that the girl might take things from them. Justin said she'd been guilty of shoplifting, although never caught in the act. Would she rob them for her own purposes?

"It is expensive," Tess replied. "We'll be putting it in storage or building a higher shelf for its protection once the baby comes."

Sherry nodded. "Yeah, a kid would destroy this place in a matter of minutes."

Tess smiled, trying not to feel offended. "Maybe you'll be able to help me figure out how to make the house more acceptable for a toddler."

Sherry shrugged. "Maybe."

Tess motioned to the balcony door. "This is our view of the ocean and our little haven in the sky. We're only five floors up, but you'll see for yourself we have quite a view."

Sherry followed Tess out onto the balcony and for the first time really got excited. "Wow! I've never seen the ocean. I tried to see it from the plane, but I didn't have a window seat. This is really awesome."

"We thought so too. We spend quite a bit of time out here when the weather is nice."

"What about when it's not so nice?" Sherry questioned. "I've heard you get a lot of hurricanes down here."

"Maybe not as many as you'd expect," Tess replied. "And Miami is seldom bothered. It's the way we're positioned. Maybe we'll study about that in homeschool."

Sherry said nothing more, and Tess could see that she'd totally given herself over to the view.

"Why don't I show you your room and then you can always come back here and enjoy the sun," Tess suggested.

Sherry reluctantly followed her back into the house, and Tess quickly picked up the tour. "This is the den, but we've made it into my little office." She opened the door for Sherry to look inside. "Then this is the bathroom. We'll all be using this one for showers and such. We have a half bath off the master room and Brad and I will be using that for our personal things. That way we hopefully won't tie up the bathroom when you need it."

Sherry popped her head in and nodded. "It's a lot bigger than I figured. Wow, is that a Jacuzzi tub?"

Tess smiled. "It sure is. Feels good after a long day, let me tell you."

Sherry smiled. "I'll bet."

"We can find out from your doctor if it's safe for you to use," Tess said before heading toward the kitchen. "This is the formal dining room and through this opening is the kitchen. There's all kinds of food in the cupboards and fridge, but why don't you make me a list of things you like to eat and we'll make sure to incorporate them into our menus."

"You'd do that? For me?" Sherry questioned, suddenly surprised.

"Of course," Tess replied with a smile. "We want you healthy and happy. A happy mother means a happy baby."

Sherry frowned and looked away. Tess wasn't sure what she'd said that spoiled the moment, but she decided to put aside her concerns and move on.

"This is our bedroom," she said, flipping on the light. "I have the drapes drawn to keep the sun from fading everything out quite so quickly."

"Is this for the baby?" Sherry said, noting a cradle at the foot of the bed.

"Yes. We have a bigger crib in the guest room, which will be the baby's room eventually. But we figured for the first few weeks we would need a smaller bed, something we could keep right beside our bed for those middle-of-the-night problems. Also, we figured it would be good for our bonding to the baby and for allowing you to have a quiet night's rest."

Sherry said nothing more, so Tess continued the tour. "Last but not least, we have the guest room and nursery. This will be your room for the time you're with us."

Tess opened the door and ushered Sherry inside. "We've put in a television and VCR, as well as a comfy chair and ottoman," Tess said, pointing out the attributes of the room. She pulled open the blinds, "You have a nice view out the window, but if you aren't going to be in the room, it's best to close the blinds or at least the drapes, okay?"

Sherry nodded. "It's nice."

"Here's the closet," Tess said, going to the door. "You can put your things in here or in the dresser." She hadn't paid attention to Sherry and when she turned, she found the girl holding the feathery afghan that Tess had purchased for the baby. Sherry had brought it up to her cheek and appeared to be testing the softness.

Without thinking, Tess rushed across the room and pulled the blanket out of Sherry's hands. "Please don't. That's for the baby and it cost quite a bit." She hated her words as soon as they left her mouth.

Sherry looked at Tess in wide-eyed surprise. The hurt was evident in her expression, but then she quickly covered it with a look of scorn.

"I guess your money is pretty important to you. Sure hope you don't plan to yell at the baby like that," Sherry said, turning her back to Tess. She walked to the window, leaving Tess consumed with guilt for her actions. She looked at the baby blanket for a moment and then decided to put it in her own bedroom to avoid another scene like this one. She wasn't entirely certain why she'd reacted as she had, but she knew it was wrong.

"I'm sorry, Sherry. I didn't mean to snap. I guess I'm just on edge about this entire arrangement. To be perfectly honest with you, I just had a friend go through a similar arrangement only to have the birth mother change her mind and take back the baby. My friend was devastated."

Sherry turned. "I don't plan to change my mind. I don't have anything to offer a baby. I'd like to finish school, maybe even go to college. Besides, they wouldn't let me have the baby where I was."

It was the most the girl had admitted to since Tess had first been introduced to her.

"I appreciate that you would share that with me," Tess admitted. "It's hard to want a baby so much and know that you have no control over whether you will be allowed to have one or not. I want you to know up front that this baby is extremely important to me. I've never wanted anything more. I'm grateful you care more about your child having the best than in keeping a baby you can't take care of."

Sherry said nothing and when she turned back to the window, Tess decided to leave Sherry alone for a while.

"I'll give you some time to get used to the place," Tess said as she went to the door. "Feel free to rest or watch television. I'll call you when dinner is ready. Do you like Chinese food? We thought we'd call out for some."

"It's fine," Sherry said, refusing to turn around.

Tess decided she'd said enough. "All right, then. I'll let you know when it gets here."

Sherry stared out of the window without seeing. Her eyes had filled with tears, to her great amazement. She hadn't thought it would be so hard to come into the home of strangers—strangers who cared only about one thing: her baby.

The incident with the blanket had really put it into perspective for Sherry. She wasn't wanted here. She was just extra baggage. She carried the child they wanted but was otherwise unimportant.

The realization hurt her so badly that Sherry crumpled to the floor and began to sob.

No one wants me. No one cares about me. They only care about the baby that lives inside of me. When the baby comes, I won't matter anymore. They'll push me out and send me away, and that will be the end of it.

Sherry rocked back and forth, hugging her knees against her chest. She rested her head on her knees and continued to cry. Her tears seemed endless, streaming down her cheeks in a heated frenzy.

The emptiness she felt frightened her more than anything she had ever known. Her life meant nothing. She might as well be dead. If she fell off the balcony, would anyone even care—if not for the baby?

Maybe I should just end it. But her thought faded quickly. She hadn't been able to end her baby's life—she certainly couldn't end her own.

Exhaustion overcame her, and dragging herself across the floor, Sherry crawled up onto the beautifully made bed and wrapped her arms around one of the pillow shams. Holding it close as if holding on to a lifeline, Sherry gradually stopped crying and fell asleep. Her only hope was that somehow in the months to come, she could figure out what she was to do and where she was to go. She had to find a place where she'd fit in.

Chapter
16

The first week of Sherry's new life with the Holbrooks passed in a series of strained activities. Tess tried to make arrangements in such a way that they didn't interfere with her business, but it was becoming very clear that her job duties were going to consume far more time and energy than Tess could give. Especially if she were to give Sherry equal time. This, coupled with the thought that when the school year began she'd be required to homeschool Sherry, caused a panic to well up in Tess.

Taking Sherry shopping was also enough to send Tess into a panic. The girl had outlandish taste and they couldn't seem to agree on anything, save blue jeans. Sherry wanted shorts that were indecently short and turned up her nose at the thought of having to wear floppy, oversized maternity tops until it was absolutely necessary. This meant that Tess had to find some regular clothes to suit the child in the meantime, and that did not prove to be an easy task at all.

"I don't like green," Sherry said when Tess held up a green-colored pullover. She continued leafing through the rack of clothes while Tess sighed and put the green shirt back. There was no pleasing the girl.

"I like this," Sherry said, holding up a white knit top.

The scooped neckline and short sleeves seemed modest enough and Tess nodded. "I think that would be all right."

Sherry threw it into their shopping cart and moved on to the next rack of clothes. "I want something red, too. I like red." She totally surprised Tess by adding, "What's your favorite color?"

"Lavender," Tess admitted.

"Why?" Sherry questioned, still considering the clothes.

"I guess because it's springy and makes me think of flowers," Tess replied.

"Makes sense," Sherry commented, seeming to give her approval. "I like lavender."

The comment made Tess feel marginally better. They'd at least connected on this small matter.

"Have you given any thought to dresses?" Tess pressed. "You'll need one for church tomorrow."

"Do I have to go?" Sherry questioned, frowning. "I mean, I can't stand all that stuff. People crying and praying and acting like a bunch of . . . well . . . I don't know, but it's stupid."

"Sherry, we love our church. We have a lot of good friends who go there. I know you don't think it's important, but we do. I'm hoping you'll have a good attitude about it and give it a try. In a few months you'll be gone and you won't have to give it another thought. Is it really that unreasonable to ask for your cooperation in this area for the short time you'll be here?"

Sherry scowled. "Yeah, it seems real unreasonable to me." She stalked off to a rack of dresses, muttering all the way.

Tess had no idea why Sherry had to take on such an attitude. It wasn't like she was being asked to endure torture. The church would welcome her with open arms, and Tess really hoped that Sherry would learn to care about God while living with them. Tess thought it would be marvelous if they could have a positive effect on the life of this child.

"Plant seeds," her pastor would say. *"You never know which ones will grow."* Tess could only hope that by living her faith in God, she'd be planting seeds in Sherry's life.

By noon, they headed over to Laura's for lunch. Laura had wanted to meet Sherry ever since Tess had first mentioned her. Lunch seemed an appropriate time and Tess was actually quite excited about the event. She looked forward to questioning Laura about the confusing mind-set of the teenage girl.

I know I was once her age, Tess thought as she maneuvered the car through traffic, *but I don't remember having such a bad attitude about everything.*

"Is this where your friend lives?" Sherry questioned as they passed into the gated community.

"Yes," Tess replied. "The work I do helps older people move down here for their retirement. I line up all the things they'll need to live in the area."

Sherry nodded and then quickly switched the subject. "Can I have some headphones? You know, a CD player and some CDs?"

Tess hadn't expected the question, but she didn't see anything wrong with the idea. She wanted Sherry to feel as comfortable during her pregnancy as was possible.

"I suppose we could check into it," Tess replied. "We'll see how much time we have after our visit with Laura and then maybe we could stop at the store on the way back to the apartment."

Sherry nodded. "That'd be great."

Tess breathed a sigh of relief. At least she hadn't irritated the girl with her answer. Tess parked the car and went to the trunk to retrieve a flower centerpiece she'd bought to welcome Laura to Miami.

"Do you always buy people flowers when they move here?" Sherry asked.

"Not always," Tess replied. "Sometimes, after I've gotten to know them, I realize they'd prefer something else. You know, a box of candy or a basket of different coffees and teas. That kind of thing."

"Why do you care? It's just a job."

Tess eyed Sherry for a moment and realized the teenager really wanted to know. "It's always been more than just a job to me. I care about these people. You can't spend that much time with folks and not come to care at least a little bit. I guess I just want them to feel at home here in Miami. With the relocation, I know they have a lot of things to get adjusted to. And usually they don't have a lot of friends or people they know." She stopped and realized Sherry was in the same position.

It dawned rather painfully on Tess that she gave her seniors more attention and more of herself than she was willing to give Sherry. The thought made her uncomfortable and she quickly added, "I'd like to make you feel comfortable too. We won't have much time together, but you're giving me a very precious gift by allowing me to adopt your child. I'd like very much to see you happy while you're here."

Sherry shrugged and turned away.

It frustrated Tess to no end to have the conversation so completely cut off, but there was nothing else to do but go ahead with her plans.

"Laura and Darren's place is over here," she said, walking past Sherry toward the row of condos.

Laura was happy to see them both. She seemed especially

pleased to meet Sherry. "I've heard a lot of things about you," she said, shaking Sherry's hand. "Tess said you were pretty, but I think that's an understatement."

Sherry surprised Tess by smiling. "Thank you. Tess said you're a good friend."

"That I am. Maybe we can be friends as well," Laura suggested.

"Maybe," Sherry replied.

"Well, then, maybe you won't mind that I bought you a present," Laura said, smiling.

Sherry looked from Tess to the older woman. "You bought me a present? Why?"

"Because I felt like it, that's why." Laura went to the hall closet and brought out a small white box. "It's really not all that much. I just wanted to welcome you."

Sherry took the box hesitantly. "Thanks." She opened the top and reached inside. Pulling out a shirt, Sherry gasped. "Wow! This is so cool."

Laura laughed. "I saw this tie-dye shop and there was this maternity top in the window. It just seemed like the perfect thing."

Sherry held up the top, admiring the crazy swirl of colors. "Now, I can see me wearing this. This will go great with my new jeans."

"Well, I'm sure you won't need the extra space anytime soon, but I'm glad you like it," Laura replied. "Would you like to come chat with us? I have some iced tea."

"If it's okay with you, I'd like to go swimming. Tess had me bring my suit."

"Sure," Laura replied. "Feel free to go change in my bedroom. It's just down the hall and to the right. I'm still trying to get boxes unpacked, but there's a path."

Sherry took off down the hallway and Laura turned to Tess. "She seems very sweet."

"She can be," Tess agreed. "Although half the time she's so moody I don't know what to make of her."

"She's had a big change in her life. Plus, she's expecting a baby. That in and of itself upsets all of your hormones and causes a great many emotions to run rampant."

Tess supposed that to be true. She'd read enough about pregnancy in hopes of conceiving that she could easily remember whole sections written on mood swings.

"Oh, these are for you," Tess said, suddenly remembering the flowers. "I always try to do something to make my clients feel welcome, and since you're a friend as well, I wanted to do something special. The flowers reminded me of the flower beds you always seemed to be tending when I was small."

Laura took the arrangement and placed it on the coffee table. "Why, they're lovely. And yes, they do look like summer in Kansas City."

Sherry quickly appeared, towel in hand. Her slender frame hardly bore any witness at all to her condition. "So where's the pool?"

"Just head out through my back door," Laura said, leading the way through the kitchen area. "You'll see the gate just down the walkway."

Sherry looked out the door. "Down there?"

"That's it," Laura told her. "Now, don't be gone too long. Lunch will be ready in about thirty minutes."

Sherry nodded and hurried out of the house as though afraid Tess and Laura might change their minds about the swim.

"She's so cute," Laura said. "Just a little mite of a girl. Hard to believe she's going to be a momma."

Tess felt a pang of jealousy and wasn't at all sure how to handle it. "Well, technically speaking she'll be a mother, but I hope to instill right from the moment the baby's born that I am his or her mother," Tess said.

Laura smiled and nodded. "I'm sure you'll do the right thing." She turned to toss the salad. "So whatever happened to your friend—the one who had adopted the baby and had to give it back to the birth mother?"

Tess shook her head. "I haven't talked to Kim in ages. As soon as she learned what I planned to do with Sherry, she wanted no part of me. I've tried calling her several times, but she's always gone and she never returns my calls."

"She must be hurting a great deal."

Tess knew it was true, but she was frustruated that Kim wouldn't allow her to help her through her bad times. Then again, Tess wondered where she'd ever find time to be there for Kim and maintain all her other responsibilities.

"I know she's in pain," Tess finally admitted. "What I don't know is how to help her. Especially when she's the one who's closed the door."

"Well, maybe God will open a window for you," Laura said with a grin.

Tess laughed. "Given my life, I'm going to need a lot of open windows."

The three women sat down to lunch on Laura's patio nearly half an hour later. Sherry looked content after her swim. Her long blond hair draped in wet folds over her shoulder as she munched on a tuna salad sandwich. Wrapped in her towel and looking for all the world like a kid without a worry, Sherry simply seemed to be enjoying the day.

She didn't know why, but Sherry's casualness around Laura irritated Tess. Sherry had been nothing but moody and tense since first coming to Tess and Brad. Tess had figured her to just be that way naturally, but seeing her so relaxed with Laura quickly gave evidence to an entirely different thought. *She just doesn't like me,* Tess decided.

"So have you given any thought to your future plans?" Laura asked Sherry. "What about school?"

Sherry took a long drink from her iced tea and shrugged. "Tess says she's going to homeschool me. I guess we're going to get some videos or something like that."

Laura nodded. "I'm sure homeschooling would be much easier than just trying to jump into a new school while expecting a baby."

"It would be hard," Sherry admitted.

"So do you have any other plans?" Laura pressed.

"No. I don't figure I have too much say in plans," Sherry said as if it didn't matter to her.

Tess took the opportunity to jump into the conversation. "Sherry has a doctor's appointment in three weeks. We're hoping to have the doctor do an ultrasound and make sure about the due date."

Sherry looked at Tess as if she'd suddenly grown a third head. "Why didn't you tell me about this?"

Tess detected hostility in the girl's question. "I didn't think you'd care about those kinds of details."

Sherry pushed back from the table. "Everyone is always making choices for me. Just once I'd like to be included in the plan."

"But, Sherry, you made the choice to come here to live with us. To have us adopt your baby. I just thought I was taking the burden off you to worry about the finer details of doctors and bills."

"Well, I don't like being told what to do. I'm finished with lunch. I'm going to change my clothes."

Tess shook her head as Sherry stormed off into the house. "See what I mean? Night-and-day differences. She can be pleasant one moment and difficult the next."

"She's had her entire world turned upside down."

"She's used to that," Tess replied. "I agree the pregnancy is a new twist for her, but she has been shuffled from one foster-care home to another since she was born."

"Exactly," Laura said softly. She reached out to put her hand on Tess's arm. "She has no stability, Tess. I know what it feels like now to be uprooted, but at least I have stability and security. I have Darren and my own things. I know you and have our friendship to rely on. But that little girl has nothing. She's all alone. Can't you understand that?"

Tess was taken back in time to when she'd first been thrust into foster care. Everything had been terribly hard. She had nothing, not even a stuffed animal of her own, to cling to. Her mother died so soon after she'd been taken that she hadn't believed the authorities when they'd first explained the matter to her.

"Your mommy went to sleep. She's sleeping in heaven now," a kindly woman had told her.

But mommies who went to sleep woke up, and Tess couldn't understand why they were all telling her that her mother would never wake up again. For weeks Tess had been terrified of falling asleep for fear she might not wake up. She couldn't fathom death, but she knew about nightmares and those always came when she was sleeping. If a person couldn't wake up, she had reasoned in her five-year-old mind, she might have to live in the nightmare forever.

"Tess? Are you all right?" Laura questioned, drawing Tess back into the present.

"Hmm? Oh, sorry. I was just thinking about something." Tess leaned back in her chair. "I know you're right. I know she's probably scared out of her wits, but I don't know how to help her. There are times when she seems to open up to me, but then something always happens. Like the other day, I snapped at her when she picked up the baby blanket I bought. I don't know why I got so upset when she picked it up, but I grabbed it away from her."

"That doesn't seem like you, Tess. Were you afraid she might harm the blanket?"

"I guess so," Tess answered. It didn't make sense to Tess, however. It was just a material object and she'd never felt overly attached to any of her things. What was wrong with her that she would react so harshly?

"Well, I'm sure this is going to be a difficult time of adjusting for each one of you."

Sherry finished changing her clothes and stuffed her wet things into the backpack Tess had purchased for her. She hated that she'd gotten so mad at Tess. After all, what would happen if she made Tess mad enough to send her back to Judge Woodsby? It was always a possibility.

Sherry stood for a moment looking around the Johnsons' bedroom. Some of the knickknacks had been put into place, but as Laura had said, a lot of stuff was still in boxes. Spying a lady's purse, Sherry realized it probably belonged to Laura. Dropping her backpack, Sherry went to the purse and opened it. The routine things could be found. Comb, lipstick, wallet. She listened for a moment to hear if anyone was coming, then opened the wallet. There were four twenties and several ones inside. Slipping one of the twenties into her pocket, Sherry quickly replaced the wallet and put the purse back where she'd found it.

She reasoned that if she were to be ready to run away after the birth of her child, she was going to have to start saving up money. Maybe she could hit Tess up for an allowance. The state was sending them money—at least, she'd been pretty sure they were going to do that. Maybe she could just insist that she'd always been given an allowance out of that money. Otherwise she'd have to start stealing from Tess and Brad as well.

Picking up her backpack, Sherry slipped it onto her back. She felt a twinge of guilt for her actions. After all, she liked Laura. The woman was kind and didn't have anything to gain by it.

For a moment, Sherry actually considered putting the money back, but her common sense told her that would be a mistake. This was a world where no one cared whether she lived or died. Well, maybe they cared so long as she was carrying a baby. But she was no fool. She knew very well that after the baby was born, she would be discarded like wrapping paper the morning after Christmas. Somehow that rationale made her actions acceptable. She was merely trying to survive. Who could fault her for that?

Chapter
17

Sherry looked at the throng of people gathered in the church foyer and immediately wished she could run away. It was just as she'd figured. Families. Couples. People who cared about one another. They were laughing, patting each other on the back, and sharing secrets. It only served to magnify her loneliness. Just as she'd known it would.

"Sherry, this is Dennis Dearborn. He and his wife run the youth group here," Brad explained.

Sherry looked at the man and nodded. He smiled at her and reached out to shake her hand. "Sherry, we're glad to have you here. We're getting ready to have the youth worship and we'd love to have you join us."

Sherry looked at Tess and felt even more panicked. Were they actually going to send her off to be with other teens? Sherry wasn't exactly sure she'd be comfortable with that. She didn't want to have to explain why she was here with Tess and Brad, and she certainly didn't want to get to know anyone when she'd just be running away in a few months.

"I think you'd enjoy the youth group if you give it a chance," Tess said softly. "Dennis is a pretty neat leader. He and his wife have some great activities going for the kids."

Just then a couple of teenage girls came up. "Hey, Mr. D,

we got our registration in for the overnight trip to Key West."

"Great. Glad you girls are going to be coming along. Say, I'd like you to meet someone new. Sherry, this is Amanda and Renee."

The three girls gave each other a shy nod. Amanda actually spoke. "You can hang out with me and Renee if you want."

Sherry didn't "want," but it seemed everyone else thought this to be a marvelous idea. Before she even knew what had happened, she found herself in the flow of teens headed for the youth room.

Amanda introduced her to at least twenty other kids. Some gave her a smile and nod; others offered a more enthusiastic greeting. One talkative girl even questioned as to where she lived, but before Sherry could answer, Dennis Dearborn called them to order.

In rapid-paced order the room settled. Kids took seats on couches, stuffed chairs, and the floor. It seemed wherever there was an empty space, kids were more than happy to fill it up.

Amanda pulled Sherry with her to an old plaid love seat where all three girls squeezed together. "This is our regular place," Amanda whispered, as if it should matter to Sherry.

Trying not to appear too interested, Sherry tried instead to focus on the flower print of her skirt. She toyed with the rayon material, wondering how long the ordeal would last, when Dennis Dearborn began to speak—or rather, to pray.

"Father God, we thank you for this day. It's just beautiful out there in the sunshine and glory of summer. The water looks so welcoming and there's bound to be all kinds of activities to distract us for the rest of the day. But for now, Father, we want to concentrate on you. Help us to keep focused. Help us to leave the world out there and to keep our mind on you in here. Thanks for everything. In Jesus' name, amen."

"Amen!" a chorus went up from the audience.

Sherry looked up hesitantly and watched as Dennis—or Mr. D, as the girls had called him—grabbed a football and called out, "Who wants to play a game with me!" Several of the boys volunteered and Dennis picked out three to come forward.

"Okay," he said in animated form. "Jimbo, you play third base. David, second base, and, Terry, you'll be on first." The guys looked kind of confused but said nothing. "Now, I'm going to need another volunteer." He looked out over the audience. "Okay, Rachel, you come on up here." A girl wearing jean shorts and a pretty ribbed-knit T-shirt came forward.

"Okay. Now, Rachel, you'll be our pitcher." He tossed her the football.

Everybody started laughing as he tried to position the kids in specific places. Mr. D took the entire matter quite seriously, however, and after approving of each person's position, he reached for a baseball bat.

"I also need some linemen." He pulled up a couple of guys who were sitting on the floor only a couple of feet away.

"Now, when Rachel pitches the ball, I'll hit it and you guys play your positions. Me and my guys will advance forward and tackle you base players while Rachel tries to field the ball."

Everyone was laughing and even Sherry was intrigued. Dennis stopped at this point and looked at the group with a dead-serious expression.

"You can't play two games at once. It doesn't work that way. Each game has different rules, and those rules tell you how the plays will be made and what your goals will be for completing the game." He motioned for the kids to take their seats.

"It's the same way with God. You can't serve two masters. You can't play the game the world offers, with its rules and goals, and be on God's team at the same time."

Sherry had never heard anyone talk like this before. Usually the sermons she'd been dragged to were boring liturgies and tiresome droning of death and destruction.

"Questions?"

No one spoke. Sherry had some questions, but there was no way she was going to voice them in this group. Probably the reason everyone else was silent was that they were already well trained in all this church stuff and knew all the answers. She certainly wasn't going to make a scene and embarrass herself.

"No questions?" Mr. D said rather thoughtfully. "Well then, I guess we can all go home." He headed for the door and Sherry's mouth dropped open.

"I have a question, Mr. D," one of the boys called out.

The man stopped and smiled. "What is it?"

"Well, like how are we supposed to live in the world and not have to do some of the things it tells us to do—you know, the rules?"

"Excellent question," Dennis said, resuming his place at the front of the room. "Anybody else want to know about that?"

Heads nodded and a few people responded with enthusiastic affirmation.

"Okay, then. Let's get down to business."

"I hope Sherry won't be too uncomfortable by herself," Tess whispered to Brad. They had just entered the sanctuary to take their regular place when Brad spotted Bartolo Aznar.

"Oh, look, Bartolo made it. I invited him last week, but I wasn't sure he'd come."

"I didn't know he was even interested in church," Tess said without giving it much thought.

Brad smiled. "Our men's Bible study challenged us to invite someone new to church. I got to talking to Bartolo and asked him if he and his family attended church, and he said they'd been looking for a church home but hadn't found anything."

"That's wonderful, Brad," Tess replied. "Guess we don't know if we don't ask."

He nodded. "Come on. Let's go welcome them."

Tess followed her husband to where the Aznar family was taking seats at the back of the sanctuary.

"Care if we join you?" Brad questioned, coming up to greet them.

Bartolo extended a brilliant smile to them both. "I'm glad you found us. I wanted to make proper introductions." He turned to a beautiful redheaded woman. "This is my wife, Emily, and our children, Stacy and Daniel."

Tess smiled and noted that Stacy looked to be about the same age as Sherry, while Daniel appeared closer to seventeen or eighteen.

"This is my wife, Tess. We're very happy to meet you all," Brad said, reaching out to shake hands with Emily Aznar.

"You have a beautiful church," Emily told Tess as she slid into the pew beside her.

"It seems to be in a perpetual state of change," Tess said, nodding to the area behind the pulpit. Heavy construction plastic had been stapled in place behind the main stage, where a new choir loft was being constructed.

"It's a good sign to see a church like this," Emily replied. "It means growth, right? Alter the old to bring in the new?"

Tess thought about Emily's words long after they'd finished singing and the pastor had begun to speak. Growth meant change, and Emily was right—the old was often discarded or remodeled to make way for the new. Some people thought that was bad. They clung to the old ways and the old things as though to lose them or change them somehow stripped away the preciousness of what they had.

I've been guilty of that myself, Tess thought. *Change has always been hard for me. I find my security in a stable routine and consistent schedules.* All of that would have to change, she reasoned, once the baby came. In fact, all of that was changing now. Ever since the arrival of Sherry, her life had taken on many changes, including one change she hadn't planned on. For some time now, Tess had hardly given any thought to getting pregnant on her own. She found that amazing. For years it had been her only consuming goal.

Tess was so lost in her own thoughts that she hardly heard the sermon. She followed Brad out into the foyer after the service and was surprised to find Sherry laughing with a group of kids. The youth group had apparently ended their worship earlier than the adults and they now all stood congregated around the front doors of the church.

"Oh, I'd like to introduce you all to Sherry," Brad said as the teen joined them. "She's staying with us for a time."

"It's nice to meet you," Emily said in greeting. "You look about the same age as our daughter."

Sherry smiled shyly and endured the introductions. Tess worried that she'd become sullen or retreat back into her shell, but she remained quite open and pleasant.

"Would you and your family by any chance be interested in an afternoon of relaxation and fun?" Bartolo questioned.

Tess laughed. "We're always up for an afternoon of relaxation."

The man's dark eyes seemed to twinkle. "Good. I would like to invite you all to join us on our yacht. The weather promises to be good and we thought a cruise might be a welcoming reprieve."

Brad rubbed his hands together in anticipation. "Sounds good to me. What do you think, Tess?"

"I think it sounds perfect. Shall we bring lunch?"

"That's a good idea," Emily said. "We already have a fridge full of deli meats and cheese, as well as several different kinds of breads, so why don't you bring salad?"

"Sure," Tess said. "What about dessert? We could bring that as well."

"If you like," Emily replied. "And we'll furnish the drinks."

Tess looked to Sherry and remembered Laura speaking about how the teen's life had been turned upside down. No one gave her options anymore. In hopes of helping Sherry feel included, she asked, "What about you, Sherry? Do you think spending the afternoon on a yacht sounds like fun?"

Sherry seemed surprised to be asked. "Yeah, I guess so." She smiled then as if she'd given the matter a more thorough consideration. "It sounds good."

It was settled then and Bartolo gave Brad directions to the marina where he kept his boat. The kids seemed especially excited by the prospect of spending the day on the ocean.

Later that day, groggy from the sun and too much food, Tess lazily drifted in and out of sleep on the deck of the Aznars' boat. She didn't know when she'd enjoyed anything quite so much. The lapping of the water against the hull and the rhythmic hum of the boat's engine lulled her into a sense of serenity. At least for the moment, she was void of problems and concerns.

"You said you wanted to talk to me," Bartolo remarked as he came alongside her lounge chair.

Tess sat up, rather startled. "Oh, I'm sorry. I've just been dozing."

"No apologies are needed," the man said, taking the chair beside her. He had dressed casually in khaki shorts and a white cotton shirt. The straw hat he wore shielded his face, while his sunglasses hid his eyes.

Tess had pushed her own sunglasses atop her head so that she wouldn't tan with the obvious marks on her face, but now as she squinted against the brilliant reflection of light on the water, she found it necessary to put the glasses back on.

"I did want to talk to you," Tess agreed, "but I don't want to do business on the Sabbath. Perhaps you would have some time for me tomorrow?"

He smiled. "I will make time. Are you reconsidering my thoughts on your relocation business?"

Tess nodded. "Yes, I am. I know Brad has told you about Sherry. Her baby isn't due until November, but with her living with us and her need for schooling, I think it would be better to turn parts of the business over to others rather than see it go completely by the wayside."

Bartolo nodded. "I'll be happy to set up a meeting for tomorrow. I'll have my secretary call you first thing in the morning."

Tess felt a strange relief at his enthusiasm. She had worried that actually speaking to him on the matter might cause her to change her mind. But instead, Tess felt a great sense of peace about the idea.

Laughter sounded from the bow of the boat, and Tess looked up to find Sherry and Stacy laughing at the antics of Daniel. He apparently didn't mind showing off for the girls.

"I'm so glad the kids are enjoying each other's company," Tess said, continuing to watch the petite blond teenager. "I'm never quite sure what Sherry will actually find favor with."

"With kids, it's always hard to tell," Bartolo offered. "Mostly they need reassurance that they are safe and that all is well."

Tess nodded. "I guess we all feel that way."

Bartolo got to his feet and added, "Oh, and I've found that a little spending money helps." He grinned mischievously and raised a brow. "And that, too, is of interest to most all of us, no?"

Laughing, a thought crossed Tess's mind. She should give Sherry an allowance. Maybe she could give the girl chores around the house and offer to pay her. Would Sherry find that offensive? After all, the idea was for Brad and Tess to take care of her and foot the bills for her pregnancy. Would she feel it unreasonable to be given responsibilities, as well?

Then again, what would Sherry involve herself with if she had money? Would she get into drugs or other kinds of destructive behavior?

Tess contemplated the matter for the rest of the afternoon. It was a real dilemma. On one hand, every kid needed a little spending money; on the other hand, she didn't know that she entirely trusted what Sherry might do if she had extra funds. The matter clearly came down to trust. Tess needed to trust Sherry, but in order to trust her, she would have to allow the child room to prove herself worthy.

Chapter 18

Weeks of meeting off and on with Bartolo and her accountant left Tess feeling very positive about her decision to expand. Bartolo had already arranged to draw up plans, detailing his ideas for Tess's approval.

Tess could find no fault with his suggestions. The office layout and plans for staffing were sensible and would easily promote positive business practices. In all actuality, Tess found it rather amazing that Bartolo had such a clear understanding of her business and the work she hoped to accomplish.

At one point, she'd even asked him why he didn't just open his own relocation business and leave her out of the deal altogether. He was, after all, wealthy and well-received in the Miami area. It wouldn't be that hard for him to arrange something on his own. His answer had been simple. He had prayed about it and felt this was the direction to take. Tess could hardly argue with reasoning like that.

The day of Sherry's first doctor's appointment came upon them the day after Tess finalized her agreement with Bartolo. Having the matter of her business resolved gave Tess a tremendous amount of relief and allowed her to focus on Sherry and the baby. Even so, Tess approached the doctor's office feeling rather apprehensive. Sherry had hardly said two words about the appointment, and Tess found it impossible to understand the teenager's silence. Was this a good sign or a bad sign? Was she excited to be going or nervous? As if reading her mind, Sherry suddenly spoke.

"I hate going to the doctor. They're always poking you or sticking you with needles or doing some other stupid thing."

Tess nodded. She couldn't help but hear the anxiety in her voice, and when Tess mingled it with her own nervousness, she felt an overwhelming urge to reassure Sherry. Reassure them both.

Tess opened the clinic door and held it for Sherry. "Dr. Zeran is a good friend. I've known him for quite a while now. He actually goes to our church, but since we have so many people and several services, I know it's hard to get to know everyone."

"I just hate being messed with," Sherry admitted in an unusual moment of openness.

"I do too," Tess admitted, following Sherry into the building. "I've been here enough times, I could walk these halls blindfolded."

Sherry eyed her quite seriously for a moment. "Were you sick?"

Tess shook her head. "No, just trying to get pregnant. The doctors couldn't figure out any reason I couldn't have a baby, so we just kept coming back and trying different things."

Sherry looked away but seemed to consider the words while Tess pushed for the elevator.

"Until I got pregnant, I'd never had a woman's kind of examination," Sherry said, shuddering. The elevator doors opened and they stepped inside before she added, "Being examined now is sure different from being examined when you're a kid. I didn't like it at all."

Tess felt sorry for the teenager. What a rude awakening to adult life. "It can be very uncomfortable and a bit embarrassing, but you have to realize that these doctors deal with people in this manner all the time. It's just their business. Dr. Zeran is very kind, and I don't think you'll have any reason to be afraid."

"I hope not. I still wish I didn't have to go through stuff like this."

Tess reached out to touch Sherry's shoulder. "I'll stay with you, if you like."

"Would you?" Sherry's voice held such hope, but just as quickly she tried to look unconcerned. "You can if you want."

"Of course. I didn't want to intrude, but I'd love to see the sonogram firsthand."

"Good. I want you there," Sherry said. Then, as if realizing she'd said too much, the girl looked at her rounded abdomen. "I'm really getting big."

"Yes," Tess agreed, seeing her discomfort in having exposed her fears. "You'll probably be amazed at how big you'll get in the next few months."

She hated herself for envying this little girl. In a perfect world it would have been Tess who carried the new life. This child would have been safely in a loving home, attending school, and having the time to grow up properly before being faced with such responsibilities. But it wasn't a perfect world.

They waited some thirty minutes in the reception area before the nurse finally called Sherry back. When Tess followed close behind, Sherry announced to the nurse that she wanted Tess with her at all times. The nurse smiled in response and told Sherry that would be just fine.

The nurse weighed and measured Sherry, got a routine work-up of blood and urine samples, then left them with the promise the doctor would be right in.

Dr. Zeran arrived in short order and within a matter of minutes had the exam completed, much to Sherry's relief. Tess had been surprised to have Sherry reach for her hand halfway through the procedure, but even now, with the exam over, Sherry was still clinging to her hand.

"You look to be in good shape," Dr. Zeran told Sherry. "Your measurements are good and in a few minutes I'll send you down the hall for the ultrasound. After you finish with that, we'll discuss the results."

Sherry and Tess were soon taken down the hall. The technician, a young blond woman who appeared to be not much older than Sherry, smiled at them in welcome.

"I'm Gail and I'll be doing your sonogram," she announced.

Sherry looked warily at the woman and then to Tess. "What do you have to do to me?" Sherry asked.

"Oh, it's simple and painless," Gail told her confidently. "I'll put some jelly on your tummy and we'll use this," she held up a long, cylindrical instrument, "to give us a picture of the baby on the screen."

This seemed to give Sherry some comfort, and Tess could sense her relaxing.

"Now I need you up here on the table," Gail instructed.

Tess stood by as Gail ran through her preparations. She couldn't help but wonder what might be going through Sherry's mind. She knew what would have been running through her own mind had she been the one under examination.

Would it be a healthy baby? Would it be a boy or a girl? How much development would she be able to see?

All of these questions flooded Tess's mind, along with numerous other thoughts. Thoughts like what it would feel like to be the one having the ultrasound.

"Have you been feeling the baby kicking today?" Gail questioned.

Sherry nodded. Tess was startled at the news. She hadn't even thought to ask Sherry if the baby had been kicking. The thought had never even entered her mind.

"How long have you been feeling the baby?" Tess blurted out without thinking how it might sound.

Sherry looked up at her and shrugged. "I don't know. A little while."

Tess felt more pangs of jealousy. *Oh, God, help me,* she prayed. *I want this to be a joyous occasion and I don't want to do anything to make Sherry upset with me.*

Gail went to work locating the baby, and within moments, she had a visual outline on the screen. It looked to Tess like a poorly tuned black-and-white movie.

"This is your baby's head," Gail announced to Sherry. "Can you see it? Here's the nose and the mouth."

"I do see it!" Sherry exclaimed.

"Yes!" Tess agreed enthusiastically. "I do too."

"Oh, look," Gail said, grinning, "the baby is sucking his . . ." She paused and added, "or her, thumb."

Sherry shook her head. "I didn't know they could do that when they were still inside."

"They do a lot of things," Gail replied. "Sometimes I've even seen them sucking their toes."

Tess and Sherry laughed and exchanged a look of amusement.

"Do you want to know the sex of the baby?" Gail questioned.

Sherry looked to Tess, giggling as she did. "It'd be like

knowing the end of the movie before you watched it."

"I agree," Tess said, reaching out to touch Sherry's hand. "But it's up to you." She thought of Sherry's feeling of helplessness—of being poked and prodded. It seemed a small concession to allow her to choose this matter of knowing the sex of the baby.

"I don't want to know," Sherry replied, suddenly seeming to remember her position. "It won't matter anyway."

Tess tried not to be affected by the girl's sudden change of mood.

Dr. Zeran came in about that time and Tess's thoughts shifted. "Well, how's it going? Oh, good," he said, noting the screen. "I see our little star is already making a debut."

"I've asked them whether they want to know the sex of the baby," Gail said, handing the doctor the notes she'd already charted.

"And?" He looked first to Sherry and then to Tess.

Tess finally shook her head. "No. Let's keep it a secret."

David smiled at Tess. "It's more fun that way." He studied the chart for a moment. "The court arranged for your records to be sent to me, Sherry. I'd say the due date is right on target for what you were already expecting from your previous doctor. Looks like November twenty-sixth, give or take." He handed the chart back to Gail. "Have you decided what hospital you'll use and how you will proceed once the baby is actually on the way?"

Tess nodded. "To a certain extent. We'll use the Aventura Hospital. It's closest."

David nodded. "It's a good hospital." He dismissed Gail and allowed Sherry to sit back up before continuing. "I hope you'll both understand, but there are some questions that I must ask. They might be uncomfortable for one or both of you, but I need to know what your plans are for the delivery of this baby."

"What do you mean?" Tess questioned.

"Well, for instance," David began, "do you plan to be in the delivery room with Sherry? Is Sherry planning to use Lamaze, and will you be her partner if she does?"

"I guess we hadn't really considered it yet," Tess said, looking to the teenager for confirmation. Sherry said nothing and looked down at the floor as if to avoid the entire matter.

"The breathing techniques taught in Lamaze will be good to help with the birthing process. There are also some good educational films shown during the class time that will give you an idea of what the process will be like once you're actually in labor."

"I'd be happy to help Sherry through the classes, if she wants my help," Tess offered.

"That's fine," Sherry said without emotion.

Dr. Zeran continued. "There's something else. I need to know what the plans are once the baby is delivered."

"What do you mean?" Tess questioned. Sherry looked up as if to see his response.

David leaned back, striking a casual pose. His words, however, were anything but casual. "This situation being what it is, I need to know what the plan is for the baby after delivery—after we've finished examining and caring for the baby's needs. Does Sherry want to have time with the baby? Is she going to be a partial caregiver? Or will the baby go immediately into your care, Tess?"

Tess didn't even look to Sherry for a response. She could allow the child a say on many things, but this wasn't one of them. "Sherry has agreed that since I'll be the baby's adoptive mother, I'll be the one to handle the baby after the delivery."

"Is that right?" Dr. Zeran asked, looking directly at Sherry.

"I didn't want the baby anyway," Sherry replied flatly.

Tess realized Sherry was upset by the situation. She could hear an edge of fear in the girl's voice.

"I'm sure you understand, Sherry," the doctor began, "this isn't going to be an easy situation. You may change your mind. You may have desires to keep this child."

"I don't plan to keep the baby or to break my agreement," Sherry stated firmly. "I just want to have it and see that it's happy with the Holbrooks."

Tess saw David raise a brow and interjected. "Sherry will be living with us for a short time after the birth."

David shook his head. "I've seen situations like this before. Are you sure this is wise?"

"It doesn't matter what she says. I have rights!" Sherry looked at the man with a fixed expression of determination. Resembling a fighter about to square off, she stood her ground. "I just want time."

Tess had never seen her quite this worked up, at least not in such a verbal manner. The statement about time permeated Tess's thoughts. Time? Time for what? What was it Sherry needed and why was time so important?

"I think we'll be all right," Tess said, seeing that Sherry wasn't about to back off. "Brad and I have arranged to keep the baby in our bedroom. Sherry won't be the one to take care of the baby and so I don't think the bonding issue will be a problem."

David nodded. "I just don't want to see either of you hurt. This isn't a simple matter. There are a great many emotional and physical needs that will come into play. You both need to keep that in mind."

Tess nodded. "I'm sure we will."

Sherry's words haunted Tess throughout the remainder of the day. Now that they were home, Sherry had hidden herself away in her room, leaving Tess alone to contemplate what had happened. More and more, Sherry's vulnerability and fearfulness were becoming apparent. And with that revelation, Tess became more uncomfortable.

She'll be gone in a few months, Tess reminded herself. *She'll leave and it won't be my problem anymore.*

Sitting down to her desk, Tess toyed with a pencil and tried to shake the thoughts from her mind. *What does she really need? Why is time so important? Are we making the right decision to let her stay?* David Zeran certainly didn't seem convinced. Could he be trying to save Tess from additional trouble? The questions stacked up, one on top of the other, like a fragile house of cards.

Tess reached for the telephone. She'd call Laura and discuss the matter with her. Laura might well be able to give her some answers or at least set her thinking in the right direction.

But before she could dial Laura's number, a knock sounded on her front door. Tess hurried to see who it might be and was surprised to find Kim on the other side.

"Kim! It's been ages. I've called—"

"I know," the woman said, seeming contrite. "I just couldn't deal with it. Forgive me?"

"Of course, come in," Tess said, pulling back. "Can you stay for a while?"

"I suppose. I just wanted to see how you were doing." She glanced cautiously down the hall. "Did you and Brad decide to go through with your plans?"

Tess nodded enthusiastically. "Yes. We have a fourteen-year-old who lives with us right now. Her name is Sherry and she's due to have her baby in late November. Would you like to meet her?"

Kim shook her head. "No. I still hope to talk some sense into you."

Tess was crestfallen. Why couldn't Kim just be happy for her? But then she remembered her own reaction when Kim had adopted Laney. She'd hardly given Kim an easy time of it.

Softly, with as much tenderness as Tess could show, she reached out to touch her friend's hand. "Kim, I'd rather you didn't see this as your personal battlefield. We've been friends for too long. Why don't you come sit down."

Kim shook her head. "It's because we've been friends that I don't want to see you hurt—like me."

"I know you don't want to see me hurt, and I appreciate that," Tess began, "but I have to live my own life the best way I see fit. You do understand that, don't you?"

"I think you're reaching for a star," Kim replied. "An unobtainable dream."

"Kim, people adopt every day. Remember, you were the one who showed me the statistics long ago when you first decided to adopt. You had a bad experience, but it was an isolated incident. That doesn't mean that when you decide to adopt again, the same thing will happen."

"I'm not going to adopt again. I'm not about to set myself up for that kind of misery and you shouldn't either. I feel badly because I know I helped to convince you to adopt, but now I'm here to help convince you not to go through with it. This girl is just going to break your heart."

"Sherry's a wonderful girl," Tess said with confidence, though her own fears were rapidly feeding off of Kim's negative comments. "She's just been put through a lot in her life. She doesn't have much of a future and she can't keep her baby with her after it's born. There's no way she can take the baby back. She has no way of supporting the child at fourteen."

"She could always find a way. She'll find someone to help her. Laney's mom did."

Tess shook her head. "Laney's mom was older, had the baby's father in her life, and had graduated from high school. She was for all intents and purposes ready to live an adult life. Sherry has no hope of that at this time. She's just a kid living off the state, has no living relatives, and the baby's father and family want nothing to do with her or the baby. They hoped Sherry would have an abortion, and now that she's going through with the pregnancy, they've shown no further interest."

"Things happen, Tess. You're just going to get hurt."

"Life hurts, Kim. But the alternative to life is not something I want to consider at this point," Tess replied, and for the first time she could honestly understand that it was true. Life did hurt. It hurt, but it also felt wonderful. It had its moments of heartache right along with its pleasures.

"I think you're crazy," Kim replied and turned for the door. "I just came to try to help you see reason. I couldn't rest thinking that somehow I had failed to do everything I could to persuade you not to let this delinquent into your home."

Tess felt defensive on Sherry's behalf. "She's not a delinquent, she's a little girl who's been caught up in a difficult situation. She deserves to be cared for and nurtured just like everyone else. How can you be so heartless?"

Kim stopped at the door and eyed Tess quite seriously. "Because *they* are heartless."

"They?"

"These unwed mothers—these girls who play around at being adults, get themselves pregnant, then, rather than do the right thing, they selfishly think once again of themselves. They don't care who they hurt, Tess. I'm telling you this as a fact of life. Believe it or not, but chances are pretty good that your Sherry will do no different. She'll break your heart. They always do."

With that, Kim hurried from Tess's condo, not even bothering to close the door. Tess stood for several minutes, staring out into the empty hall. Kim's words had affected her sense of peace more than Tess wanted to admit. Closing the door, Tess turned and found Sherry standing in the hall. She had no idea how long the girl had been there, but apparently she'd been there long enough. Without a word, Sherry turned away and went back down the hall to her room.

Tess thought to call after her, but hesitated, replaying the conversation in her head. Maybe Kim's pain would sear Sherry's conscience, and if there were any thoughts of being deceptive with the adoption, Sherry would now think twice. Perhaps Sherry had even heard Tess's confidence and support of her and would feel less anxious about her stay with them.

Tess bowed her head. "Please, Lord," she whispered, then continued silently, *please show me what to do and what to say. I can't stand the thought that Kim might be right. I don't think I could bear it if Sherry did the same thing that Laney's mother did.* She lifted her face and sighed. "Please, Lord."

Chapter
19

Sherry gave Brad and Tess very little trouble during the months that followed. She'd had her moments of moodiness and even minor rebellions when they'd set curfews and insisted on knowing where she was at all times. After a while, however, everyone eased into a daily plan that quickly fell into a routine. The worst and best day were the days Tess took Sherry to the doctor. She loved hearing the baby's heartbeat and all the positive things Dr. Zeran had to say about Sherry's condition.

Tess had decided to keep a journal about the events. She started at first only writing about the doctor's visits, but soon, without really intending to, Tess wrote in the journal on a daily basis. She wrote about her feelings and thoughts concerning the arrangements she'd made. She wrote about her fears and her growing faith in God—faith that was born out of knowing she had to either trust God for the situation with Sherry or go mad.

Sitting down to take up her journal once again, Tess startled at the sound of breaking glass. Rushing from her office into the living room, Tess was stunned to find Sherry attempting to pick up the pieces of a broken crystal vase.

"What in the world happened?" Tess exclaimed, looking

to see if there was anything left to salvage.

"I don't know, I guess it fell off," Sherry said, sounding rather indifferent. Now in her seventh month of pregnancy, the petite teen was beginning to struggle under the added weight of the baby.

"You don't know?" Tess replied. She was heartbroken over the loss. Her mother had given her that vase on her eighteenth birthday. "That's no answer, Sherry. I want to know what happened."

The girl looked rather indignant. "I said I don't know. Why are you yelling at me?"

"I'm not yelling, not yet. But I do expect a decent answer." Tess tried to calm herself. The last few weeks had been especially stressful for her, with the added work of blending her business with new employees and homeschooling Sherry.

Steadying her nerves, Tess took a deep breath. "Now, will you tell me what happened?"

Sherry looked at Tess and rolled her eyes. "It's not that big of a deal. I don't know how it broke. It just did."

"Crystal vases do not just jump off the table, Sherry. Besides that, what are you doing in here? I thought you were watching your algebra video."

"I finished it," Sherry replied. "I was going to sit outside on the balcony and read my Shakespeare."

"That still doesn't tell me what happened with the vase."

Sherry shrugged and started to walk off. "I told you, I don't know."

"Get back in here," Tess said, and this time she did raise her voice.

Sherry halted in her steps and turned around. "Are you going to yell at my baby like this?"

Tess sobered at the question. "Sherry, I expect a certain

amount of respect from you. You have broken something special to me. I would at least expect an apology."

"So I'm sorry," Sherry replied. "That still doesn't mean you can yell at me. I don't want my baby growing up being yelled at."

"Are you threatening me?" Tess questioned, her whole body shaking from the ordeal.

"Get real," the girl answered, shaking her head. "Do I look like I could be very threatening to you?"

"Look, you've been sulking around here all week. I don't know what the problem is, but I'm getting tired of it."

"You're tired of it?" questioned Sherry angrily. "I don't see where you get off being upset. I'm the one who's being bossed around day and night. 'Do this, Sherry.' 'Don't do that, Sherry, you might hurt the baby.' 'Eat this.' 'Take this vitamin.' I'm getting tired of being told what to do. You aren't my mother, so stop acting like it."

"Given your inability to be civil and respectful, I'm certainly glad I'm not your mother," Tess snapped back. She instantly regretted the words when she saw the painful flickering of understanding in Sherry's eyes.

Trying to mend the situation, Tess sighed. "Look. We're both just on edge. Everything has been stressful. Living here with us, the homeschooling and the chores . . . well, I know it's probably more than you're used to. I wouldn't have given you chores if you hadn't agreed that you wanted an allowance."

"I don't know why the state can't just give me the money and leave me alone," Sherry muttered. "I don't need them, and I sure don't need you."

Tess felt a twinge of fear ignite. Sherry's statement reminded her of Kim's warning. "I'm sure you think you're capable of taking care of yourself, but you're just a kid. Just four-teen years old. That doesn't lend itself to a whole lot of life experience for taking care of yourself."

Sherry looked at her as if Tess had lost her mind. "I have more experience than you could ever dream of. I can take care of myself."

"That's how you got in the condition you're in right now," Tess countered. "Didn't it ever dawn on you that there's a reason we have laws about kids marrying or age limitations on driving and drinking? You're a smart kid—didn't it ever occur to you that the reason adults are allowed to do certain things that kids aren't is because they're more capable of handling the consequences and the responsibilities?"

"What do you know? You've never lived like me. You don't know anything. I hate being treated like some kind of crimi-nal! I'm blamed for everything wrong that happens. I hate it, and I hate you!"

She stormed off to her bedroom and let the door slam good and hard. Tess cringed and turned to face the broken vase. It was all too much. With tears in her eyes, she knelt down to pick up the pieces.

"You're no good," she could hear her birth mother say. *"You're worthless, Tessera. Worthless and stupid. I don't know why God gave me such a stupid child, but I wish you'd never been born. I hate you for the burden you've put on me."*

The words rang in Tess's ears as she picked up the shards of glass. Her biological mother had hated her. The only rea-son she hadn't deserted Tess on some street corner was be-cause Tess was good at working the pushers and getting her mother a quick fix.

Tears mingled with the glass. The emptiness inside her heart threatened to eat Tess alive. *Oh, God,* she began to pray, *where are you in all of this? Why do I have to hurt so much? Why can't I just let go of the past?*

From that moment on, the day went downhill. Sherry refused to speak to Tess and refused to come out of her room. It was only when Tess was tied up with a phone call that she heard Sherry's door open. Glancing down the hall, Tess saw Sherry clad in a maternity bathing suit. She was out the door before Tess could get off the phone and call to her.

She wanted to apologize to Sherry and tell her that the vase was important to her because of her mother. She thought to follow after the girl and corner her at the pool, but the telephone rang again.

"Hello?"

"Tess, it's Laura."

"Oh, it's good to hear a friendly voice."

"I just heard your message on my answering machine. You sounded completely done in. Are you okay?"

"Not completely. I had a bad fight with Sherry this morning. She broke a vase and that just seemed to trigger all sorts of anger. We yelled at each other and said things we didn't mean. Oh, Laura, it was just awful."

"I'm sorry to hear that. Where's Sherry now?"

"She just took off for the pool. I was going to talk to her and then you called."

"Well, I don't need to keep you, but I wondered if you'd like to come over for supper this evening."

"That would be wonderful. Brad is out of town, and with Sherry so hostile toward me, it will be nice to be with friends."

"Well, why don't you bring Sherry and come around seven," Laura suggested.

"Sounds like heaven. We'll be there," Tess replied.

Tess had just managed to bury herself in a client's request

list when she heard the front door open. Surprised that Sherry had returned so soon, Tess got up to go see if anything was wrong.

Sherry, wet from head to toe, padded across the carpet, leaving a water trail as she went.

"You're getting water everywhere!" Tess declared, running to the bathroom for a towel. "Why didn't you change in the pool house?"

"Why don't you stop yelling at me?" Sherry demanded. "I left because I didn't feel good. Now you're just making me feel worse."

"Is it the baby?" Tess questioned, forgetting about the floor.

"That's all you care about, isn't it?"

Tess felt guilty for her obvious omission of Sherry's feelings. "I just wanted to know how to best help you."

"No, it isn't the baby," Sherry replied snidely. "I just have a headache from all this yelling and the sun didn't make it feel any better."

"I didn't mean to yell," Tess began. She figured to apologize, but Sherry gave her no chance.

"Well, you did. Now leave me alone. I'm going to take a shower."

Tess felt tremendous irritation with Sherry's dismissal. "Don't order me around, Sherry. You aren't the grown-up here."

"Well, if yelling and being bossy is being a grown-up, then count me out. I'd rather be a kid any day than act like you." For the second time that day, Sherry went storming off to her room and Tess was left gritting her teeth.

Why was this so hard? What was happening to her patience?

Cleaning up the water from the carpet, Tess tried to rationalize the events of the day. Both times she had reacted poorly. Maybe that was the key. Hadn't the pastor spoken on the positives of action versus the negatives of reaction? She tried to remember the specifics of the sermon.

"Trouble comes when we react to a situation rather than act. Reacting involves emotions, and that lends itself to irrational thinking and motivational issues," Tess recalled. It perfectly summed up the way she'd responded to Sherry on both occasions.

Walking out onto the balcony, Tess gripped the rail and studied the pale blue of the ocean. The water crossed a vast expanse and faded into the horizon, where it met the darker blue of the sky. Where they touched, Tess could see a thin, translucent line. It was the tiniest reminder that the two elements would forever remain separate bodies.

"Just like Sherry and me," Tess muttered.

Laura watched Tess and Sherry with the experienced eyes of a mother. She could see the pain in Sherry's eyes and the closed, almost protective expression on Tess's face. They were both hurting and Laura didn't know exactly how to help.

"I hope you like spaghetti, Sherry," Laura said as she put down a huge pot in front of the teenager.

"I love it. Especially with meatballs," Sherry replied.

Tess seemed to open up a bit. "Laura always makes the best spaghetti. My mom even said it was the best."

Sherry made no comment, but Darren joined in the conversation. "My Laura has always known how to cook. Even when she was a kid, she could whip up a batch of brownies that would just melt in your mouth."

"How do you know that?" Sherry questioned.

"Because she made me a batch when we were younger than you."

"You were allowed to cook when you were just a kid?"

Laura laughed. "*Allowed* is hardly the word. I had to help in the kitchen from the time I was big enough to stand on a milk crate and reach the counter."

"Wow, I wish I knew how to cook."

"Well, Tess is a pretty fair cook herself. I'll bet she'd teach you if you ask her."

Sherry clammed up and focused on dishing out a portion of the spaghetti. Tess said nothing.

"Why don't we offer thanks for the meal," Darren suggested. They all bowed their heads and while her husband asked blessings on the food, Laura felt compelled to silently ask blessings on her guests.

Father, they're hurting so much. There is a great deal of pain in the lives of these, your daughters. Heal their hurts, Lord. Hear their hearts and speak to their spirits that they might know the kind of calming love that only comes from you.

"Amen," Darren said in his booming voice. "Let's eat!"

They dug into the food, each one commenting on the taste and aroma. Laura noticed how Tess picked at her plate while Sherry ate like a horse. The old expression "eating for two" came to mind and made Laura smile.

"You know, when I was pregnant with our son, I could eat three regular meals a day and three irregular meals on top of that."

"Sometimes I get so hungry," Sherry told them. "It's really weird, but sometimes I just want to eat certain things. Like boxes of crackers or chocolate chip cookies."

"What? No pickles and ice cream?" Darren teased.

"What do you mean?" Sherry questioned.

"Well, that's the standard craving for expectant mothers," he replied.

Sherry laughed. "I've never heard of that."

Laura smiled. "It's just an old wives' tale. I never craved either of those things. I wanted bananas. I could have eaten entire bunches of bananas in one sitting."

"I can vouch for that," Darren replied. "She was always sending me out for them."

Laura sensed that Tess was withdrawing even more into herself. Poor thing. She had tried so hard to have a baby and now she was clearly an outsider in the conversation.

"So, Tess, tell me how the relocation business is going. Has the new arrangement caused you any concerns?" Laura asked.

"Not anything of major importance," Tess replied. "The fact that Bartolo is a Christian helps a lot. He and his family have joined our church and they're already very active. We both have the same ethics for business and we value the lives we touch."

"That's what makes you good at what you do," Laura replied, offering Tess a plate of hot garlic bread.

Tess took a piece of bread and added, "I know my biggest fear of taking on a partner and expanding the business comes in the form of losing control."

Sherry looked at Tess but said nothing. Laura nodded and smiled. "It's hard to feel like we have no say over our lives or the things that are important to us. Feeling out of control is a terrible way to live."

She hoped the words would touch the hearts of both Tess and Sherry. "Ultimately we have to remember that God is in control. Once I came to realize that, it took a big burden off my shoulders. With God taking control, I didn't have to." Laura watched their expressions to see how they received her words, but both women kept their expressions veiled.

The rest of the dinner passed in lighthearted conversation about Sherry's schooling and Darren and Laura's new home. After dessert, Darren suggested that Sherry come play his newest computer game while Tess and Laura began to clean up.

It was as they stood loading the dishwasher that Laura braved what was on her heart. "Tess, may I ask you something rather personal?"

Tess looked at her rather oddly. "You know that you can. We're friends, after all."

Laura nodded. "I hoped you'd feel that way." She wiped her hands on a dish towel and offered Tess a glass of tea. She poured the tea and cocked her head in the direction of the patio. "Shall we go outside?"

"Sure." Tess followed her outside and took a seat at the table. "So what's this all about?"

Laura sat down and sampled the tea before speaking. "I'm worried about you, Tess."

"Why?" Tess asked with disbelief in her voice. "Things seem to finally be coming together."

"Yes, but after all this time of you and Sherry living together, you still hold her at arm's length."

"What do you mean?"

Laura put her hands around her glass but didn't drink. Staring down at the table, she prayed for the right words. "I see you treating Sherry as a non-person. You exist with her, but you don't really interact. Do you understand?"

"Not really," Tess replied. "After everything I've been

through today, I feel that I've definitely interacted with Sherry."

Laura looked up, shaking her head. "You only care for her because she will bear the child you have so long awaited. I don't say that to hurt you, but I can't shake the feeling that it's true. If you could have sent Sherry packing after day one and still retained rights to her unborn child, you would have done so. I think you'd do it still, if it were given as an option."

Tess stared hard at Laura for several minutes. Laura could see that she was giving honest consideration to her words.

"I suppose there is some truth to that," Tess finally admitted. "I guess I've never seen it as a big deal. Sherry will only be here for a short time and then she'll be out of our lives."

Laura shook her head. "No. Sherry will never be out of your lives so long as you have her baby."

"But the baby will belong to us. We will bond with it and raise it as our own."

"But Sherry will still be its biological mother. Tess, I believe adoption is a wonderful institution. You know that. I've encouraged you to adopt, and I even applaud the good you've done in the life of this wayward child. You've given her a safe haven, a roof over her head, food on the table, a doctor to care for her needs. But you refuse to give her anything more."

"What more do you suggest? I give her an allowance. I homeschool her. I've bought her just about anything she asks for, within reason," Tess argued.

"Yes, but you give her nothing of yourself. You refuse to share your heart with her," Laura said softly. "She's just a child. She has no one in the world to care for her. The only way she could get anyone to care for her was to barter the life of her child. Can't you understand?"

Tess shook her head. "She doesn't want me to be close to

her. She pushes me away at every turn."

"Isn't it possible that she's pushing you away because she's afraid of getting too close? Of caring too much?"

The realization seemed to sink in all at once. Tess's expression changed. "We're both doing that. That's what you're trying to make me see."

Laura nodded very slowly. "You're both terrified of caring about the other because you know the day will come when you will go your separate ways. But, Tess, how can your heart not go out to her? She's so needy and sweet. She's just a little girl."

"I know," Tess answered softly. "Sometimes I see myself in her."

"Don't push her away," Laura suggested. "Reach out to her. Help her. Love her."

"But what happens after the baby is born and she leaves? She's already fourteen, and in a few short years she'll be released from state care and out on her own."

"So you refuse to invest anything of yourself or your time in her because you don't want to be heartbroken in a few months when she goes away?"

"Well, that's reasonable, isn't it?" Tess questioned. "I mean, why should I set myself up for such hurt? Worse yet, why should I set myself up for that kind of rejection? I could reach out to Sherry and have her throw it all back in my face."

Laura nodded. "That's true, but just remember what the Bible says. 'Whatever you do unto the least of these . . .' "

" 'You do unto me,' " Tess filled in. Her shoulders sagged a little as she sank back against the chair. "Oh, Laura, I just don't know if I can do it. I do care about her, maybe more than I want to admit. I wanted to make a difference in her life, to show her the way to God, to help her see a different path. What do I do?"

"Let Jesus love her through you," Laura suggested. "Let Him show you how to care for her . . . even if it means having Him show you how to let her go when the time comes."

Chapter
20

Brad came home two evenings later and Tess was still contemplating Laura's words. She had tried hard to keep a gentle peace in the house, but Sherry continued to act like a wounded animal.

"So what happened while I was gone?" Brad questioned as they slipped into bed.

"Oh, the usual roller coaster," Tess replied. "Sherry's been in a mood ever since I got after her for breaking my Waterford vase."

"Was it an accident?"

Tess pulled the covers high and wrestled with her answer. "I'm sure it must have been, but she wasn't at all repentant. She didn't even act sorry, just indifferent."

"She was probably embarrassed," Brad suggested.

"I'm sure, but she could have at least acted like she was sorry."

"So what happened?"

Tess plumped her pillow and leaned back against the headboard. "Well, we started a yelling match. She told me to stop acting like her mother, and I told her I was glad I wasn't her mother. I knew it was a horrible thing to say even as the words came out of my mouth, but it was like I couldn't stop them."

"Did you just say them to hurt her as much as she had hurt you?"

Tess bit her lip and nodded. "I'm so childish. How could I have acted that way? I'm a grown woman. How could I so completely disregard her feelings?"

"You were upset. I can see that you still are. Wanna talk about it?"

Tess nodded. "Laura said I'm pushing Sherry away for fear of getting too close to her. She thinks that I feel out of control with Sherry, that my emotions are threatened."

"And is she right?"

Tess looked at her husband and reached out to touch his bare shoulder. He knew her so well. She knew he didn't need to ask the question—knew that he already understood the answer. He might even understand the answer better than she could.

"I don't want to hurt her, but neither do I want to be hurt. Oh, Brad, what am I supposed to do? I want the baby. I want to be a mother. Sherry seems to take pleasure in hurting me, in defying me. She seems to push me until I reach a limit, then she stands back just to watch me fall apart. I think it's a game to her."

"Maybe she's testing you to see if you'll go the distance with her," Brad said softly.

"Maybe, but why? Why, when you've pushed yourself off on total strangers, do you then put them through the wringer as well? Why would you jeopardize your own well-being by threatening theirs?"

"Maybe she's just tired of having no say over her life. She's finally found a bit of leverage, and desperation causes her to use it."

"I don't know," Tess said, her emotions running rampant. "Laura said I need to love her—to let Jesus love her through me, but, Brad, I just don't know if I can do that. I don't want to risk the pain."

Brad reached out and pulled Tess into his arms. As she slid down in the bed and rested her head against his chest, she felt at least a bit of her peace return.

"Justin and I have been talking and praying about this situation. I know you don't like Sherry, but—"

Tess pushed away. "That's not true. It has nothing to do with like or dislike. Sherry defies me at every turn. She is the one doing the rejecting. She wants nothing to do with our ways or beliefs."

"And why should she?" Brad asked. "She has no investment in us, short of giving us a child she never intended to have in the first place. We've made it clear that she'll be leaving once the baby is three months old. We even made it clear that we didn't care for that provision to begin with. It's obvious to her and to everyone else that Sherry is only here because that was her condition for us to be able to adopt her child."

"Maybe we shouldn't have agreed. Maybe we should have found another unwed mother."

"It's a little late for that now, don't you think?"

Tess felt a kind of hopelessness sink over her. "I know, but maybe we could talk to Justin about the arrangements. Maybe we don't have to let her stay here after the baby is born."

"Break our word?" Brad questioned. "We signed an agreement."

Tess nodded and let out a heavy sigh. "I know. I know."

From the hallway, Sherry heard every word of Brad and Tess's private discussion. They hated her. They hated her as much as everyone else did. Never in her entire life had she known anyone who cared about her and loved her just for being herself.

Sniffing back tears, Sherry hurried back to her room. The last thing she needed to do was break down in a loud display of emotion. She closed her bedroom door and contemplated what she should do. She rubbed her protruding stomach and felt the baby kick against her hand. This only made her tears come faster.

It hurt so bad to be alone—knowing that no one in the world cared about you. Sherry had lived this way for fourteen years. She felt tired and hopeless.

I'll leave now. The thought played in her mind for a moment. *If I take the money I've stashed, I could buy a bus ticket and . . .* No, that was no good. A pregnant teenager on a bus was certain to be remembered, and once she was listed as missing, it would be easy enough to trace where she'd gone.

Sitting on the edge of the bed, Sherry tried to devise a plan. She had nobody. No friends. Nothing. Well, there was Laura Johnson. She had said Sherry could call up anytime, but Laura was also Tess's friend, and that would hardly serve her needs under the circumstances.

She liked Stacy Aznar, but Stacy's father was working with Tess and that might cause the same kind of problems that going to Laura would cause. Reluctantly, Sherry faced the truth. There was no one to turn to.

"I have to do this myself."

She dried her tears and hurried to pack her things. Tess had bought her a backpack for those times when they went to the beach, and now Sherry stuffed it as full as she could with her clothes. Next, she went to the dresser and pulled out several pairs of socks. One pair contained the money she'd been saving faithfully. Tess had been giving her twenty dollars a week and that, along with the money she'd managed to steal, gave her a grand total of two hundred and thirty dollars. It wasn't much, but it was enough to start on.

She started for the door, then realized she was still wearing her pajamas. Hurrying to the closet, she threw off the gown and pulled on a pair of maternity shorts. She finished dressing and pulled on her sandals. Lately her feet had been swelling and the sandals were a bit tight, but she reasoned they would just have to do. She wasn't about to spend more time finding her tennis shoes.

Finally ready to leave, Sherry tried not to think of the task at hand. She thought only of her freedom—of being on her own. She opened the door and listened carefully. Everything was quiet. She started to leave her room, but something on the table beside the bed caught her attention.

The Bible.

Mr. D had given it to her. It was the first and only time someone had gifted her with something without expecting something back. It wasn't given out of obligation or state mandate, it was simply given because he told her the contents would change her life and make everything better.

Grabbing the Bible, Sherry forced it into the backpack with her clothes. For some reason, it gave her comfort to know she'd at least have this small connection to God.

Tess sat down to breakfast as soon as Brad took off for work. He'd let her sleep late as a gesture of comfort and had even gone so far as to fix her pancakes.

Picking at the stack, Tess looked over her monthly bills and began sorting them into piles. She figured once Sherry got up they would hit the books, then see where the day led them.

What Tess really wanted was simply to talk with Sherry. She felt the need to try to explain some of her feelings, even if it meant having those feelings completely walked on by the teenager. Brad had convinced her that the answer wasn't in sending Sherry away, but rather in trying to resolve the differences between them. Even so, Tess couldn't help but wonder if some differences weren't insurmountable. A sort of Mt. Everest in the middle of a winter blizzard.

When she glanced up at the wall clock, Tess was startled to see that it was already nine. Apparently Sherry had overslept again. Tess sighed. She had tried to keep the child on a regular school schedule starting at nine and ending at three, but Sherry was continually bucking at her suggestions of order.

Getting up, Tess feared she would have to face another battle of wills with Sherry. She knocked lightly on the guest room door, then opened it. "Sherry? It's time to get up."

Tess was instantly greeted with silence. The room showed no sign of the teen. The dresser drawers and closet doors were left open in a haphazard manner that suggested something Tess didn't even want to consider. Going to the closet, Tess began a mental inventory and realized that many of Sherry's things were missing. Checking the drawers confirmed her suspicions. Sherry was gone.

Feeling a panic rise up within her, Tess ran to the phone and punched in Brad's number. *Oh, God*, Tess began to pray as the telephone rang, *where is she?*

"Brad Holbrook speaking."

"Brad, Sherry's gone!" Tess exclaimed without introduction.

"What?" His tone of disbelief set Tess's stunned emotions into motion.

Sobbing, Tess broke down. "I don't know where she's gone, but she's taken her things. Clothes are missing and so is her backpack and her makeup."

"Calm down, sweetheart. Are you sure she didn't just go down to the pool or the beach?"

"I can't see her hauling all that stuff with her to the beach," Tess answered. "I'm telling you, she's gone."

"All right. If you're certain, call Justin. He'll know what route to take. I'll be home as quick as I can get there."

"Hurry, Brad," Tess said. "Please hurry."

She hung up the phone and dialed Justin's office number. After speaking to his secretary and assuring her it was an emergency, Justin finally came on the line.

"Tess, what's wrong? My secretary said you were having an emergency."

"I am. Sherry has run away."

"Are you sure?"

"Well, I think that's what's happened. A bunch of her clothes are gone and some of her other things. Justin, Brad told me to call you. I don't know what else to do."

"Well, you need to calm down, for one thing," Justin replied. "You won't find her by working yourself into a breakdown. Look, why don't you try to think of some special place she might have gone. Sherry must have had places she liked better than others. Maybe she would go to one of those places for a little rest and quiet. Also, call downstairs and ask if any of the doormen saw her leave."

"All right. I'll do that," Tess agreed.

"I'll finish up here and get over to your place as soon as I can. If you find her in the meantime, just page me."

"I will," Tess replied, though she was doubtful she'd find Sherry anywhere nearby.

She had no sooner hung up the phone, however, when it began to ring. Anxious that maybe Sherry had decided to call and let her know where she was, Tess grabbed the telephone on the first ring.

"Hello?"

"Mrs. Holbrook?"

The voice wasn't at all familiar. "Yes, this is Tess Holbrook."

"Do you have a young pregnant teenager living with you? Goes by the name of Sherry Macomber?"

"Yes!" Tess declared excitedly. "Who is this? Where is she?"

"My name is Mrs. Riley. I'm with hospital patient relations at Aventura."

Tess felt her knees grow weak. Sinking to a nearby chair, she barely managed to question the woman. "Hospital?"

"Yes. I'm sorry to tell you this, but Sherry was brought in early this morning. She was found near one of the marinas. She's been badly beaten."

"How's the baby?" Tess questioned without thinking.

The woman paused for a moment. "Mrs. Holbrook, the baby appears to be just fine. Sherry, however, needs some attention. The police believe she was mugged. She gave your name and address and told us you were her legal guardian. I'm calling to let you know that we need you here." Her clipped tone was no-nonsense.

Tess realized the woman was put out with her and she didn't blame her. She was disgusted with herself for having seemed so indifferent to Sherry's condition. It only proved Laura's point more clearly, making it impossible for Tess to ignore the obvious. She didn't care about Sherry like she should.

"Will Sherry be all right?" Tess finally asked.

"She's still being evaluated. How soon can you come?"

"I'll be right there."

Chapter

21

Tess didn't wait for Justin or Brad. In a mad dash, she raced to the hospital. Her mind and emotions were overcome with guilt and grief.

"Oh, God," she prayed, "I've really made a mess of things."

She thought of her heartless inquiry about the baby rather than asking about Sherry. What had happened to the compassionate human being that Tess used to be? What had happened to the kindness and love?

The old Tess would never have treated anyone as badly as I have that child, she reasoned. *The old Tess knew how it was to be treated like that—to be rejected and held at arm's length. So why did I act like that with Sherry?*

The thoughts tormented her.

Traffic crept at an unbearably slow pace, giving Tess even more time for personal evaluation. She hated what she saw.

"Lord, I've been callous and mean-spirited," she said. "I never meant to hurt Sherry. I never meant to get myself into this situation. Kim warned me. I should have listened, but I so selfishly wanted a baby. Now Sherry is injured, and who knows what will happen?"

Tess had never known a stronger conviction for her wrongdoing. What had started out as a simple plan to keep herself from further pain had unwittingly led her to more heartache.

This triggered thoughts of what must have happened to send Sherry packing. Yesterday had been a typical day, as far as Tess could remember. They had worked together on some new algebra techniques. Sherry had quickly picked up on the logic and reasoning and Tess had even commented on how smart she was.

Later, they had shared lunch on the balcony while Tess went over the geography lesson slated for the day. Nothing there to cause any real problems. Sherry had been tired and rather irritable, and Tess had finally sent her to rest after they'd finished the lesson.

Tess reviewed the events one by one as if picking through a file cabinet, searching for a single document. There had to be some reason that Sherry chose last night to run away.

Then the answer came. Her talk with Brad. Sherry must have overheard her discussion. It was the only reasonable explanation. With a groan, Tess tried to recall her every word.

With each remembered phrase, however, Tess only felt worse. She had said things that would no doubt have cut Sherry to the bone. The words became a blur as Tess tried to battle her emotions. *How could I have been so cruel? She must have been terrified.*

Her cell phone rang, nearly causing Tess to jump out of her skin.

"Hello?"

"Tess, where are you? I tried to call the house, but you didn't answer."

"Oh, Brad, I'm sorry. I meant to call you the minute I got into the car. I'm heading over to Aventura Hospital. Sherry's been found. She was beaten up and the hospital called to tell us."

"Is she all right?"

His immediate question piled guilt onto Tess's fragile state of well-being. "I don't really know. The woman said she was injured and needed us to come."

"I'll get there as quickly as I can. Did you call Justin?"

"He's supposed to be on his way to the apartment. Could you call him and let him know what's happened?" Tess questioned.

"Absolutely. We'll get folks praying too. It's going to be all right, Tess," he said reassuringly.

"I hope so."

At the hospital, Tess nearly went mad trying to locate where they'd taken Sherry. When she finally caught up with someone who actually had seen the child, Tess begged for information.

"She's in X-ray right now, Mrs. Holbrook," the nurse said after Tess's hasty introduction.

"Is she going to be okay?" Tess questioned.

"I'll let the doctor know you're here," the nurse replied. "He'll be able to tell you more." She looked almost conspiratorial as she glanced over her shoulder and added, "I do know that she's going to need stitches on her forehead."

"Stitches?" Tess barely spoke the word.

"She suffered a blow to the head." The nurse lowered her voice and added, "The wound isn't all that bad, but it will have to be stitched. We're also pretty certain her wrist is broken. Apparently she was defending herself by putting her hands up to ward off the blows of some type of weapon. Probably a pipe or something similar."

Tess felt her stomach begin to churn. "Oh, Sherry," she

said, sinking down into the waiting-room chair.

"Are you going to be okay?" the nurse asked sympathetically. "Would you like some water?"

Tess shook her head. "No, I just want to see her."

"Well, as soon as they're finished with the X-ray, I'll arrange for you to join her."

Tess knew it was the best the woman could do. "Thank you."

She watched the nurse stride off and felt helpless. In spite of the crowded conditions of the waiting room, Tess bowed her head and began to pray.

Father, I know I haven't been the woman you would want me to be. I know I've failed to share Jesus' love with Sherry, and I know I've done this purely out of selfish concern for my own pain. Please forgive me and please let that little girl forgive me. I should never have written her off the way I did. I feared her power over my life. I feared her taking away the baby I had waited so long to have. I feared everything about Sherry Macomber. But, Father, I know my fears are wrong. I know they aren't healthy, productive, or in any way related to you. I know that I have to be willing to let go of those fears in order to find the spiritual maturity and love that I have so long craved.

She paused, straining to keep her emotions under control. *But, God, I don't know how to let go. I'm back to being that scared and brokenhearted little girl whose mother didn't love her. I'm back to picking up the pieces of my handmade flower vase.*

She thought of the Waterford vase Sherry had broken and instantly realized that it was this memory and not the sentimental value of the vase that had so devastated Tess. Why hadn't she seen it then? She remembered her biological mother's hatred for her in light of Sherry's angry and pain-filled words, but she hadn't put the two events together.

Broken pieces. Tess had had a lifetime of broken pieces.

Now Sherry lay somewhere down the hall, possibly fighting for her life and the life of her child. More broken pieces.

"Tess?"

Tess looked up to find Laura Johnson. "What are you doing here? Did Brad call you?"

Laura looked confused. "No. We're here for Darren's lab work and chest X-ray. What's wrong?"

Tess broke down, her shoulders trembling as her tears fell. "It's Sherry. She ran away last night and someone beat her up."

"Oh no," Laura said, sitting down beside Tess. She put her arm around Tess's shoulder and hugged her tight. "Is she going to be all right?"

"I don't know. I only know that she took a blow to the head, and her wrist might be broken. Oh, Laura, this is all my fault."

"How so?"

Tess looked into Laura's concerned face. "She probably overheard my conversation with Brad. I said some awful things."

"What makes you think Sherry overheard?"

"It's the only thing I could come up with that would send her away. We didn't have any fights yesterday. Sherry was tired and feeling irritable, but I swear I didn't pick at her for it. I sent her to bed to rest, and I didn't ask her to help with the laundry or—"

"Calm down, Tess. I believe you," Laura interrupted. She patted Tess lovingly. "You can't blame yourself for what has happened."

"Oh, but I can and I do. None of this would have happened if I hadn't kept Sherry at arm's length, like you said. If I'd done things differently . . ."

"You'd have no way of knowing that the scene would be any different than it is," Laura replied. "Tess, instead of wasting time blaming yourself, just put it to prayer. Sherry is now in the best possible place, with all the care and attention she could need. The only thing you can do to help the situation is pray."

Tess nodded. She knew Laura was right.

"Mrs. Holbrook?" The same nurse who had disappeared moments before, now reappeared. "Sherry is out of X-ray now. You can come sit with her if you like."

Tess nodded. "Yes, I want to be with her." She looked to Laura. "Please keep praying for us."

"Of course. Let me know what happens. I need to go figure out what they're doing with Darren, but I'll try to locate you afterward."

"Thanks, Laura." Tess suddenly realized that God had perfectly ordered Laura's appearance at the hospital. Laura's companionship and promise to pray gave Tess a peace she'd been missing since the hospital had first called.

Following the nurse into a small room, Tess found herself unprepared for the sight of Sherry's beaten face. Tears instantly came to her eyes.

"Oh, Sherry. You poor baby," Tess said, reaching out to touch the girl's arm.

Sherry looked up at her through swollen eyes. Puffy and bruised, her face hardly resembled the angelic features Tess knew to exist.

"Are you the mother?" a man said, coming into the room. "I'm Dr. Bervert."

"I'm Sherry's legal guardian," Tess replied.

"We have paper work for you," the man told her, motioning to the nurse. "And right now I need to get her head wound treated. So if you'll just step outside . . . ."

"No!" Sherry moaned out the word in a desperate manner. "Don't go."

Tess reached for her hand. "I won't leave you." She looked to the doctor. "I want to stay. I'm not weak stomached, and I won't cause you any problems."

He looked at Sherry and then to Tess and nodded. "Okay by me."

Tess squeezed Sherry's hand and felt flooded with concern for this wounded child's fears. "It'll be all right, Sherry. I'll be right here. I'll hold your hand the entire time. You just squeeze my fingers when you're afraid, and I'll pray extra hard. Oh, and Laura is praying. I just saw her outside."

"Laura's here?" Sherry asked. Her swollen lips caused the words to be mumbled.

"Yes." Tess decided not to explain the situation further. Let Sherry assume they were here for her all along. There would be time to explain later.

The stitching went quickly and Sherry hardly flinched when they stuck her several times to deaden the area. Next, the doctor moved Sherry to a different area and yet another physician came in to address the problem of Sherry's wrist.

"I've arranged with a good orthopedic doctor, Dr. James Seymour, to see her and set the wrist. She's in a temporary splint right now. The break isn't bad—in fact, it should heal rather quickly; however, we need to let the swelling go down before we can put on a permanent cast."

"I'm so glad," Tess said, breathing a sigh of relief.

She felt a strange protectiveness for the child. Sherry was her responsibility, and to see her so wounded, so pained, caused Tess to completely reevaluate the situation and her own emotions. She did care about Sherry. She cared about her suffering and her fears.

By the time they'd finished, the doctor announced that Sherry looked to be in good enough shape to go. A nurse walked in as if on cue and handed the doctor some papers. She started to say something to Tess, but Sherry interrupted.

"What about the baby?"

"Sonograms look good," the doctor replied. "You're a very lucky girl."

Sherry looked away and said nothing. Tess knew her heart—knew that she felt anything but lucky. "My husband is somewhere here in the hospital," Tess said, realizing that she'd given Brad very little thought.

"He's outside," the nurse offered. "He got here just a minute ago."

Tess breathed a sigh of relief. "Thank you." She looked at Sherry. "I'm going to go get Brad. I know he's worried about you."

"You won't be gone long, will you?" Sherry asked, the fear still evident in her voice.

Tess smiled. "No. I won't be gone long."

She was as good as her word, bringing Brad back with her. He looked at Sherry with such a loving look of concern that Tess momentarily wondered if he'd come to care for the child more than he'd let on.

"You look like you went ten rounds with the local boxing champ," he offered with a smile.

"I wouldn't have lasted ten rounds," Sherry said, trying to smile. "Agh. That hurts."

Brad looked to the doctor. "Can you give her something for the pain?"

"In her condition, we don't want to give her anything too strong," the doctor replied.

Sherry frowned and looked away. The action wasn't lost on Tess. She fought to understand what Sherry was feeling. Was she angry because the baby caused her to be in pain, or was it something more? Tess thought of her own lack of concern when she'd first heard of Sherry's mugging. Hadn't the baby been her first thought? Hadn't knowing that the baby was safe been more important than knowing of Sherry's condition?

"We'll just have to do whatever it takes to make her comfortable," Brad said, reaching out to give Sherry's good hand a squeeze. "Won't we, Tess?"

"Absolutely," Tess replied in a strained voice. "Whatever it takes."

Sherry settled into her own bed with a sigh of relief. Her head was killing her and Brad had just gone to the store to buy tea bags and Tylenol. He and Tess were being so nice to her, and because of her injuries and weakened condition, Sherry didn't have time to question their motives.

"Are you hungry?" Tess asked.

Sherry shook her head. Food didn't even sound good.

"Would you mind if I sat with you for a few moments?" questioned Tess. "There are some things I'd like to say—to explain."

"Sure, go ahead," Sherry replied. She couldn't help but be curious about what Tess wanted to say to her.

Tess sat down on the edge of the bed. "Does this cause you more pain—I mean, if I sit here?"

"No, it's okay."

Tess nodded. "Good. I want to talk to you about last night."

"I already told the police that I can't remember much. I was going to find the Aznars' boat and see if I couldn't sneak on board and spend the rest of the night. After I got down to the marina, I really don't remember much else."

"I understand," Tess said. Her expression was sympathetic. "I don't want to talk to you about that. I want to talk to you about what made you leave. I have a feeling you left because of things you overheard me say. Is that true?"

Sherry didn't know whether to admit it or not. She didn't want some big lecture about eavesdropping, and neither did she want Tess lying and saying she didn't mean any of it.

"Please, Sherry. Just tell me the truth."

Sherry nodded. "Yeah, I heard you talking with Brad."

Tess looked down at her folded hands. "I kind of figured that. I owe you an apology. I should never have said those things. It's important to me that you understand why I said what I did." She looked up at Sherry and for a moment said nothing more. Finally she took a deep breath and continued. "I want to be completely honest with you. I cherish honesty, and I feel that people need to be open and honest in order to better their relationships.

"The things I said last night were completely related to my fears. I know you overheard some of the conversation I had a while back with Kim. She thinks our arrangement is a horrible mistake. I guess down deep in my heart I've worried about it being a mistake as well. Then Laura made me see some things that I didn't want to see, and now that I see them, God won't leave me alone about them. Last night I was really struggling with my conscience, my heart, and even my soul."

"Why?" Sherry asked. She couldn't imagine that this

woman with her husband and pretty things should struggle with much. They had plenty of money and a really nice home—why should she have any worries?

"I had to come to terms with the fact that I was afraid of you. I've been afraid since we first heard about you."

"Me? Why are you afraid of me?" Sherry questioned. The very idea seemed laughable.

Tess smiled. "I know it might seem silly, but believe me, it's a very real emotion in my life right now. I know I've held you at arm's length. I know I've done nothing to help you get close to me or me to you. I figured it was best for all parties concerned, but mostly I figured it was better for me that way."

Sherry knew exactly what she was talking about. She had learned to protect herself from others long ago. The thing that surprised her, however, was that this woman felt the same need that Sherry had felt.

"When you came here, I knew you wouldn't be here for long. I knew that if I cared about you—really cared—it would break my heart when you left. I figured if I could keep a distance between us, it wouldn't hurt at all. I'd have the baby to raise and you'd have the rest of your life to focus on. I thought it to be a rather simple and neat little package. Now I see that's not the way it was ever meant to be."

"Why not?" Sherry asked.

"Because I know God doesn't want me to be like that. He brought you into our lives for a reason. He knew you needed us and that we would need you. I don't know all the whys and wherefores, but I do know that this entire matter is something that God has controlled from the start."

Sherry had been doing enough soul-searching of her own to know that Tess was right. She had listened to the weekly sermons at youth group and honestly believed that God did have a reason for everything that He allowed to happen. She hadn't been able to figure out the reasons for her own life and the problems she'd had, but Sherry was certain that God really did exist and that He really saw it all.

"Look," Tess said as she got to her feet, "I just want you to know that I intend to stop being so childish. I don't want to keep putting a wall between us. I do care about you, and if that gets me hurt, then so be it. I want you to be healthy and safe and I want you to be able to talk to me and share whatever thoughts you have. Can we possibly agree to start over?"

Sherry felt as if the wind had been knocked out of her. No one had ever truly cared what she thought or how she felt, and nobody had ever asked Sherry for a second chance.

Words failed her and all she could do was nod. She was afraid if she did try to speak, she might start crying, and her head already hurt bad enough.

Tess smiled. "Thank you. Look, when Brad gets back I'll bring you some pills and hot tea. For now, just try to rest."

Again Sherry nodded, even though she had no real intention of resting. She had a great deal to think on and rest seemed the least of her worries.

Brad accompanied Tess when she delivered Sherry's tray. "You sure took a beating, kid," he said, his voice full of affection mingled with relief. "You worried at least ten years off my life, too." He smiled, hoping she wouldn't feel chastised.

Sherry nodded. "I'm sorry."

Brad could see she was sincere. "I hope you won't feel the need to leave again. We might not have done everything right, but we're just human. We're trying, Sherry." She looked up at him and nodded again.

Tess handed her two pills and a glass of water. "Look, the doctor said these should help with the pain but not hurt the baby. If they—"

"I never wanted to hurt the baby," Sherry interrupted, as if suddenly needing to explain herself. "I wasn't going to keep the baby even if I had stayed away."

"Sherry, we don't want you to feel the need to stay away," Brad replied. Tess had told him about the talk she'd had with Sherry, but he felt it necessary to reinforce her words. "Please don't do it again. If you feel so upset that you want to go elsewhere, Laura and Darren have said they'd be happy to have you spend some time with them."

Tess nodded. "That's right. We don't want you to feel like we don't care. We've handled this all wrong, and we're willing to admit our mistakes. Please give us another chance."

Sherry nodded. "I won't run away again."

Smiling, Brad took the glass of water and set it on the nightstand beside her bed. He motioned to the tray. "Drink your tea and get some rest. We can talk more in the morning."

Tess followed him out of the room and down the hall to their own bedroom. He closed the door before saying, "She's really swollen. I can't believe anyone could do something so inhumane."

Tess began unfastening the barrettes that had held her hair back. "I know. I just want to cry when I see her lying there so helpless and small. Oh, I'd give anything if I could take back what I said last night and turn back time."

Brad came to her and put his hands on either side of her face. Tenderly he rubbed his thumbs along her cheeks. "I know you would, but we can't change the past. Only the future."

"Oh, Brad, I really want to change—for the better."

She put her arms around his waist and lifted her face. Brad lowered his lips to hers, knowing after all their years of married life that this was what she desired. Better yet, it was what he wanted as well. She responded warmly—eagerly—as if his touch might somehow heal her of her regrets.

"I love you, Tess," he whispered, pulling away just enough to see her face.

She opened her eyes to him and he lost himself in their depths. "I love you, Brad. I'm sorry for all the wasted years—for my blindness. I don't want to be the cause of anyone else's pain, yet I know I'm bound to make mistakes."

"We both will," he said, stroking her hair, "but as long as we keep trying to change . . . to make it better . . . I know God will bless us."

Tess nodded. "I know He already has."

Chapter
22

"Are you sure she doesn't know anything about this?" Laura asked Tess several weeks later.

"No," Tess said excitedly. "Sherry thinks we're just here to visit you like any other time." Tess threw a cautious glance over her shoulder, to where Sherry and Brad stood talking to Darren.

"I think this surprise party will make her feel very cared about," Laura admitted. "It's hard to believe she's fifteen—she looks twelve."

"I know. It makes it even harder when people see her in her condition," Tess replied. At nearly eight months along, Sherry's pregnancy could not be mistaken or hidden as it could have been in the early half of her pregnancy.

"Poor little mite. It's not going to be easy on her."

"No," Tess admitted. "But David said she's in good health and the baby is as well."

Laura shook her head. "I keep them in my prayers constantly—you too."

Tess smiled, reassured by Laura's deep commitment to pray for them. "Thanks. I know it's making an impact. Since Sherry ran away, things have been different."

"When does she get the cast off?"

"Another week. The doctor says she's doing just great, but I know she still has bad dreams about that night."

"If I were her, I'd have bad dreams about my life," Laura said without thinking. Realizing her words, she shook her head. "That wasn't very nice of me."

"Maybe not, but it's true. I've thought the same thing. She's resilient, you have to give her that much."

They walked up the lane to Laura's condo, and Tess noticed the curtains flutter as if someone had been peeking out.

"You're awfully brave to leave the house with ten teenagers hiding inside."

Laura laughed. "Mr. Dearborn is also in there."

Now it was Tess's turn to laugh. "That might just make it worse." She turned around to call to Brad and Sherry. "Come on, you slowpokes. I'm hungry."

Sherry left the men and waddled after Laura and Tess. "I'm hungry, too. Let's eat!"

It was only as they came to the door that Tess began to worry about the shock Sherry might sustain when everyone yelled, "Surprise."

Turning to Laura, with Sherry right beside them, she said, "Laura, do you think our plans will cause problems for Sherry and the baby?"

Laura cocked her head to one side and threw Tess a questioning look. "Huh?"

Sherry looked at Tess with the same puzzled expression. "What are you talking about?"

Tess fumbled for words. "Well, it's just that I made some plans, and, well . . . I don't want you to be too startled."

Sherry looked at Laura and shrugged. "What's she talking about?"

"I think she's worried," Laura said, seeming to finally understand, "that surprises might cause harm to the baby or even send you into labor sooner than you expect."

"Why would I be surprised?" Sherry asked, looking first to Tess and then to Laura.

"Oh, just don't be," Tess replied. "What I mean is . . . well . . . when we go inside, be prepared for a surprise and don't get too worked up."

Sherry laughed. "You guys are goofy."

Tess nodded. "Yes. Yes, we are."

She opened the door and allowed Laura to go in first, then Sherry stepped inside to a rousing chorus of "SUR-PRISE!"

Then, without waiting for the shocked teen to recover, the group began to sing "Happy Birthday."

Sherry turned to Tess. "How did you know it was my birthday?"

"I asked," Tess said rather smugly. "I figured a party might be fun, and I wanted the day to be special for you."

"So this is why I wasn't supposed to get too excited," Sherry said, smiling. "A birthday party. Wow, I sure never expected this."

The kids rushed up to Sherry as soon as the singing stopped. Brad and Darren stood in the doorway behind Sherry and were nearly forced back out of the house at the onslaught.

"Wait until you see the cake!" Stacy Aznar declared. "It's huge."

The group pulled Sherry toward the kitchen, but not before she glanced over her shoulder at Tess. For a moment, their eyes met and Tess knew without words that Sherry's heart was full. Tess couldn't help but smile. "Happy birthday, Sherry."

Sherry crawled into bed that night with her mind still reeling from the day's events. She had a pile of unexpected presents, and to her surprise, not one thing was for the baby. She'd figured they'd give her things that the baby could use—after all, the baby was staying and she'd be going.

Now, too big to sleep comfortably on her back, Sherry rolled to her side and stuffed a pillow between her legs. This helped her with the back pain she was always suffering.

Just a few more weeks, she thought. A few more weeks and she would have the baby and everything would go back to the way it was. She would be slender again and . . .

"And what?" she whispered. "What then?"

She thought of the party and all the fun she'd had. Everyone had been so kind. She had laughed and eaten, played games, and even joined in some impromptu singing. It had been like nothing she had ever known. Sadly, she faced the fact that she would probably never know anything like it again.

She had broken her own cardinal rule: Never get close to anyone. She had done that before, with Joey, but she'd vowed she'd never again give away her heart. Now she found herself in jeopardy once again.

Sherry admitted she cared about these people. She enjoyed their company and loved being with them. Ever since the mugging, Tess had treated her with an open warmness that had made her long to be with her, share everything with her. Sherry had told herself that it was all right, that she was only allowing it for the sake of her baby. But now she couldn't lie to herself any longer.

She had friends at the church, people she liked to be with.

Mr. D had helped her to understand more about herself and God than anyone else had ever even attempted. She knew she was on the verge of deciding to accept Christ as her Savior, but there were still lingering fears that if she did accept Him, He might not accept her.

Beyond this, Sherry knew that she cared deeply about Laura and Darren. They were like the grandparents she had never known. She remembered once when Joey's grandparents had come to stay with them around Christmas. They fussed over the grandchildren and played with each one— even the younger foster kids were lavished with attention. Sherry had avoided any contact, but even watching from afar, she knew that what they offered was something she wanted. Laura and Darren fussed over her and made her feel like they really cared—maybe even loved her.

That's a lie! a voice seemed to call out in the recesses of her mind. *No one loves you. You aren't worth loving.*

She hugged her pillow and tried not to hear the ugly thoughts. *Your mother didn't love you. Your father didn't love you. Joey didn't love you. There's no way that Laura and Darren love you.*

Sherry closed her eyes and thought of Tess. Tess had said she cared about Sherry, but no doubt that was just because of the baby. Sherry knew the baby was everything to Tess. Tess fussed over the nursery and the baby clothes, and while she often included Sherry in some of the choices, Sherry knew she was no more significant to the scheme of things than the doorman downstairs.

Tears came to her eyes and oozed out from behind her closed lids. Silently, Sherry cried. She thought of God and how Mr. D said you could talk to Him anytime. She thought for a moment that she might talk to God and explain how much it hurt to feel this way—how scared she was. But even as she considered it, her heart told her she would never be good enough to talk to God. And so she tried her best to sleep.

Sometime in the night Tess awoke to the sound of crying. She had thought it was a dream at first and then she realized it was real. Yawning and trying her best to wake up, Tess realized it had to be coming from Sherry's room.

It wasn't the first time. Sherry was always trying hard to put on a front of indifference or strength, but Tess had heard her muffled cries on more than one occasion. Always before, Tess had whispered a prayer and left the girl alone. After all, she didn't want to embarrass her or make her feel worse. Then, too, as ashamed as Tess was to admit it, she knew that she had often left Sherry to cry alone for fear of letting down her own defenses. It had terrified her to see Sherry so vulnerable and needy.

But this time was different. This time the sobbing sounds cut clear through Tess's heart and there was no way of avoiding it. Getting up, Tess pulled on her robe. She knew she should go and confront Sherry, but still she hesitated.

"What if she doesn't want me there?" she questioned to the darkness. "What if I only make it worse?"

But Tess didn't want Sherry to bear her sorrow alone, even if it meant Tess would pay for her actions later on. For the first time since deciding to adopt and learning of Sherry's plight, Tess cared more about the lonely teenager than she cared about herself.

Silently she crept out of her bedroom, down the short hall, and, without knocking, entered Sherry's room. No matter what Sherry did or said, Tess would help in whatever way she could.

"I heard you crying and thought you might need help," Tess said as she switched on the lamp. "Are you all right?"

Sherry buried her face in her covers. "I'm fine. Just go away."

Tess didn't think the words sounded very convincing. "Sherry, you don't have to bear this alone. Whatever is troubling you, I want to help."

"Nothing is wrong. Go back to bed," came the muffled response.

Tess knew she couldn't leave. She sat down on the bed and laid an arm on the form beneath the covers. "Sherry, just talk to me."

Sherry struggled to sit up. She looked as though she might say something in anger, then her expression contorted and she burst into tears anew.

Tess did the only thing she knew to do. She opened her arms and pulled Sherry close. Stroking the girl's hair, she spoke soothingly. "I want to help, but I don't know how."

"I'm so afraid," Sherry said, clinging to Tess's neck.

"Of what?"

"Everything," Sherry replied. "The future."

The future? Tess couldn't help but wonder what she meant by that. Was she afraid of having the baby?

"Dr. Zeran thinks you'll do just fine when the baby comes. He says you're strong and healthy and so is the baby. It'll pass before you know it. Don't worry about the future."

Sherry pulled away. She looked at Tess with such longing that for a moment Tess thought she might open up and speak about all of her concerns.

But the moment was gone in a flash. Sherry suddenly

seemed embarrassed by her tears and her actions. "I'm sorry for waking you up. Really, I'm okay."

"I know you're okay," Tess said, disappointed that Sherry was hiding her feelings. "I just didn't want you to think you couldn't talk to me. We have a new friendship going, right?"

Sherry sniffed and turned away. "Right."

Tess lingered for a moment, disheartened because she couldn't seem to break through Sherry's tough façade. "I'm just down the hall if you need me."

But despite the sincerity of her words, Tess knew Sherry had no desire to hear them. She was closing herself off again—protecting herself from further hurt.

The next morning Sherry acted as though nothing had happened the night before. She took up her studies and devoted herself to her books in a manner that made it clear to Tess that the subject was not open for discussion.

Tess, in turn, buried herself in her work because she had no idea what else to do with herself. She was troubled that Sherry was suffering, but she knew she could do very little unless the girl opened up to her.

Bored with issues of retirement communities and their benefits, Tess finally took a break and went into the living room with a new catalog from her favorite mail-order store. She stretched out on the sofa and began flipping through the pages.

She found herself in the teen section and saw a darling dress on a model whose features were not too unlike Sherry's.

That would look perfect on Sherry, she thought. It would be great for next spring—maybe an Easter dress. Then it dawned on Tess that Sherry wouldn't be with them next spring. The thought brought a cloud of gloom over her.

When a knock came upon her door, Tess was happy for the distraction. Getting up, she opened the door to find Kim.

"Hi."

"Hi, yourself," Tess said, smiling. "Come on in."

"I can't stay long, but I had to see you. Tess, I feel just terrible about the way things stand between us."

Tess shook her head. "You've endured a great deal. I've been praying for you—hoping you would come."

Kim surprised Tess by hugging her tightly, then just as quickly she stepped away. "I was wrong to be so horrible. It just hurt so much. I haven't been myself at all and it took Travis leaving me to make me realize how far down I'd sunk."

"What? You and Travis are separated?" Tess asked in disbelief.

"We were," Kim replied, "but we're back together now. He made me see that I needed help to get past my depression. He made me realize that I couldn't do this alone."

"I'm so glad you listened. I'm just sorry I wasn't there to help you. I wanted to be," Tess said softly, "but I figured under the circumstances I would just be a painful reminder."

Kim shifted and looked down the hall. "Is everything going all right? Is she still going to let you have the baby?"

"Everything is fine," Tess replied. "We still have our own brand of stress going on, but I figure that's just part of living together as a family." The words pricked Tess's conscience. It wasn't the first time she'd thought of their life with Sherry as being that of a real family.

"Well, like I said, I can't stay. Travis is waiting for me in the car. We're heading over to the Faith Family Church for some counseling. My aunt Ida goes there and said they were really good. So far, I have to agree. I just wanted you to know how sorry I am for acting the way I did. I want to be there for you, but it may take some time."

Tess was the one to initiate the hug this time. "You take all the time you need, so long as you don't shut me out."

Kim pulled back, nodding. "I promise."

Kim's visit had given Tess just the right lift for her afternoon. By four o'clock, Tess realized she needed to start thinking about something for dinner. Brad had promised to be home early and she had figured to fix something simple for the trio. But before she could even get up from the sofa, Tess heard the front door open.

"Brad? Is that you?"

"Yes, it's me. Justin's here, too."

Tess grinned. It was just like her husband to bring home strays. She went to greet them. "Well, you caught me off-guard. I knew you said you'd be home early, but I never expected it to be this early."

Brad nodded. "We've got problems, Tess."

She looked to Justin, whose expression confirmed this. "What's wrong?"

"I think we'd better sit down together with Sherry," Brad suggested.

Tess felt her stomach tighten. "All right," she said, turning to go get the girl.

Sherry was just as surprised as Tess to be called to the gathering. She eyed each of the adults almost fearfully, then settled on Tess. "What's going on?"

"I don't know, but Brad and Justin are about to tell us."

Justin cleared his throat. "I'm just going to lay this out on the table, but I want you to know I'm already taking care of matters."

Tess nodded. "All right, so go on."

"The Delbertos were not happy to learn that Sherry opted to have the baby instead of an abortion," Justin began. "Mrs. Delberto in particular is afraid that Sherry will change her mind and keep the baby and she wants no part of that. She has petitioned for custody."

"What!" Tess exclaimed. "How can this be? She has no right."

Sherry sank into the nearest chair with a look of complete shock on her face. "She can't take my baby, can she?"

"She has certain rights as a grandparent," Justin replied. "But ultimately it will have to be decided by the courts."

"But she wanted the baby dead," Sherry countered. "She said she didn't ever want to see us again."

Justin nodded. "Look, I don't want you to worry about this. It's just something that you needed to know, and other than that, all you need to concern yourself with is that I'm on the job and will take care of all the details."

Tess refused to be comforted. "I can't believe this. I read the report. She didn't want anything to do with this baby. She didn't even believe it was her son's child."

"I know," Justin replied. "But now she does and now she wants the baby to be raised as a Delberto."

When Sherry got up in her awkward slowness and headed for the balcony, Tess couldn't help but follow her.

"Please try not to worry," Tess told her, even though her own heart was tight with concern.

"That woman is just doing this to get back at me," Sherry said, looking out at the ocean. "I know I did wrong. Mr. D helped me to see how it was a sin to do what I did, but I'm sorry for that." She turned to Tess. "Is this God's punishment?"

Tess shook her head. "I can't explain why things like this happen, Sherry, but what I do know is that in spite of how things look, we have to trust God for the outcome."

"Does He really care about me?"

The words nearly broke Tess's heart. Partially because she felt guilty for never having really shared God's love with Sherry, and partially because the longing she heard in Sherry's voice was no different that the longing in her own heart. *Could God really care about me?* was a question Tess had often asked herself as a child and then as a young adult and even now. Now, when she couldn't conceive the child she so longed to have. But the peace that settled over her heart after prayer told her that God not only cared—He was already tending to the problem.

"Sherry, God cares," Tess finally answered. "He's already seen the future—He knows how this will all turn out. He has a plan and we have to trust that His plan is better than our plan."

"Would you pray with me?" Sherry asked, her voice sounding awkward and weak.

Tess held open her arms and without hesitation, Sherry came forward. "Of course I'll pray with you," Tess whispered. "I should have been praying with you from the start."

Chapter
23

The first of November arrived with the Delbertos as determined as ever to fight for custody. Sherry and Tess waited daily for reports from Justin, but they still hadn't heard the words they wanted to hear. Tess was nearly beside herself, but she wasn't about to let Sherry know. She had worked too hard to calm Sherry's fears. The teenager had asked repeatedly for prayer, and now it had become a part of their daily routine.

The stress had been enormous on the trio. Brad had buried himself in work and when Tess finally got him to talk to her, he admitted that he was terrified of losing the baby to the Delbertos. Tess hadn't even considered how hard the entire affair might be on her husband. Huddled together in the darkness of night, they had prayed for over an hour that God would deliver them from this nightmare. After that, they had lain awake—wrapped in each other's arms until dawn. This and prayer were their only comfort.

Sherry was holding up no better. She couldn't study and she couldn't eat. Tess tried everything from cajoling to promising the teen the moon, all in hopes of keeping mother and child healthy.

"You're just nagging me because of the baby," Sherry said. "That's all anybody cares about! The Delbertos want the baby.

You want the baby. The baby is all anybody wants. I wish I'd never gotten pregnant! I wish this baby had never existed!" With that outburst she doubled over as if punched in the gut.

Tess was used to her tirades. The last few weeks had them all on edge, but it was clear that this outburst had caused Sherry some kind of physical discomfort.

"What's wrong? Did you pull a muscle?" Tess asked, moving toward Sherry.

"No." The teen straightened. "The baby just kicked me extra hard." She hung her head. "He hadn't been kicking at all since early yesterday. I figured he was mad at me." Sherry shook her head. "I didn't mean what I said. I'm just so tired."

"I know you are. But it won't be long until the baby's here—"

"Then what?" Sherry questioned, moving away from Tess to pace the living room. "What do we do after the baby is born? I don't want that woman raising my baby. She's mean and she's only in foster care for the money."

"Sherry, all we can do is pray and trust God. Trust that God will show Justin the right way to handle this case, and even trust that God will change the hearts of the Delbertos."

Sherry started to say something, then held her hand to her stomach. "I don't feel good," she said, looking up at Tess. "Maybe it's the baby."

Tess felt her breath catch in her throat. "Do you really think so?"

The child's face blanched as she held her stomach. "I'm all crampy. I have been all morning."

Tess nodded, trying her best to stay calm. "That sounds like you could be in labor. I'll call Dr. Zeran." She went to the telephone and dialed the number. Her heart was racing in fear. *It's too soon*, she thought. Sherry isn't due for another three, almost four weeks. It's too soon.

The receptionist came on the line and Tess quickly explained the problem.

"Let me have the nurse talk to you. Just hold for one moment."

Tess waited impatiently. "Sherry, why don't you sit down and rest. You don't want to bring this on any faster than necessary."

"This is Sarah, Tess. What's going on?"

Tess was relieved to hear the familiar voice of one of David's nurses. "I think Sherry might be in labor, but it's early—about three and a half weeks. What should we do?"

"That's not so bad. Look, have her rest and keep track of the pains. If they get to be five minutes apart and last at least sixty seconds, then head for the hospital."

Tess helped Sherry to stretch out on the couch. "You rest here and I'll get the stopwatch. We'll see if this baby is serious or not." She smiled and tried to sound reassuring.

"But it's too early," Sherry said, rubbing her swollen abdomen.

"Three and a half weeks isn't too early—the nurse said it's just fine."

"Are you sure?"

Tess reached out and pushed back a strand of blond hair. "I wouldn't lie to you, Sherry."

"Promise?"

Tess cocked her head to one side. "What?"

"Promise you won't lie to me, even if it's hard to tell me the truth?"

Tess sat down beside Sherry and took hold of her hand. "I promise not to lie to you. I know that it's important to you that someone be open and honest, and I promise to be that person."

"Thanks, Tess . . . aghhh," Sherry moaned in pain. "This really hurts."

Tess looked at her watch, knowing full well it hadn't been five minutes. She tried to mentally keep track of how long the pain lasted. Thirty seconds, forty, forty-five. This wasn't how it was supposed to be, Tess thought, remembering back to the vast number of books she'd read regarding labor.

Tess saw the teen's face relax a bit. "Is the pain fading?" Sherry nodded but said nothing. Tess got to her feet. "Look, I'm going to get the watch. You just try to rest."

But neither one had much of a rest. Before Tess could return with the watch, Sherry was crying out for her to hurry.

"Oh, hurry, Tess," Sherry said, struggling to get up. "I think that water sack the baby's in is leaking. Oh, look. I got the couch wet." Sherry's misery sounded in her voice. "I'm so sorry, Tess."

"That's no matter," Tess said. "If your water has broken, we need to get to the hospital. I'm not even going to bother calling back. Let's just get your stuff and go."

Tess drove like a madwoman through the crowded streets, then finally she pulled into the emergency-room drive and hurried to get the attention of the staff.

Sherry remained in misery, although the pain was irregular and often not that bad. At one point Tess had even thought the pains had stopped, but she knew from things David had told them that they would still need to come to the hospital if Sherry's water broke.

Sherry allowed the emergency-room staff to put her into a wheelchair while Tess parked the car. Tess prayed fervently as she searched for a space. It was only then that she realized she hadn't called Brad. Knowing she wouldn't be able to use her phone in the hospital, Tess grabbed her cell phone. Dialing as she walked, Tess paused outside the emergency entrance. She felt only a moderate amount of relief when Brad answered after the first ring.

"Honey, we're at the hospital. Sherry was having pains and I think her water has broken."

"It'll take me a little while to get there," Brad answered. "I'm just about to start an important meeting."

"Don't worry," Tess countered. "We probably have lots of time."

"I'll get there as soon as I can. This is really happening, huh? We going to have a baby." He sounded so pleased.

"I know," Tess whispered. Her dreams were coming true and soon she'd hold a child in her arms and know the feeling of being a mother.

Sherry found herself hustled through a maze of people and corridors. Without saying a word or instructing anyone, the orderly had brought her to Labor and Delivery. A woman probably a little older than Tess smiled and welcomed her.

"I have some paper work for you to sign," the nurse said. "My name is Mary and I'll be helping to get you checked in. I'm going to need a urine sample from you. Do you think you can go for me?"

Sherry nodded, wishing Tess was here with her. She knew her baby would be born soon and it terrified her. What if it was a boy and looked like Joey? Would it be like the doctor had warned? Would she suddenly find herself wanting to keep it?

Sherry got up out of the wheelchair and started to step toward the counter where Mary held out a urine cup. All at once the sensation of warm, wet liquid flowed down her leg.

She looked to the floor and then to Mary. Stunned, she was speechless. The nurse immediately assessed the situation, but frowned. Sherry knew she'd made her mad and waited for the older woman to chew her out, but instead she very gently took hold of Sherry's arm.

"Don't worry about that. We'll get it cleaned up. Let's get the papers signed and get you into a bed."

Sherry nodded and quickly did as she was instructed and then Mary directed her to a room. "I want you to get undressed in the adjoining bathroom. Give me a urine sample if you can and then we'll get you into bed." Just then another nurse, this one younger with a bouncing red ponytail, came and conversed with Mary in hushed tones while Sherry headed into the bathroom.

The pain came again as she tried to pull off her wet jean shorts. It felt as though she were being torn in two and all Sherry wanted to do was run away—away from the pain and the misery of what was to come.

"Are you doing okay, Sherry?"

"I'm fine, just having more pain."

"Sherry, has the baby been very active?" Mary called through the door.

"No, not really. He hasn't been moving much at all."

"Oh, so you've decided it's a boy, have you?" Sherry thought the woman's voice sounded less than relaxed. Maybe the nurses got uptight when people were in labor.

"Well, when was the last time you felt the baby kicking?" Mary called again.

Sherry wished they wouldn't ask so many stupid questions. She was hurting and this wasn't helping at all. Feeling more than a little irritated, she replied, "I don't know, okay?"

She finished pulling off her clothes, got the urine sample, and put on the hospital gown before opening the bathroom door. "Here," she said, shoving the half-full cup toward the nurse.

Mary took the cup and set it aside. "Let's get you into bed and hook you up to the fetal monitor. We'll want to keep track of you and the baby."

"Sherry?"

It was Tess. Sherry felt a whole lot better just knowing Tess was there. Funny. A few months back she wouldn't have wanted to admit that. Now she knew she didn't want to have this baby alone. Tess and Brad were both supposed to help her in the labor and delivery of the baby, but it was Tess who offered her the most comfort.

"We were just getting Sherry hooked up to the fetal monitor," the nurse announced. "I'm Mary, and I'll be working with you through the delivery."

Tess smiled. "I'm Tess Holbrook, Sherry's guardian. We're just so excited, aren't we, Sherry?"

Sherry caught Tess's enthusiasm and forgot to be afraid. She was about to have a baby—her own baby. Sherry frowned and looked away as Mary led her to the bed. No, it wasn't going to be her baby. This baby belonged to the Holbrooks.

"Okay, let's get you hooked up," Mary said patiently. She worked over Sherry while Tess came to take hold of Sherry's hand.

"Do you remember the Lamaze classes?" Tess questioned.

"I remember, but I don't think they're going to help much," Sherry replied. "I never thought it would hurt so much."

"Well, it won't last forever," Tess replied, looking happier than Sherry had seen her in weeks. The smile seemed to radiate out from her lips and flow right up into her eyes. Sherry thought she had never seen Tess look prettier.

Tess looked up at the nurse, who continued to fuss with the fetal monitor. "How's it looking?"

Mary seemed preoccupied. "Hmmm, well, I'm not sure what's happening just yet."

"Don't tell me the machine is broken," Sherry said, remembering another time when the nurse had tried to listen to the baby's heartbeat in the doctor's office, only to have to change equipment. "I'm comfortable here, so please don't make me go to another room."

"Is something wrong?" Tess asked, her hand suddenly letting go of Sherry's.

At just that time, Dr. Zeran walked into the room. His face revealed concern as he looked first to Sherry and then to Tess and finally to Mary.

He went immediately to the machine and looked to Mary for information. "I'm not picking anything up," Mary replied.

"Is something wrong?" Tess asked again, this time her voice more frantic.

Sherry took immediate notice of the tone. The look on Tess's face had changed from happy to worried. "What's going on?"

The doctor worked with the monitor for a moment, then asked, "Sherry, when did you last feel the baby moving?"

Sherry felt the pain of contractions beginning again. The tightening in her stomach was nothing, however, compared to the tightening in her chest. Something was wrong. What weren't they telling her? Why were they all acting suddenly so serious? She licked her lips and turned to Tess.

"I don't remember when the baby stopped moving. I told

you I thought he was mad at me because I wished him away—
I wanted him to be gone. It's been at least a day, maybe two."

Tess gently patted her shoulder. "It's okay, Sherry. You're
in the best place if there's a problem. David, what is it?"

"I'm afraid we've got some complications." He looked to
Sherry. "Remember when I saw you last, I told you the baby
was lying sideways?" She nodded and he looked to Tess, then
back to Sherry. His expression said it all. "The baby is still
transverse, but it's dropped since I saw you a week ago.
There's no way you could deliver naturally."

"What else?" Tess asked. She took hold of Sherry's hand,
while Sherry fought back the urge to cry.

"Yeah, what's going on?" she finally asked.

"I'm afraid we're not getting a fetal heartbeat," the doctor
finally replied. "Mary said your water broke and the fluid was
green in color. And now you're telling me you haven't had
movement in one or two days."

"My baby doesn't have a heartbeat?" Sherry questioned
frantically. "Well, cut him out. Save him. Don't you have those
machines where you can shock their hearts and make them
beat?" She looked desperately to Tess. "Make them save our
baby."

Tess bit her lip and nodded. She looked at the doctor, em-
ulating Sherry's desperation. "Save him, David."

"I can't," he replied flatly. "It's been too long. The baby's
probably been gone for a day or more. The color of the am-
niotic fluid suggests fetal distress."

"No!" Sherry screamed. "Don't say that! My baby isn't
dead! Tess!" She looked to Tess for hope. Tess had dissolved
into tears and stood there shaking her head slowly back and
forth.

"He's not dead. You just have a broken machine. Get another one," Sherry said, trying to get out of the bed. "I'll walk to another room."

The doctor put his hand on Sherry's shoulder. "Sherry, I know this is difficult to understand, but these things happen sometimes. We're going to prep you for a Cesarean and take the baby out, but I can't bring the baby back to life."

Sherry looked into his eyes and fell apart. She hurt so badly inside. Falling back against the pillow, she shook her head from side to side. It was just a bad dream. That's all it was, she told herself. It had to be just a bad dream.

David ushered Tess outside while a nurse worked to put an IV into Sherry's hand.

"Where's Brad? He should be here with you."

Tess felt her world falling apart. Numb from the shock of the moment, she asked, "David, what happened? Why is this happening?"

The baby she had dreamed of was gone in the blink of an eye. Dead for a day or more without anyone even knowing. How could she have sat so casually at breakfast and not have known? How could she have gone about her routine, all while her baby was dying?

"Did we do something wrong?"

David put his arm around Tess's shoulder. "There's no way of knowing for sure what happened. You took good care of that girl, though. I know that and you know it too. These things happen sometimes."

"But you said she was healthy," Tess sobbed. "You said the baby was healthy." She buried her face in her hands. "Oh, God, please don't let this be true."

"I'm so sorry, Tess. You can be with her during the C-section. In fact, I think both you and Brad should be with her. It will help to keep her mind occupied. If Brad's still not here by then, we can break the news to him and have him join you when he gets here."

Tess looked up, barely registering all the words. "What do you mean? Does Sherry have to be awake for this?"

"I'm afraid so. It's safer than risking a general anesthetic. She'll be given an epidural and we'll deliver the baby and let you hold him or her."

Tess knew that she wanted to be with Sherry—knew she had to be with the girl. This wasn't the kind of thing that she'd be strong enough to endure alone. Tess wasn't sure she could bear it alone, herself. *God, give me strength*, she prayed and squared her shoulders.

"Brad will be here when he can, but I need to make a phone call. Do I have time?"

"Sure. It's going to take at least twenty-five minutes for the epidural to take effect after they administer it. I can't operate until then."

"I don't want to use the phone in the room, but I don't want to leave her alone." Tess kept remembering the anguished expression on Sherry's face. Compassion and mercy flooded Tess's heart. She had to help Sherry bear this devastating news.

"She'll be all right. Just make your call and then the nurse will have you change into scrubs."

Tess found a phone and dialed Brad's cell number. He didn't answer, but then, she hadn't really expected him to. He generally turned it off for meetings. Still, she had hoped he might have left it on, knowing the situation as it was. She left a message, hoping he wouldn't be too upset to drive.

"Brad, David thinks something horrible has happened to the baby." She couldn't say the word *dead*. Somehow telling him this softened the blow. "David's going to do emergency surgery on Sherry. I'll tell you more when you get here. Please, Brad, hurry." Then she called Laura Johnson. Laura had been such a pillar of strength and Tess needed her most desperately now.

"Laura, it's Tess. I need you to pray."

"Tess, what's wrong?" Laura asked without hesitation.

"I'm at the hospital with Sherry." Her voice broke, and for a moment, all Tess could do was cry. "Oh, Laura, the doctor thinks the baby is gone. They're going to operate to take the baby out, but they think it's too late."

"I'll be over as soon as I can," Laura replied. "In the meantime, I'll be praying. You just sit tight. Maybe the doctor is wrong."

"I don't think so, Laura. I don't think so."

Chapter
24

Tess felt awkward in the hospital scrubs. She tried hard to concentrate on the sights and sounds of what was happening around her and Sherry in the operating room, but her mind kept freezing on the words, *"The baby is dead."*

There were no words for the way Tess felt. The emptiness she'd known as a child seemed diminished, almost foreign, compared to the vast wasteland left in her heart after Dr. Zeran's announcement. How could it be? How could the baby be gone, just like that?

David said the baby had been dead for a day, maybe even two. Tess thought back on the events of their last week. There was nothing there that should have indicated a problem. Nothing happened out of the ordinary. Of course, they had been enduring the stress of the Delbertos' custody claim.

The Delbertos. Tess realized they would no longer be a problem. What would they say or think when they learned of the death of their grandchild?

"Tess, will you pray with me?" Sherry asked softly.

The question brought Tess out of her labyrinth of thoughts. She leaned down. "Of course. I've been praying all along."

"I know, but I just want to hear the words," Sherry replied.

Tess closed her eyes. "Oh, Father, our hearts are so broken. There are no words. No words at all." She drew a ragged breath and held it a moment. Letting it out slowly, Tess continued. "The pain is so great, but we know you still love us. We know you're watching over us. Oh, Father, be merciful, ease our suffering."

She opened her eyes to see Sherry's closed eyes swamped in tears. Reaching out, Tess gently touched the child's face with a tissue.

Sherry's eyes opened and her expression was one of gratitude. "I know this changes everything," she whispered. "I know it ends all your plans. It ends mine too." She looked away and added, "I don't know why I can't die with the baby."

"Oh, Sherry, please don't say such things," Tess declared. "I don't want you to die."

One of the nurses brought a bundle to Tess. For a moment, Tess feared what she might see. Would the baby be deformed? Would it be too difficult to look at?

"It's a boy," the nurse said softly.

"I knew it was," Sherry said, nodding slowly.

Tess looked down as she received the bundled baby. Oh, but he was beautiful. Wisps of blond hair so downy fine crowned his perfectly formed head. Light brown eyelashes lay against his cheeks. He looked as though he only slept.

Tess did the only thing that seemed natural. She kissed the tiny forehead, her tears flowing down upon the baby's pale face.

"Oh, Sherry. He's lovely. He's got such tiny little fingers."

"Let me see him."

Tess lowered him to where Sherry could look. "He's blond, just like you."

"I want to hold him," Sherry said, her voice breaking.

"The doctor has to stitch you back up, Sherry," the nurse announced. "But as soon as he's done, we'll put you both in a private recovery area. You can hold him all you want then. I promise."

Sherry and Tess both looked to the woman as if to ascertain the truth of her words. Slowly, Tess nodded and handed the baby back. She realized there would be plenty of time for good-byes.

Nearly an hour later, they were in the recovery room. Sherry held the baby close to her heart while Tess waited eagerly for Brad to join them. The nurse had just announced his arrival, as well as the news that David had gone to let him know what had happened.

Sherry and Tess had both thought it better that David break the news. Neither one felt up to the strain of the announcement and neither one wanted to leave the baby.

"What shall we name him?" Tess asked, reaching out to touch Sherry's cheek.

"I never really thought about it," she answered. "After all, he was going to be your baby."

Just then Brad came through the doors. His eyes were red with tears and his expression broke Tess's heart anew. Leaving Sherry's side momentarily, she crossed the room and fell into his arms.

"I'm so sorry," he said, barely getting the words out. "I'm so, so sorry you had to go through this alone."

Tess pulled back, feeling a strength she hadn't known she possessed. "I wasn't alone. I had Sherry and Sherry had me, and we knew you were coming and we knew Laura was praying . . . and we knew God was with us."

Brad drew her back to him and cried softly against her hair. Tess wrapped her arms around him and held him tight. Shared pain was so much less hurtful.

"Come on," Tess said softly. "I want you to see our son."

Brad straightened and wiped his eyes. "He's gone, Tess. He's not ours anymore."

Tess drew him to Sherry's side. "He's no less ours now than he was when he was alive."

Sherry lifted the baby up to Tess. "He still needs a name."

Brad looked down at the baby and shook his head. "He's so little." He glanced to where Sherry lay. "He's blond, just like you."

Sherry nodded. "The nurse took his hand and footprints and she snipped some of his hair—once for me and once for you and Tess. She took two pictures, too. That way we'll always remember him. But he needs a name."

Brad nodded and seemed to consider the matter for a moment. "My grandfather's name was Davet. It's a French name. My mother used to tell me it meant beloved."

"Davet," Sherry said, trying out the name. "I like it."

"I like it too," Tess said, looking to her husband with great pride. "Davet would be fitting."

They spent another ten minutes sharing their grief and the baby. When the nurse came to take the baby away, Sherry announced that she wanted to sleep.

"I just want some time alone, okay?" she said in a voice barely above a whisper.

"Come on, Tess," Brad encouraged. "We need to go tell Laura and Darren anyway."

Tess looked up at her husband and nodded. She felt so tired her bones actually seemed leaden. Her mind still reeled from the news, but her ability to sort through it seemed to have nestled deep into some strange, protective sleep. There would be time later to realize the full impact.

"Are you sure, Sherry? I could stay with you. We both could."

Sherry looked to Tess, her face void of emotion. "I'm really tired, and I just want to sleep. I'll be okay."

Tess nodded. She could understand how Sherry felt. She herself wanted nothing more than to curl up in a bed and forget this ever happened. She longed to wake up and realize that they were still safely back in the apartment and that the events of the last few hours were nothing more than a bad dream.

Silently, Tess and Brad walked to the waiting room. Laura and Darren immediately got to their feet and joined Tess and Brad. Tess saw movement to the right of her and realized Justin had also come to share their vigil.

"What's happened?" Laura asked. She put her arm around Tess as if knowing that the news wasn't good.

"The baby didn't make it," Brad answered.

"Oh, I'm so sorry," Laura said, squeezing Tess's shoulder. Tears came to her eyes. "What happened?"

Brad shook his head and Tess felt as though she were a spectator watching the entire matter from some far-removed place.

"The doctor isn't entirely sure. He said they sometimes never know exactly what went wrong. They think the baby died a day or two ago."

"Oh my," Laura replied, shaking her head slowly.

"Brad, Tess, I'm so sorry," Justin began. "Is there anything I can do?"

"I don't know what it would be," Brad answered, breaking

down. Tess watched as Justin embraced him for support. It was all like some strange theatrical play.

Tess continued to hear them talk about the situation. Justin and Darren asked their questions and Brad gave the only answers he could. Tess felt almost light-headed. She tried to focus on the conversation but found it impossible.

"Come over here and sit down," Laura said, leading her to one of the waiting-room chairs. "Do you want some coffee?"

Tess looked at her. *Coffee?* She shook her head.

"Bring her one anyway," Laura suggested to Brad. "Bring her something to eat as well. Maybe some cookies."

Brad knelt down beside his wife, his eyes still edged with tears. "Tess, I'm going to go with Darren and Justin to get some coffee. I won't be gone long." He got up, then leaned over and kissed her head.

Still Tess said nothing, fearful that if she spoke, the pain might very well consume her. Her strength was fading in the presence of others who could be strong for her. A tightness formed in her chest, making her breathing more difficult. Her throat ached with a strange gripping kind of pain. She wanted to cry, but the tears would not come.

A memory came to mind. It was the moment she had finally understood that her mother was dead. She could see herself as a child, standing in the middle of an unfamiliar school playground. One of the kids came up to her with something in his hands. Other children gathered around, their curiosity washing over Tess in waves of conversation. Chattering, really. Nonsensical words that meant very little to the confused child.

The boy opened his hands to reveal a dead bird. *"It's dead, just like your mother,"* he had said in a cruel, mocking tone.

Tess had stared long and hard at the lifeless creature. *Dead—like my mother?*

The teacher had come then to chide them all for their actions. The boy and the bird were quickly taken away and Tess was left to figure out what was to become of her. Suddenly death seemed more understandable. Her mother hadn't gone to sleep. Her mother had died and would never come back to life. Her mother was gone forever.

For a moment Tess had been terrified, but then something strange began to happen. If her mother was dead, then Tess would never again have to go out on the streets in the middle of the night. She would never again face the drunken woman who belittled Tess for her meager attempts to please. Without realizing what had brought about the change, Tess remembered being glad that her mother was dead. Her death meant freedom for Tess.

"Tess, darling, are you all right?"

Tess looked up and found Laura looking at her with a gravely concerned expression. "I just can't believe this. It's not real."

Laura patted her hand. "What will happen now?"

Tess shook her head. "What do you mean?"

"To Sherry. What will happen to Sherry now that the pregnancy is over and the baby is gone?"

"I don't know," Tess replied, unable to think past the moment.

"What do you want to happen?"

Tess couldn't understand why Laura would ask her such a question. Worse still, Tess didn't understand how to answer the question. Finally she said, "I don't know."

Another fifteen minutes passed and soon the men returned with the coffee. They talked in hushed whispers while

Tess mechanically sipped from the foam cup. The numbness was easing, but behind it came a rush of pain-filled emotions.

Then something in Tess ignited and began to grow. A maternal feeling like she'd never known started to warm her senses and clear away her shadowed thoughts. She thought of the baby she'd held in her arms. Even dead, the baby was so very precious to Tess. But then her heart began to focus away from the child they'd lost. Instead, she thought of Sherry. Something had happened between them in those moments of absolute despair.

Tess had realized a strong desire to protect and nurture Sherry. She wanted to spare the child from any further pain— she wanted to love away the hurt that had crossed two generations of damaged children. Suddenly she knew the answer to Laura's question.

"She needs me," Tess whispered. "I need her. I love her."

"What was that, dear?" Laura questioned.

Tess looked up and met the older woman's eyes. Brad was absorbed in conversation with Darren and seemed not to have heard his wife's murmured words. Shaking her head slowly, Tess gripped Laura's hand.

"I love her. I love Sherry."

With Laura and Darren's promise to stay at the hospital, Tess and Brad were finally persuaded to go home. Sherry had been given something to help her sleep and reduce the pain of the C-section. They weren't really needed at the hospital, and yet Tess didn't want Sherry to wake up and be alone. Laura understood perfectly.

"You go home, have a shower and nap, then come back.

We'll stay here for as long as it takes."

All the way home, Tess couldn't help but think of what had happened to her that day. She thought of her life since Sherry had come to live with them. Sherry had worked her way into Tess's heart without her even suspecting.

"Brad?"

"What?"

"I want to ask you something," Tess replied. "Something very serious."

He continued focusing his attention on the road but nodded. "Go ahead."

Tess didn't hesitate. "Brad, you know I've always wanted a baby. We've always planned to have a baby of our own."

"I know, sweetheart. I'm so sorry. I know you're hurting—I'm hurting too," he said softly. "This isn't at all how either one of us pictured this whole adoption thing. I guess I'm sorry now that I pushed you into the idea."

Tess reached out and took hold of his hand. "Brad, have you ever considered adopting Sherry?"

This caused him to look away from the road. "What?"

Tess repeated the words. "Have you ever considered adopting Sherry?"

He turned onto a side street and pulled the car over, nearly driving onto the front lawn of someone's yard. "Are you serious?"

She began to nod, praying he might understand. "I don't want to let her go." She paused and looked into her husband's face. "I love her, Brad. Seeing her so hurt, so lost—it was more than any child should ever have to endure. I don't want to let her go back to the state. I love her and want her to be our daughter."

He nodded. "You know, I feel that God has laid this child

on my heart since she first came to us. I thought maybe it was a simple matter of seeing to her well-being while she was with us, then later I wondered if God didn't want me to do something more. I never said anything because . . . well . . . you two didn't seem to like each other much and I couldn't see making you miserable with yet another of my suggestions. I hope you aren't mad at me."

Instead of feeling angry, however, Tess felt energized by his confession. "We could adopt her, couldn't we? She has no one, and now even the Delbertos can't hurt us."

"We'd have to discuss it with Justin, but I don't know why it wouldn't work. Do you think she'd want to have us adopt her?"

Tess considered his words for a moment. "I don't know. I guess we'll have to ask her."

"Are you prepared for her answer?" Brad questioned. "She might say no."

Tess shook her head. "I don't think she will. I think she needs us as much as we need her. I think God has brought us together for this purpose. We'll grieve the loss of the baby together and we'll share a hope for the future together."

"Then I suppose," Brad replied, "we should talk to her about it."

"Let me talk to her about it," Tess said. "At least let me bring the idea to her first. We can sit down as a family after that and discuss it in detail."

"As a family, huh?" Brad replied. "I like the sound of that."

Chapter
25

A few hours later, Tess and Brad headed down the hall to Sherry's room. The hospital had secluded Sherry away at the far end of the hall in a private room. Tess was glad for the privacy. What they had to tell Sherry was not something she wanted to share with others—at least not yet.

Pausing at the door, Tess whispered a prayer and looked to Brad for encouragement. She was trembling from head to foot. What if Sherry rejected them? Could Tess bear the pain of yet another person she loved refusing her love?

"It's going to be all right," Brad assured. "Either way, God brought us to this place."

Tess knew he was right. She started to say something to that effect when she heard the sobbing that emanated from the room. The sound broke her heart. Sherry was weeping for her baby—for the loss of the child's life—perhaps even the loss of her own innocence.

Tess forgot her fears and pushed open the door. "Sherry?"

The teen hurried to dry her eyes, but it was a futile attempt to hide her emotions. She lay back against her pillows and eyed Tess warily.

"What are you guys doing here?" Sherry asked. "The baby is dead."

Tess came to her side, surprised at the teen's cool reception. "We're here because of you."

"Well, you don't need to be. Just go back to your life. I don't have anything to give you now." Sherry faltered and looked down at her hands. "Just go."

"Sherry, we want to be here with you."

Sherry looked up in surprise. "Why? You don't owe me anything."

"We know that, Sherry," Brad interjected, "but we care about you."

"We don't want you to go through this alone. We're in this together." Tess's voice was strong and sure. She could feel God giving her strength.

"I can take care of myself. You've done your duty. Now go," Sherry demanded.

Tess sat down beside the girl and put her bag on the floor. "Sherry, please. I want to help you. I made you a promise to be a friend."

"That was just for the baby's sake and now the baby is dead." Her voice cracked. "My baby is dead."

Sherry burst into tears anew and buried her face in her hands. "He's dead. He's dead."

Seeing Sherry so broken, Tess, too, began to cry. She reached out, uncertain if she would hurt Sherry by taking hold of her. It was a risk she had to take. Pulling the girl slowly and carefully into her arms, Tess embraced her.

Tess's tears wet Sherry's hair. The pain of their loss was shared by both of them, binding them together. When Brad encircled them with his powerful arms, Tess knew they were a family. Sherry just had to see that.

Sherry seemed to realize all at once what had happened and pulled away. She grimaced as she fell back against the bed and Tess knew she must have hurt from the C-section incision.

"You're only here because you feel sorry for me. Don't," Sherry said. "I hate it when people feel sorry for me."

Tess looked to Brad, trying hard to battle her own emotions. Brad took over and reached out to take hold of Sherry's hand.

"Sherry, I can't say that we don't feel sorry for you, because we do. But that's not why I'm here. I'm here because I know it's where God wants me to be."

She looked doubtful. "How would you know what God wants?"

"I've been praying about this since we first learned about the baby. I've tried to understand the baby's death. Maybe I won't ever understand it, but that's not why I came here right now." His voice was gentle and Tess could see Sherry softening under his spell.

"Then why? Are you going to tell me how God loves me and cares about me?" Sherry questioned. "Are you going to tell me how much better off the baby is in heaven than here with us?"

Tess shook her head. She felt an overwhelming surge of guilt. She'd really never tried to make Jesus real to Sherry. Even after Laura had told Tess to let Jesus love Sherry through her, she felt she'd done her part to see that Sherry was exposed to spiritual matters by taking her to church on Sundays and praying with her.

"We'd all be better off in heaven," Tess replied. "But selfishly, I would rather he be here. Sherry, I'm so sorry Davet's gone to heaven. I'm sorry that you had to go through so much this past year. I know you feel alone and hopeless, but I don't want you to feel that way. *We* don't want you to feel that way. We want you to know that there is someone who cares. Someone who loves you."

"I know all of that," Sherry said, looking away from Tess. "God loves me. Mr. D is always telling me that."

"God isn't the only one, Sherry," Tess declared. "We love you too. We're here because we want to adopt you."

The words rang in Sherry's ears. She had lived her entire life hoping to hear those words, but now they weren't welcome or believable. They seemed instead to be cruel. Sherry's head snapped back and her eyes narrowed. "Don't joke about that. You don't mean it. You're just feeling bad because of the baby. You'll think differently in a few days."

"No, we won't," Tess replied.

"We love you, Sherry," Brad stressed. "There's no reason to think differently."

"You probably didn't even think of it until you came here and saw me like this. Well, I don't need your pity. Just go back to your perfect life. There'll be another kid getting pregnant—another girl who stupidly believes somebody loves her."

Tears streamed down her cheeks. She hated herself for being so weak. Why was this happening? She'd lost everything—nothing remained. Not Davet. Not the Bible Mr. D had given her. Not the home she had come to love.

Sherry turned away from the Holbrooks, this time rolling gingerly over onto her side. "Please just go," she sobbed. There was no way she wanted to allow anyone to see her so weak, so vulnerable. *I wish I'd died with the baby. It would all be so easy if God would have just taken me away as well.*

Tess got up from the bed, and for a moment Sherry was certain they were leaving. *Good. Let them go. I don't want to think about her or Brad. I don't want to remember their home and their kindness, and I don't want to think about how much I'll miss them.*

Her tears flowed even harder. The hopelessness of her situation settled upon Sherry's shoulders like a heavy mantle of truth. She had no future.

But just as the imaginary mantle weighed her down, the covering that Sherry felt placed upon her shoulders by Tess seemed feathery light.

Startled, Sherry realized Tess and Brad hadn't gone. Instead, Tess was covering Sherry's shoulders.

"We want to adopt you, Sherry. We want you to be our daughter." Tess's words burrowed into the wall around Sherry's heart. "I'm not here out of guilt or sorrow. I'm here because I finally see the truth of why you came into my life."

Sherry reached up and touched the blanket. The delicate softness brought back a memory. Opening her eyes, Sherry realized it was the white crocheted blanket Tess had purchased for the baby. She looked at Tess, her face contorting in anguish.

"This belongs to him," Sherry said. "To Davet."

"I bought this blanket for my long-awaited child," Tess said, reaching out to touch Sherry's wet cheeks. "You, Sherry, are that child."

"No," Sherry said, shaking her head. "I didn't want the baby. I wished the baby dead and now he is. It's all my fault. You can't want me—I'm evil. God hates me."

She tried to pull the blanket off, but Tess pushed her hands away and wrapped it even more snugly. Enfolding Sherry in her arms, she said, "Nothing that happened was your fault. Davet didn't die because you wished him gone. Life and death don't work that way. Besides, you didn't mean those words—they were spoken in pain."

Brad came along the opposite side of the bed. "God loves you, Sherry. Tess and I love you too. You have only to accept our love—God's love."

Sherry's heart longed for the words to be true. "I don't . . . know how," she finally said, her voice coming out in whimpers.

Tess reached up to put her hand against Sherry's tear-stained cheek. "You start by acknowledging your need. You let God know that you see yourself for the person you are—lost and alone without Him."

"Mr. D said we had to turn from our bad ways and ask forgiveness, but what if God can't forgive me?"

Brad shook his head. "There is nothing too big for God to handle, Sherry. He's God. What could be too hard for Him? A teenage girl? A thirty-something woman? Are those the monumental kinds of things that would stop God?"

Sherry had to admit it sounded silly. "I want to believe it. I've wanted to believe it for a long time."

Brad gently pushed back her blond hair. "Then do. God won't force you. He wants you to come willingly." Tess nodded reassuringly.

"I'm willing," Sherry replied, her heart suddenly free. To believe that God really loved her and wanted her as His own was too wondrous to believe.

"And what about the other?" Tess questioned.

"What do you mean?"

"What about Brad and me adopting you? What about believing that our love for you is just as real?"

She was serious. Sherry could see that as clearly as she could the truth about God. Tess and Brad really loved her—really wanted her.

Sherry slumped against Tess. She felt so weak and tired.

Almost as if she'd run a long-distance race and could finally rest. She knew in her heart Tess wasn't joking—she really loved her. She had placed her expensive, hand-crocheted baby blanket around Sherry's shoulders. The blanket that only months ago she had snatched out of Sherry's hands. The meaning was not lost on the teen.

Lovingly, Tess cradled Sherry against her. "Will you please agree to be our daughter? I won't promise to be the best mother in the world—I can't even say that I'll always do the right thing. But what I can promise is to care for you, see to all your needs and some of your wants, and be a mother who loves you with all of her heart." Tess choked on a sob. "Please say you'll be our daughter."

Sherry cried softly and wrapped her arms tightly around Tess. She couldn't speak the words, but it was all right. She knew Tess could hear the cry of her heart. And her heart said yes.

They waited to have the funeral until Sherry could be out of the hospital and was strong enough to stand at the grave.

The little white coffin didn't seem as frightening and imposing as Sherry thought it might. She felt the edges of the wood while Mr. D talked about Jesus welcoming the little children to him. He led the congregation in a prayer, but she didn't bow her head or close her eyes.

Sherry felt the heated tears fall against her face. The winds picked up and blew her hair back, and she thought of something the pastor had once said about the breath of God blowing life into Adam and Eve. Looking up to the skies, she thought of God blowing life back into her baby.

Leaning down, she kissed the coffin and hugged it for a moment. She was saying good-bye in the only way she knew how. "Go home now, Davet. Go home to Jesus," she whispered softly.

She straightened and looked back up to the skies. Tess took hold of her hand and looked into her eyes. "We'll see him again," Tess murmured. "He's waiting for us and he'll know us when we come there."

"Will he know that I really loved him?" Sherry asked.

Tess smiled broadly. "He knows. He knew when he was still inside you. He had a mother's love and no one can take that away from him or from you."

Sherry hugged Tess close. "He had two mothers. He'll always have two mothers." She pulled back to make certain Tess knew how much she meant the words.

"Thank you, Sherry. Thank you for giving him to us and thank you for giving yourself as well."

The services were over and everyone was invited back to Laura and Darren's for lunch. Barbara Woodsby had flown down to join her brother for the funeral, but now she came to speak to Sherry.

"Sherry, I just want you to know how sorry I am that things didn't work out the way you planned."

Sherry looked to the woman. She had been one of the only adults in her life, besides the Holbrooks, to ever really care.

"My plans weren't the best," Sherry said softly.

Barbara nodded knowingly. "We all have those times, but God's plans are always perfect. Ultimately, I know He has great things in store for you."

Sherry smiled. "He gave me parents—people who really love me. I don't care what else He has planned. I already have the best."

Chapter
26

"This is so exciting!" Seventeen-year-old Sherry fairly danced while Brad worked with the lock on the door. "This house is so cool. I still can't believe we're really going to move here."

Tess laughed as Brad finally managed to unlock the door. "I'd stand back if I were you, Brad. Otherwise, Sherry will mow you over."

He gallantly stood to one side. "Your palace, milady." He gave a sweeping bow as Sherry scurried inside.

She gave a squeal of girlish delight. "Oh, it's just so big. I wasn't sure it was as big as I remembered, but it's huge."

Tess and Brad followed her into the entryway, completely amused at Sherry's animated laughter.

"I'm going to go see my room," she hurried off down the hall.

"I think she likes it," Brad said with a grin. He put his arm around Tess's shoulders. "But what about you, Mrs. Holbrook? You've hardly said a word."

"I found this place to begin with," Tess replied. "You already know I love it."

"I just want you to be sure. I mean, we'll probably be here for a long time."

Tess smiled and touched her husband's face. "It's perfect. It's everything I'd hoped for, right down to the flower garden around the backyard patio."

"It's going to be a whole lot more work," he said, looking around the great-hall-styled living and dining room.

"I don't care. It's exactly what I want out of life. A lovely home, a family, and a loving husband. It's exactly what I prayed for," Tess said, bestowing a kiss on her husband's cheek. "Now, come on, let's go see where Sherry is."

Tess preceded Brad down the hall and found Sherry checking out every nook and cranny of her new bedroom.

"Look here," Sherry declared, "I'll have enough bookshelves for about a million books. And since I plan to live at home and go to college, it will be ideal."

The built-in shelving was one of the reasons Tess had thought the room perfect for Sherry. Sherry loved to read and Tess already had plans for buying her a wonderful study library.

"I'll put the bed here and my desk over there," Sherry said, waving her arms. "Oh, can we still put up wallpaper?" she asked Tess.

"I don't see why not. We can go tomorrow and pick out what you like," Tess replied. "Well, within reason. I don't want anything too wild and crazy."

"I don't want anything wild and crazy," Sherry admitted. "I want it to look like those Victorian rooms in your magazines."

"Look, we'll have plenty of time for this later," Brad said, looking at his watch. "If we don't get a move on, we're going to be late for your graduation ceremonies. Laura and Darren are probably wondering where we are."

Sherry laughed and gave Brad a hug. "You're not going

to be one of those worrywart fathers, are you? I mean, I am almost eighteen. And we all agreed it's time I learn to drive and, of course, date Daniel Aznar. . . ."

"You can do both of those things when you're thirty," Brad replied. "Eighteen still seems too young."

The ladies laughed and Tess felt an overwhelming happiness as Sherry gave Brad a playful nudge. "No fair, Dad. I want to be just like all the other kids."

"I'd rather you just be yourself," Brad replied. "Now, I'm going to head back to the car. You ladies hurry it up."

Sherry released him and nodded. "We're coming." She waited until Brad had stepped down the hall to look to Tess. "I love it here. I'm so glad you picked this house."

"I like it too," Tess admitted. "It feels like home."

Sherry nodded and came to where Tess stood. She hugged Tess tightly. "You're the best, Mom." She stepped back and grinned. "I love being able to call you that. Mr. D always says what a privilege and joy it is to call God 'Abba-Father,' and I agree with that, too, but there's nothing in the world like having a mom."

Tess felt tears come to her eyes. "There's nothing quite like having a daughter, either."

Tess reached her hand up to brush back an errant strand of Sherry's hair. "I'm so proud of you, Sherry. You've come so far and had to deal with so much. You've worked hard on your studies and now you're graduating with honors and getting ready for college. I know it hasn't always been easy for you, and sometimes I haven't handled things as well as I had hoped to. But I love you. And I consider myself the most blessed woman in the world."

"I love you too," Sherry said, beaming with happiness.

Tess knew that no one else in Sherry's life had ever praised her like this. Tess thought of her own adopted mother and how good it felt to be recognized as having worth. Suddenly the past seemed so unimportant. The pieces all fit, and each one held equal value.

Tess had known security and love in her adopted home. Her birth and the difficulties that followed were of little consequence, because what man had meant for evil, God had worked for good. She couldn't help but fervently hope that her own children would feel the same way one day.

"Come on," Tess said, reaching out for Sherry's hand. "Laura and Darren are probably half crazy trying to keep up with your brother and sister."

Adoption had proven such a blessing with Sherry that Brad and Tess had found four-year-old twin siblings to add to their family. "We'll be lucky if they haven't turned the entire retirement center upside down. I've never seen two kids with more energy."

Sherry laughed and the sound rang through the empty house like a song. It was a melody Tess hoped to hear many times in the years to come. It was a song of hope and joy. It was a song of home and family.

ENJOY TWO OF CHRISTIAN FICTION'S FINEST!

A Spine-Tingling Escape From a Love Gone Dangerously Wrong

To the outside world, Dr. Russell Koehler was the ideal catch—charming, attentive, and attractive. And life in Serenity Bay offered the perfect setting for a young family. But eight years into marriage, Patricia knows her world is crumbling fast. With two children and no one to trust, Patricia faces the most frightening decision of her life.

Serenity Bay by Bette Nordberg

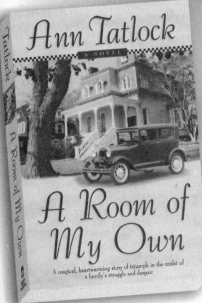

A Story to Stay With You Forever

The daughter of a physician, Virginia Eide has known only an idyll world until the Great Depression descends onto her community. Soon she begins accompanying her father into worlds of poverty and hunger, giving medical aid to those most in need. As she reaches out, Virginia develops a compassion and strength of character that changes the very direction of her life.

A Room of My Own by Ann Tatlock

BETHANY HOUSE
www.bethanyhouse.com
1-800-328-6109